The Berserkers

The Berserkers

Vic Peterson

For Tracy, Reid, and Royce
~ Voyagers ~

The great god's men went armor-less into battle and were as crazed as dogs or wolves, and as strong as bears or bulls. They bit their shields and slew men, while they themselves were harmed neither by fire or iron. This they called *going berserk.*

—Yngalinga Saga

Contents

Part I: The Flyting

1: Valkyrie

Snorri cackled and sucked at his teeth. The wind blasted across the lake, cutting the snow into sharp ridges. He hurled instructions at me as if he were whipping a husky, and I spun the wheel according to Snorri's command. Our tires rolled off the beach onto the thick ice cap that froze over the lake in Winter, clods of snow drumming the floorboard from underneath, like the rapping of the dead. Somewhere in the endless white lay our destination.

"I'm a records clerk," I said.

"A noble profession."

"I shelve file folders and fuss with index cards. I'm not trained as a crime scene technician."

"I'll bet the Constable doesn't get out of his vehicle," Snorri laughed, no longer having to be discrete. Despite having left the force more than a year before, he came around the stationhouse to harvest gossip and otherwise pierce the tedium of his days. Today, he had come to *us* with the news. With a grunt of satisfaction, Snorri shot an index finger under my nose. "Over there."

Three precinct cars tailed us in caravan style, a procession blind to its destination and deaf to the admonishing wind. A knot of veins flared between Snorri's eyes. We had found the hillock of snow Snorri wanted. It was the sole hillock of snow on the frozen lake, and he had scraped it up himself, a bier to mark the spot. His face twisted with exhilaration.

The remaining vehicles slid into place, a break against the gusts. Engines were cut, with more boots hitting the ice. Flipping the door handles, we stepped out and gathered in a ring. I looked around, first at Snorri and then at Bergthora, the sole remaining sergeant detective in our precinct. She was a wary creature whose penchant for vigilance had by slow degrees surrendered to grievance, just as her husky frame had given over to butter. The circle was completed by Patrolman Jerker, whose crisp azure uniform seemed ridiculously cheery.

Snorri muttered, "You see, what I said is true."

Yes, we finally saw what we had come to see. I gazed down at the exploding nova of hair through the window of ice at our feet. The girl seemed to float in a cauldron of glass. She had been there for a while, days at least - her eyes rolled back, her arms spread in pirouette beneath the translucent dome, a distorted shadow in the watery darkness.

"Always a female," said Bergthora.

þ

I am a musician. I work as a records clerk at the police station for the paycheck. Fulaflugahål is a modest harbor city on Lake Munch that insists on its image as a dour commercial town, a solemnity underwritten by the beautiful dark secret of Scandinavian contentment. The unwritten code: conform, conform. Do not stick out, do not be different. Do not behave as if you have something unusual about you.

The day job suits me. By nature, I am an observer, a listener, absorbing all. When I am not toting sheaves of paper for cases or denying access to miscreants, I work on my music. At night, keyboards, band rehearsal. During the day, I get my musical fix while doing something else. I might give the impression of being unusually fidgety, but what I'm really doing is ensuring I understand. I work on a tricky spot in a song and run my hands over an imaginary keyboard as fast as I can — on the dashboard, on a lintel, on my thigh. Insanely fast. Hammering every single note. If I can do that, I'll completely own the sound later.

Snorri picked at his eyebrows, then applied his blunt intellect like a pair of industrial tongs. "Lots of people walk out on this ice, hiking, or skiing, or chasing a pet, or drunk.

Once every few years, some poor idiot breaks through." The little man's eyes flitted over the rim of the frozen grave. After a considerable pause, he remarked: "But this girl, uh, she didn't just break through."

A perfunctory *hup* echoed through the group, our signal for agreement. Snorri continued examining the scene as if he was parting the bones of a herring. He noted the thinness of the ice cap trapping her and that the surrounding ice was clear, with stress fractures that shot through the surface like the tails of comets. The surrounding sheet was the kind that takes months for nature to build, yet the mirror-smooth surface directly over her was less than a few centimeters thick. The new ice was recent and terribly precise.

Snorri tapped his nose. "Made for the purpose."

Jerker nodded tentatively. "I know what to call it—a lid."

Snorri beamed. "Exactly, it is a lid." Flushed with overconfidence, however, he pushed his logic too far, supposing this or that, extrapolating any tenuous connection, nattering on and excluding only what his spirit impelled him to exclude. Finally, he arrived at a Zen-like impossibility: Someone had welded the ice cap in place.

"Welded?" Bergthora snorted.

"Welded," Snorri insisted.

Jerker said, "I have heard of carving ice, but not welding ice."

Bergthora rolled her eyes at the circus. "Welded with what?"

"A culinary torch."

Bergthora wheeled on Snorri, a wave of flesh rolling across her gut. "This isn't wagering on a Sunday match. You are beyond your depth, Sturlusson."

"I have been known to beat the odds."

"What are you even doing here? You were forced to retire."

Snorri's squint at me was as bitter as the one I received from him the morning the file had landed on the desk of the director-general for internal affairs. "Everything was fine for forty-five years until *someone* toted the wrong file from the archives."

Bergthora interrupted him. "Back in the car, Sturlusson."

Snorri planted his heels and said, "I found the body." Bergthora hitched her thumbs into her belt. A standoff. Jerker used the backs of his trouser calves to polish his boots. I studied the lace of fractures in the ice.

Meanwhile, Bergthora tugged a thread on her sleeve and hinted she might lodge a complaint with the justice ministry. Recalcitrance hung heavy on the moment. Snorri spat at a snowbank.

With our alternatives rapidly diminishing, the rest of us turned practical. We documented, made shaky videos, tapped notes into our electronic devices. Jerker took countless photos with great care and paced off the perimeter distance. Bergthora broke the stalemate to produce a thermos of black coffee, dispensing it in paper cups.

Having otherwise wordlessly dispatched of our duties, we gathered again around the dead girl. Snorri said we needed a way to extract the body. Bergthora declared a chainsaw the best tool. A rectangular swathe would be cut around the corpse, a process she had read about in an article on corpse recovery. Or was it a circular swathe? She could not remember. While she thought about it, she ordered Jerker to fetch equipment from the vehicles.

Jerker trudged off, shoulders sinking. Hefting surely was the lowest job on an investigation. I was surprised Bergthora had not assigned it to me.

þ

Grumbling with discontent, Bergthora then began to second-guess her own decision. She muttered that a chainsaw would disturb evidence and, even so, a rookie knew the cut should be rectangular. Snorri countered with a long-discredited theory that the body could remain as it was until the spring thaw. Bergthora retorted that vinyl fishnets were superior in every way for retrieving corpses from water. Dogmas mounted, spread, ossified.

Jerker returned empty handed. "Fine preparations here. The car boots are empty. No chainsaw or any other equipment to fetch a body from the lake."

Bergthora smiled sharply. Her all-purpose pessimism was vindicated. Snorri and Jerker debated who should go back to the Fulaflugahål station. The dispute led to accusations. Meanwhile, the wind whipped the snow into miniature whirlwinds that blasted themselves back into powder against the car doors. We huddled and quarreled, oblivious to the nightmare beneath our feet.

As predicted, the Constable had remained in his car, engine cut, sheltered from the wind while consulting his ancient manual on investigative science. I had seen the book open on his desk; it was almost a century old, filled with dense, hand-wrought diagrams and complex tables, and with guidance surely obsolete.

I had seen the Constable around the precinct but did not know him well. His inky wool suit, cuff-linked shirts, cravats and wingtips, the heavy cloak and ever-present manual, were relics of long-gone salad days and fodder for pub hour mockery.

The Constable stepped from his car onto the lake, one exploratory foot after the other. He wore heavy-rimmed glasses, the left lens blackened to disguise an old wound that had taken his sight in that eye. At some angles, the black disk seemed to absorb all light falling upon it; at others, it glinted like a scythe of obsidian.

I didn't know the Constable, but he knew me. He marched straight toward me. "You are Kolbitter?"

It had been the Constable himself who had insisted I accompany the squad. I was baffled when I saw the request. And though I dared not confess it, for fear of insolence, I had better things to do with my life than play at cops and robbers.

"Yes," I said.

"Jerker informed me they found no tools. You loaded the vehicles?"

"You mean today?"

He cut me off. Wiry gray hair jutted in sprigs around his ears. I slipped my hands into my parka, wary. My fingers worked at a song.

"Check the glove box of your vehicle for the aerosol snow wax, Kolbitter."

I fetched the can. Bending and marking the icy grave with waxen x's and o's, the Constable hunched over his work as a shaman at his symbols. He seemed to detect things the rest of us could not as he crouched in the wind, cloak fluttering.

"It's too stupid. Terrible. Hopeless." His lips paled with pressure. Then, the Constable stooped and lifted something from the ice. He handed me a shaggy brown clot of hair.

"Human hair?" I asked.

"No," he blasted back. "Can you not tell human hair from animal hair, boy?"

I glanced at Snorri, then back at the Constable.

"I'm just a records clerk, sir."

The Constable went back to spraying, wandering the ribs of the shoreline, an ever-lengthening trail of forensic wax dropping like spoor along his path. I looked back down on the frozen cloud of hair about the victim, bewildered, inexplicably embarrassed, listening to the crepitating ice.

Snorri shattered the moment with a plea.

"Constable, the sun is well past overhead. Our shift is almost over."

Bergthora laughed with a sputter. "You don't have a shift, Sturlusson; you don't work anymore."

The clouds had dropped and thickened. The sun was lost in grey. I did not want to be there; my heart was elsewhere. I dug my gloves further into the trenches of my parka and began again to finger an unheard chord. My head bobbed with a chord transition, a vexing shift I'd been laboring over. As my glove bumped into something hidden, a mechanical rumble started somewhere nearby. But I dismissed the noise as being incidental. I might have seen puffs of smoke wafting toward shore and misconstrued them as the handiwork of my wracked imagination, a prefiguration of dry-ice fog and lasers in a roaring stadium.

The Constable had loped almost a kilometer away to pursue something unknown to us, a detail, a pattern. Snorri drew a hand over the spade of his beard; our quarrel resumed within no time. Ours were the uncompromising disputes of those who treat delay as an entitlement and guesswork as science. At the Fulaflugahål precinct, few things were as deeply satisfying as a procedural victory.

The sun sank toward the hills. An hour later, everything had been posited, nothing resolved. We had lost sight of the Constable. The wind moaned, the heavens darkened, and time disappeared, like a continental shelf into the sea.

þ

Then we saw the Constable's flagging greatcoat and heard his cries across the frozen lake. He sprinted toward us over the ice, legs pumping. He had a long way to go, a kilometer perhaps, as we watched him tip and right in mad measures, waving his hands overhead. His screams seemed to perish on the wind like the cannonade of a losing army.

"What's he saying?" Snorri fingered the skin flakes beneath his beard. "What do you think, Grammaticus? You're a young man, and you have good ears."

I leaned toward the Constable's shouts. After much consideration, I said, "I don't know."

I sensed a tide of resentment in the silence of those around me. I shrugged, "I'm only a records clerk." As it turned out, my shrug inspired their mutual incomprehension. They all shrugged, too. None of us could decipher the Constable's caterwauling.

Slowly, the bounding man's cries collapsed into meaning. "Turn it off!"

Too late. An enormous snap thundered a dozen yards behind us. We pivoted as smoothly as the chorus in a Wagnerian opera, gawking as a precinct wagon lurched. The rear axle spasmed; the front bumper yawned at the sky. Steam shot from beneath the vehicle, the frame shuddered, a fissure opened, and the wagon slipped through the ice into the boiling deep.

Rafts of ice closed over the water, that is, over the wagon I had driven with Snorri beside me gabbling directions. My gloved left hand wormed deep into the folds of my coat pocket, hunting. And there it was: an electronic ignition key that could start a car from a dozen meters. A vehicle that, with a running engine, would melt the ice underneath.

The Constable reached us, huffing. He halted, toes digging like crampons into the snow, his one good eye fixed on the bubbling gap in the ice. Tremors of outrage propagated over his face.

"Kolbitter."

I quailed. "Sir?"

There I stood before them all, helpless. A tide of blood throbbed in my ears. My hand stopped twitching. I freed the key from my pocket and dangled the fob before them. The Constable plied the scar beside his eye patch. Jerker kneaded the back of his neck, and Bergthora frowned grimly. Snorri sat on the snow, placing his head in his hands.

"Usch," Snorri moaned.

Pellets of snow streaked from the demolished sky.

A pale tangle lay beside the hole the girl had been sunk in. It then dawned on me that the pale tangle *was the girl*. Her body lay sprawled on top of the ice, displaced by the minor tsunami of the sinking car, and ejected from the ice like the cork from a champagne bottle. Her clothes spread about her in wet snarls lurid under the dim sun, a cape and corset and stockings.

The girl's pallor was blue and ruinous. My jaw slackened. I tried to utter some words, any words, whether of shock, wisdom, or warning. No sound emanated from my lips. For a pair of large wings had begun unfolding around the corpse, beautiful, wispy, shivering with each gust like the pinfeathers of a hatchling drying in the dying light.

2: Grimke

A kind of delirium haunted the moment. The feathers spread until every barb of every plume fluttered. A harness of leather straps bound the wings over the girl's shoulders. The wind gusted and wracked the vision. With a hollow snap, the delicate contrivance crumpled as swiftly as a kite in a gale.

I approached the dark sight half under its spell. The Constable shouted, "Boy!" I halted, yards from the corpse. The message was clear: I was not to advance. The Constable then divided the crew among tasks. Bergthora and Snorri secured the wings by packing them down with snow; Jerker circled the body, snapping photographs. I remained alone on the ice without an assignment, bouncing on my toes to keep warm, a trick taught the children of our town in grade school. Finally, the Constable handed me a paper pad and pen.

"Make yourself useful, Kolbitter."

"Sir?"

"You are a records keeper. Keep records."

"I will, sir."

The Constable withdrew the antique investigative manual from an inner pocket of his cloak, a reflex. It seemed he found on those pages not the debunked scientific folklore of an earlier time, but wild apparitions of truth longing to be revived. The officers fell again to their tasks. After a while, Bergthora mumbled a half-baked excuse, detached herself from the group, and shuffled behind the vehicles.

"Yes, yes," I heard her rasp.

Marching around the wall of wagons, Snorri found Bergthora muttering into a precinct cell phone.

"Calling your sweetheart?" he asked.

Bergthora snapped the device shut. "At least I have a

sweetheart, Sturlusson." The shine in Snorri's eyes disappeared, and he grew sullen. He was a widower. The two returned to clapping snow around the feathers. I wrote it all in the notepad.

þ

"You think the wings were on the girl when she went in?" I wondered aloud.

Snorri kept his voice low. "I should say so. Whoever is responsible must have known her, that is what I believe."

I was about to ask why he was whispering when the scrutinizing eye of the Constable fell upon us as if we were convicts on line detail. Snorri hunched back to his task. I turned away, continuing to scribble on in my exile.

The Constable's head bobbed between the dead girl and the antique pages of the manual. Then, a low barbed whine echoed across the ice. Snorri lifted his eyes to a black shape driving over the horizon.

"A helicopter," he said in an undertone. The rhythmic whopping became more discrete, a small craft striped blue and red and yellow swooping down from beyond the mountains. It sped with ominous precision toward us, like a glass wasp. Soon, I could decipher the letters on the undercarriage as it circled overhead though I already knew what it said: G-R-I-M-K-E.

Jerker uttered the word like a terrible curse. Things were going from bad to worse. It was the violence squad from Grimke, the big city beyond the mountains, an arm of the national force deployed only for the most aberrant crimes.

"Who called Grimke?" Snorri knit his brow.

The flint in Bergthora's eyes betrayed her. "So what."

Snorri kicked at a ridge of ice, "You're right. I'm not the one who has to worry. I'm not on a police force that Grimke might see as tiny and superfluous, and shut down."

Grimke was purposeful, prepared, and efficient. Grimke had funds. Grimke had respect. Grimke was everything we from Fulaflugahål were not. The Constable stepped into the whirlwind of the descending machine. The skids were set with professional skill upon the ice, sufficiently far from our labors to prevent disturbance. The rotors spun to a halt, and the Constable's cloak fell still.

Two officers dressed in black livery filed out: black boots, black combat pants, black parkas, black batons, black holsters, raked black side caps. A straight-shouldered female approached us, with sleeves laced with gold piping. She was about six feet tall with yellow hair that hung midway down her back and violet eyes under clipped bangs. Her presence relayed a sense of robotic precision. When she moved, the force was as fluid as the wheels of a locomotive connected by powerful bars; when she did not, her arms fell, inert at her sides.

The male officer, shorter, sporting fewer brocades, crossed his hands before his groin and waited valet-like by the aircraft. I braced for a harsh polemic toward the approaching officer from the Constable. Instead, I heard him intone, "Welcome, dear Freja," as if this were some private soiree. The two old colleagues bent over his handbook. He drew his hand in a strange rite from top to bottom and side to side over the illustrations, stabbing an index finger at graphs. Freja lowered her nose to the leaves, quizzical yet non-committal—again, the robotic perfection.

Freja signaled the male officer, who then walked along the helicopter tail, opened a compartment hatch, and unloaded supplies, including a chainsaw. We were ordered back to shore. Bergthora whimpered about her loyalty and the unfairness of her treatment. Under Freja's impassive gaze, a windshield tent was erected around the dead girl, a stretcher unfolded, and the victim smocked in a white tarp.

Snorri and I huddled in the rear seat of a parked wagon. Bergthora and Jerker sat together in front. Through the transparent plastic barrier, Bergthora pantomimed her throat being slit. I said to Snorri, "What can happen to me for putting the car through the ice, Snorri?"

The little man considered the possibilities. "Sticklers they are for administrative procedure. Reprimand. Maybe suspension without pay, or you get fired."

He grimaced, then said, "Worst case, jail time."

"Jail!" I cried.

Snorri sat watching Bergthora knot an imaginary noose and hang herself. Jerker's brow wrinkled in consternation. Bergthora straightened an index finger, cocked her thumb, and shot herself in the temple. When the dumb show ended, Snorri said, "You're a good kid, Grammaticus."

"Incarcerated for an accident," I muttered.

Snorri patted my knee. "I promise to visit you."

The rap of a baton on my side window made me jump. The male Grimke officer ordered me back into the searing cold. He grilled me with questions, seemingly intrigued by me triggering the key fob. He was keen to know why I had been fidgeting so absent-mindedly. I started to explain, tried to. "You see, sir, I have to practice because I'm. . ."

"Because you're practicing to be a cop. No amount of practice will ever make you a cop. Look at your scraggly hair, clothing like a hobo; no discipline whatsoever. Why were you even present at the crime scene?"

I wiped my nose on my sleeve. I told him the Constable had ordered me, and I followed because I'm an obsequious records clerk, and obsequious records clerks obey their superiors.

The officer blinked, said, "Ja," and then blinked again.

Jerker, Snorri, and Bergthora suffered the same debasement, piling back into the vehicle afterward, despondent, fretful, scolded to remain quiet on the matter. The Constable, though, appeared to be permitted to roam about as if under some magical dispensation. He joked, he advised. He blandished the archaic volume. Once the field protocols were dispatched, the corpse was lifted on a stretcher into the helicopter. Freja swept her violet eyes over us, her swift mechanical eyes, an automaton doing her best to go undetected among humans. The rotors chopped, the craft rose in a straight line from the ground, its nose dipped, and its tail tilted up. The grim cargo was spirited back beyond the mountains.

The Constable pressed his blind lens to the door window of our wagon. He crooked his finger at me; I stepped out again. "Give me your notes," he instructed. A sense of impending doom growing in my heart, I handed him the pad of paper.

"My handwriting is miserable. The cold made it worse."

The Constable peeled back the pages, scrutinizing them. The pad was a welter of fragments and jottings, sketches of what I thought I saw, erasures, revisions, anything that might pass as a note. It was fear that had driven my pen. I had filled seventeen pages. On the bottom of the last page, I had outlined a sequence of minor chords ending in an F# that would be held for twenty-three stupidly long seconds, leaving me mortified.

The Constable tore off the swatch, crumpled it, and handed the lump to me.

3: Memory and Thought

The Constable let out a sigh that transformed into a groan. "This is all too half-witted, beyond speaking."

It was late March. Six weeks had passed since we stood on the ice of Lake Munch. Since then, there had been an unreal mood about things I could not put my finger on. The Constable himself seemed to take on a more outrageous, even fantastic quality and a sense that invisible machinations were occurring as the days passed.

The six-week period would have been far shorter, but for the extra work the forensic lab had to do in light of my catastrophe with the key fob. Jerker, Bergthora, Snorri, and I hunkered at one end of a long table in the cavernous hall where we gathered like knights of a vanquished tribe. The Constable crouched in his chair at the head using a laptop to flip through images on a standing screen. These images were of the crime scene, the first from a distance in a car, more approaching on foot, then scores close up of the disgorged body, focusing finally on the strange wings. The Constable jerked abruptly to his feet.

"We are fortunate that Patrolman Jerker took a lot of photos. At least there is a record of unsullied facts." The black lens fell upon me. My hours at work shuttling dusty files were anguishing as I awaited the lab results, whatever consolation I might derive from my music. Had my clumsiness ruined evidence that could identify a culprit? This wasn't an inquisition, yet I started to apologize again. The Constable cut me short. "You are a wretch, Kolbitter, a calumny. How old are you, boy?"

"Thirty-one."

"A lifetime squandered."

I squirmed in my seat, "I am a late bloomer."

Bergthora let out a guttural noise, savoring my humiliation. I asked the question I had asked since that day on the ice. "Why am I here? I'm not even a policeman," I implored.

All was stillness, disrupted only by the Constable's breathing. "You're here now because you must clean up the mess you made."

We all had been summoned earlier in the day, told to leave off our duties, and gather at the Constable's home. The house sat far up a narrow lane. The distant clash of ice floes as the lake's frozen surface broke up in the late days of March intensified the somber mood about the place. I arrived just before twilight guttered out. With the high roof looming before me, I now fathomed why the Constable's home stoked rumor. Thick whitewashed granite walls overlooked Lake Munch, shadowed by narrow windows and oak columns blackened by time. The door hinges whispered of baroque intrigues. It had been the western outpost of some ill-fated, forgotten kingdom; now, the footsteps of the Constable echoed through its corridors, and his oaths rang through its vaults. How such an estate had come to a man on the salary of a civil servant, none of us dared ask.

A fire was jumping in a hearth as we entered. I positioned myself close to it, hoping to snatch its comforts. Plates of cheese and bread sat on the sideboard, along with two clear vessels of a snuff-colored drink corked like old apothecary bottles. One of these bottles was freshly open.

"A cognac of a closely held reserve," the Constable offered. We received our goblets and drank. The richness of the flavor was beyond my understanding other than it must have been expensive. Meanwhile, two large black birds squatted on open perches on either end of the hearth, tranquil and uninterested in us, black feathers glistening.

The Constable bowed while introducing us to the birds. "She is Minne; he is Tanke." Minne had a single white feather in her tail. Tanke was grave and serene.

Jerker clapped his hands, "You have named them *Memory* and *Thought*. How charming, sir."

Bergthora tasted from her snifter and coughed. "I didn't know that was possible for ravens to be domesticated. These birds live indoors with you, Constable?"

"These birds are far better disciplined than you lot," he replied.

I glanced all around the room. The paintings on the wall were intact. None of the books betrayed tears from their hard bills.

"I hear you can teach a raven to speak. True?" asked Snorri.

The Constable tapped his chest, suggestive of some sort of greeting ritual, and said, "Tanke?"

"Tanke," croaked Tanke.

He addressed the other bird: "Minne?"

"Minne," rasped Minne.

Jerker giggled with delight. "They look so dignified, like wise old people."

Our host swung back to the screen, the subtle reproval unmistakable. He advanced to the last picture. The victim was a desolate beauty, her lips purple as beetroot, torso sagging over the ice. I now saw her hair was not standard issue Nordic blond. It was dyed yellow, a bit wiry, with her deep brown eyes being wide-set, pinched at the interior. Her cheeks were dusted with russet freckles, and her face formed a kind of inverted teardrop, a shape seemingly hinting at a home, a people, very distant from Fulaflugahål.

Snorri ventured back into the black tide of the Constable's temper. "What is the meaning of the costume wings?"

The Constable snorted. "Isn't it obvious?" He plunged on, redirecting our attention to marks above the corset, zooming in to make the three small puncture wounds midway between the left collarbone and breast visible. Bergthora's face darkened; Jerker bent forward. The Constable said, "Stab wounds. It must've been a long, skinny blade to pierce the artery. The work of an experienced hand."

Jerker ventured the next question cautiously, his tone impossibly polite. "This is the conclusion of Grimke? A stabbing with a long skinny blade by someone who knows how to kill with a long skinny blade?"

Bergthora worked herself into a fury. "Grimke bastards. They have all the money. They have the lab and even a helicopter. In their eyes, we're babies playing with our poop."

"It's a wonder any of us still has a job," Jerker offered.

Snorri slurped at the remaining portion of his drink. "Heh," he declared.

The Constable looked around the table at the composed, fearful faces. "Hiding by the fire, are you, Kolbitter?" he said to me. He tucked his ascot between the lapels of a wasp-waisted dinner jacket and then fetched the electronic remote, thrusting it at the screen until the screen turned black. His good eye narrowed to a cold gleam.

Our host then reminded us that solving a murder was not just a procedural achievement for the best inspectors; it was also an intellectual enterprise, a discipline. This group had failed on the first account; it could perhaps redeem itself on the second.

Bergthora tapped her pink snout. "We need more evidence, Constable. You can't come to conclusions without more evidence. Conjectures are not going to work."

The Constable gave a dry laugh and insisted we had seen enough evidence on screen for now. "It's time for intellect. Cognition. Examine this well." We needed to look closer. For our purposes, the enigma of the dead woman in the ice could be reduced to three elements. The first element was the costume with the wings. The second was the stab wounds. We would advance through them in that order. With a bombastic twirl of a remote, the Constable said, "Let us proceed with exhibit one, the costume and wings."

Jerker's voice went high and sharp. "You said three

elements. The costume and wings are the first elements, no? The second element is the stab wounds, right? You left out the third."

I pushed my long hair back over my ears. "Her face. Her eyes and hair," I suggested.

The Constable looked pained. "Blunderers. First, the costume."

"Yes, the costume," Snorri urged in an undertone.

The Constable informed us the stockings and corset's lacework were a run-of-the-mill pattern found anywhere across Europe, but the harness straps, now those were interesting. These leather thongs were braided in a style reflecting a deft craftsperson's handiwork familiar with remote rural folk methods. And the leather, yes, that was unusual too, probably reindeer.

Bergthora sputtered, "Decent, law-abiding local folks don't kill reindeer; it's illegal." Then she leaned back in her chair. "Wait; there is a cluster of foreigners living in a small section near the harbor. Aliens bring crime and leave dead bodies in their wake."

Snorri plied the thicket of whiskers on his chin. "But what is the purpose of the wings?"

Bergthora sneered, "Because perverts love dress-up."

"Facts," the Constable insisted. "Start with facts." The feathers were swan feathers; the wings had expanded in the wind because they were intended to fold in and out for display. Removing a small object from his waist pocket, the Constable tossed it onto the tabletop's planks. It landed with a soft clap. He explained the item was a label that had been affixed to the interior of the wing harness. I could see the stitching and loose threads.

Jerker pointed at the ragged edge of the cloth. "Look here."

The Constable whirled his hand as if encouraging a poor student. Tell us all, what did he see? Jerker slouched, repeating the rough edges somehow looked suspicious. The Constable noted the short rough strokes could mean the label was hastily clipped from its place, with scissors with a very short blade. From another waistcoat pocket, he produced a pair of fingernail clippers. "Perhaps like these."

Jerker puffed out his lower lip, concentrating. "The killer was so confident he paired his nails on the job."

Our host pounced with cruel relish. "You are like an acrobat too lazy to reach for the trapeze. See how quickly the ground comes rushing up?" Grimke, too, was obtuse, failing to grasp the wings' significance; thus, when consulting at the Grimke lab, he had removed the label with the clippers. "Perhaps we may unearth the answer to the question of the significance of the wings by asking the proprietor of the firm that owned the wings."

I saw his index finger come to rest, between the clipped edges, upon the words *Kvasir Mead Company*.

Snorri shifted his weight from one buttock to the other. "I volunteer to go there," he said.

The Constable stared in brute silence.

Jerker asked, "What about the stab wounds?"

The Constable produced an imaginary dagger which he held inches below the patrolman's left clavicle, narrating a scenario in which the wounds were inflicted with a thin, long blade, punched rapidly. Even a strong assailant can't pierce the breastbone with ease, he grinned. The target was the wide-open terrain above the ventricle of the heart and the forest of vessels arching out to the lungs. He pantomimed three hair-trigger jabs. Jerker flinched, gasping.

"The victim would have only seconds to live." The Constable gently withdrew the invisible weapon from the patrolman's flesh and sheathed his imaginary blade. Tanke fluttered down from his perch and ambled over the floorboards. Snorri extended a hand and shook the bill of the raven before caressing his fuzzy head. The raven tilted his head sideways and fluffed out his feathers. Jerker leaned from his seat and, following Snorri's lead, extended his hand in welcome too; the bird folded his shoulders forward, widened his wings, and darted his bill. The patrolman snatched back, yelping, blood seeping from the heel of his thumb.

"That creature is a wicked devil," Jerker protested.

The Constable crossed his arms. "You must be allowed into their world."

"Their world," Bergthora scoffed. "As if we lived on different planets."

The Constable's hand fell to the ancient investigative volume on the tabletop, an unconscious gesture. I understood then the book was not merely a refuge of techniques; it was a dimension of his presence that promised worlds and withheld them. It was an avatar of himself and an entry into his universe.

Tanke crowed like a rooster, wingbeats ending in a tumult of sound.

Bergthora began tossing chunks of table bread to Minne and watched the bird catch them in her beak. While the mechanical fluidity of the interaction seemed most engrossing to the sergeant detective, she said, "Are we going to finish analyzing the evidence? The so-called third important element? After all, this is a murder investigation."

"I want to know about that infernal harness," said Snorri.

I felt compelled to press my point as well. "And her eyes, Constable, the corners of her eyes."

The Constable unfolded his arms and rested his right hand on the computer keyboard, lightly pressing the keys as if he were an undertaker probing a body. "One feels these elements are intertwined, does one not? One feels they are connected in some essential yet undiscovered way." The image of the leather harness came back on screen. Snorri, Bergthora, and I studied the brown thongs in search of some unholy truth.

Jerker propped his chin in his hands, still riveted by the birds. "What magical things can Minne and Tanke do,

Constable?"

Tanke croaked in a manner hoarse and far off. The Constable bowed his head, though to camouflage an expression I could not discern.

"Very well," he said, seemingly in reply to the bird.

The Constable closed his eyes and drew together his brows. "Winter. Countless years, the Finland border. An immense forest. Fevered action, quick decisions. Minne and Tanke were perched on my shoulders. Arcades of black spruce rising fifty meters high. Great snowflakes drifted down between the towering trees."

"What were you doing way up near Finland?" Jerker asked.

Bergthora paused, lobbing crusts to Minne. "Good question. That is not our jurisdiction."

"You assume I am at liberty to say."

The Constable's tale played in my ears. I listened to him weave his pursuit of an old nemesis, a figure known for his fugitive arts and vast astuteness.

"Within an hour," said the Constable, "the snowfall had piled over the tops of my boots. The shadow flitted far ahead beyond the curtain of branches."

My hand began to thrum across several bars. The Constable liberated the cognac bottle from swaddles of linen and dolloped again until our goblets brimmed. The label peeked beneath the Constable's grip, but all I saw was a year, 1928, realizing that the drink's value would surely top months of my salary.

With his knuckles, Snorri rapped a tattoo on the table. "The Cold War. Power, statecraft. Stealth and brinksmanship, spy versus spy. Those were the good old days."

The Constable continued, "My foe fled into the unearthly whiteness. His boot prints appeared and then disappeared on the drifts at inexplicable intervals. Nightfall threatened; no village dared to present itself."

Jerker's cheeks had grown apple-red from the heat of

the hearth, "A tipping point?"

"Yes, patrolman, a tipping point. I released Minne and Tanke to flight, hoping they could locate safety. They raced among the snow-laden trees. Pumping their wings, they then darted up into the blurred immensity overhead. Minne and Tanke had disappeared. I conceded defeat."

The Constable stared fixedly upon an imaginary spot just before the hearth flames. "Then, after what seemed like an anguish-ridden eternity, my loyal ravens returned, black feathers streaking by me, leading me to shelter." The Constable and his bird-guides reached a high hill, which he climbed. At the top was an old, corroded but sturdy metal rod anchored on the top of the rise. The birds slid on their backs down the long slope to the bottom, followed by the Constable. He crept forward, pressing ice-hard arms of the spruce apart, swiftly dug a cave in the deep snow and nestling within, swaddled in his cloak. "Then I slipped into a void of sleep. Outside my shelter, the wind raged throughout the night."

Bergthora snorted. "What happened to the fugitive?"

"His footprints," the Constable said, pausing to let us savor the image. "His footprints had long disappeared."

A tiny, inarticulate bleat of pleasure escaped from Patrolman Jerker's lips.

"No fugitive, no clues. Sounds like failure to me," said Bergthora.

"My saga is not over. Morning came. The storm had passed, and the sun pierced a brilliant blue sky. The snow had been swept away by the storm revealing a structure. I found myself under the eve of a barn. I sheltered within until Minne and Tanke were prepared to lead me back home, which they did two days later with great cunningness."

Jerker laughed and hugged himself, giddy. "That was a magnificent escapade, sir."

Bergthora resumed delivering portions of the loaf to the birds. "If this country's police had been allowed pistols back then, you'd have made short work of that escapee."

Minne and Tanke squawked like disapproving gentry.

The Constable's black lens gleamed up into the rafters. He was striding somewhere very far away from us in the sparkling light of a distant vale on a lost day in a forgotten world. Though I took the Constable's tale to be nothing more than a fabrication, I understood Jerker's excitement. Perhaps it was the Constable's silent laughter or forbearance, as Snorri helped himself to a second brimming portion of cognac. There was something profoundly unreal about the man. I found myself rising to my feet involuntarily, clapping applause. The menagerie of dreams had lifted me—a feeling eerily similar to when I have assembled a worthy song.

"Ah, sir. Like a fairy tale, a poem."

Bergthora stared at the torn clumps of bread.

"Sycophant," she growled at me.

4: Surly Gang

Bergthora suspended the decanter punt-end up over her goblet, drip, drip, drip. Primordial dismay ensued in her when the upturned bottle yielded no more. The sergeant detective shuffled toward the kitchen as discontent churned in the muscles of her back. I heard her clattering around the cabinets for a corkscrew.

Bergthora charged back into the room, laughing harshly. Pinched between her fleshy fingers was a metal cylinder tipped with a nozzle, long and hooked, which she waved about, crowing, "Behold, boys, exhibit one."

Snorri popped his head back, eyelids flattening with scrutiny. "A culinary torch. Perhaps one like the killer used to seal over the dead girl."

The Constable raised his fingertips to his temples and began to massage them slowly. The silver helixes of his hair flashed in the firelight. He then closed his eye, purposefully, as if debating with inner phantoms. He spun on Snorri. "This isn't wagering on a soccer match outcome. Do you want to know the meaning of the girl's costume? We must start the fact-gathering phase of this case. Follow my instructions."

The Constable issued directives rapid-fire, flinging vituperation to every point on the compass. "Snorri, I grant your desire. You will go to the Kvasir Mead Company, the establishment whose label was on the wings, and get what you can there about the victim."

"And you," he thundered at Bergthora. "Go to the immigrant quarter near the docks."

Bergthora slumped.

An agonizing moment persisted until the Constable reached a kind of fragile composure. "Patrolman Jerker, you will go to Grimke to grovel before the magistrate. While you're there, you'll do additional reconnaissance as

I instruct."

The Constable managed to subdue his agitation again, and his dinning diminished our objections.

"Now, all of you get out."

The Constable tugged the sleeve cuffs of his waistcoat. The surly gang gathered overcoats and gloves. At the threshold of the hall, Bergthora's mouth fell open slightly. "Grimke approved this?"

Receiving no answer from the Constable, Bergthora slogged on her heavy coat. Snorri emerged with a large fury hat.

"You look like a Cossack in that thing," said Bergthora.

Ignoring her, Snorri asked, "And you, Constable? What will you do while we're off working?" Under Snorri's arm was tucked the second, unopened bottle of cognac.

Our host suddenly became jovial, even winking at the theft.

"Other duties call. I must assist the king in finding some of his lost love letters. A dire matter of state, and the king, the king is very needy."

I made a sharp intake of breath, "Oh, my. The king."

"Other duties my foot," Bergthora scoffed.

Tanke tipped his head to one side, and Minne bowed and fanned her tail. The Constable flung the door wide and pointed into the black void beyond. Having received no assignment and hoping to escape ahead of the others, I started up, but the Constable pressed his bony fingers on my chest, much to my chagrin.

"You will ride along with the others on every assignment. Continue to take notes."

"Constable?"

"You are a scribe, their scribe, boy, for all of this. Keep a record."

A thick, inexorable silence ensued. Finally, I pierced it with a statement. "Constable, her face, the girl's eyes, her hair. They seem so different for around here."

Once again, the Constable swung down his black lens,

an ax to the block.

"Go, now go, go."

There were the customary terse farewells. Jerker, the last one to depart, clicked his heels the old-fashioned way, still accepted as good manners here in the hinterlands of Fulaflugahål.

I stepped from the darkened door, and the air swirled with a chill mist from the lake. Snorri stood beside his car, exuding an aroma of bargain pipe tobacco and admiring his appropriated bottle of cognac.

We stood there in the carriage breezeway, saying nothing. I thought back to the slides of the victim and saw her face once more in my mind: her freckles, and the white wings, a swan. I tried to piece together some notion of who she was. I imagined her lost from a distant land, trying to get back. A person, a real person, yearning. Was there some greater meaning hidden in the Constable's bedlam? If I could somehow be instrumental in making sense of the death of this forlorn soul, even as a bit-player, I had a duty to do so, did I not? I also knew that if I leaped in, I would be overmatched by the Constable's erratic temperament and consumed at the expense of what truly mattered to me, my music. I, too, would become lost.

"Snorri, did you ever want something that seemed impossible? Something you'd risk even your reputation and be a fool for?"

"You mean, this cognac."

"No. Something meaningful you *do*. Something you would do even on the worst day of your life."

A flame was visible in Snorri's eyes. "I would buy a cheap rail pass and chase the soccer matches all over the continent, penniless, with lots of lagers. Mirth and spectacle. An old man's hopes."

I concurred. "It is 'the beautiful game.'"

"You're never too old for a top-notch derby," Snorri said, then slid into his car, mimed a toast with the unopened bottle then drove away.

5: Small Beer

Climbing in my vehicle, a tumbledown mini, I headed back downhill. The stars pawed their footprints overhead, and hours would lapse before morning. I drove to Fadlan's flat for band practice, pulling to the curb at his flat bloc. I felt oddly upbeat, tapping a spot on my knee in the blue light of the dash. Fadlan played guitar in my band, The Berserkers. He roomed with a dozen of his countrymen in quarters approved for four by council housing. Exhaust simmered from the tailpipe of my mini. I flicked off the engine and mounted the council bloc steps.

When I opened the door, a warm rush met me, a mix of grilled lamb and human sweat. Egil, the lead singer, was already there along with Gudrid, our drummer, the only female member in the group. We practiced at Fadlan's because no neighbors complained about our noise at public flats.

I unhitched my shoulder-strap keyboard, and we got to work. Fadlan banged the strings of his v-body guitar with his palm. Gudrid beat time on a snare as Egil roared meaningless scat vocals to hold a place for real lyrics. Meanwhile, I lay down the song's direction, whirling my key fingers and transcribing what came out, which was my job as the song writer. Undeniably, the work was grueling, and I was surprised I could rise to the effort after that fiendish evening with the Constable.

Gudrid rested her drumsticks. "It sounds like old pensioner music."

Ever pressing at a boundary, Fadlan found a screwdriver someone had left beside the TV set and wedged it beneath the strings of the v-body. I had seen him do this before.

"No screwdriver, please," I said.

"I make a unique sound."

"Punk rockers do that; we are metal. Minor chords.

Eight at most. Fast."

Fadlan was not protesting; he was a craftsman experimenting. Nonetheless, this drew us to an old impasse. I threw my shoulders back. "What kind of people are we?"

Egil grinned, homely as an ogre in a folk tale. "Vikings."

"What kind of band are we?"

Gudrid gave a tribal smack of her sticks. "A heavy-metal band."

"And what kind of heavy-metal band are we?"

Fadlan's pleasure was rich and contagious. "A Viking heavy-metal band."

I spread my arms and intoned the familiar words. "We are metal Vikings. We are The Berserkers." I used this routine to pump up the band whenever we stalled.

Of course, none of us knew what Viking heavy metal music was, other than a backwater that ostensibly suited our mashup of talents. But mashup was what we did best. On stage, we wore helmets and chainmail and bellowed songs about raids, treasure, and dragons. On good nights, we got a cut of the bar.

Fadlan withdrew the screwdriver from the strings. Gudrid pushed her straw cloche hat back off her ears. "Grammaticus, you're practically a metalhead genius, everyone here knows it, but this, um, thing. You are working too hard at the station to focus."

Egil grimaced. "What happened to the old Viking song-writing wonderkid?"

I stared at the blue tendons of my hands. I told them a little about the murder case, but not the things that would get me interrogated by Grimke again. In my mind's eye, I once more saw the corpse on the ice. Snarled rags. The golden blaze of hair. Was I obsessing? I said, "I should quit my job at the precinct."

The flat grew silent. Gudrid swept off her cloche. "That's not what I meant."

Fadlan thumped the thickest string. "If you quit your job, how will we get petrol money to go to the gigs?"

"I must write the music *and* front the money?"

Egil shrugged. "That's the way it's always been."

Fadlan slid his long hand down the neck of his base, revisiting some of the more difficult moments of our song. "I tended bar at the canteen by the dual carriageway. Then, they asked for my work permit, and I no longer tend bar there. Grammaticus, you are skinny and pale, you can get a job anywhere in this country."

I turned to Gudrid.

"No one hires a woman with a record of petty theft and a rap sheet like mine," she moaned. I recalled seeing her file once at work. It was prodigious.

Egil doled out bottled lagers. "Sorry, mate. Anarchist. I shun toiling for the global corporate cabal."

"You would sign a recording contract in a heartbeat, Egil," Gudrid said.

"The drummer girl is right; I can't wait to be compromised," Egil said.

We sipped our lagers and traded notions about lyrics. Gudrid insisted, "We will never win RagnaRock with this song, Grammaticus."

The RagnaRock festival, a song contest celebrating a rogue's gallery of taste and talent from Viking geekdom, had been held every summer for two decades. It was an eddy of dreck that every few years washed up a nugget of golden amber. Sometimes, a lucky band signed with a recording label. Every practice session led one way or another to my impossible hope, winning RagnaRock. Right now, however, I questioned whether I had it in me.

I ordered a break and stepped onto the balcony, where the sky was a mash of rain-clouds. The wind whistled between the nearby buildings; a spring storm loomed. Out there in the wind, stirred in my baroque way by Gudrid's peace-making reproof, I set down some lyrics:

Listen to the darkness
Crackling with fear
In the afterglow
A silver tear—

> *Small beer*
> *Small beer*

You leap to reach
But miss the hitch
And dangle there
A cosmic-jest
A fool at rest

> *Small beer*
> *La, la, la*
> *oo-loo-looo-laaaa-loo…*

Listen to the darkness
Whisper in your ear
Hum and sing
Laugh and cling
Let me dry that tear
That silver tear
My dear.

> *Small beer*
> *Small beer*
> *La, la, la*
> *oo-loo-looo-laaaa-loo…*

Upon returning indoors, I passed a second sheaf among my mates. I had added a melody and set it drifting above the commotion. I put my finger on the paper to show an F# held for twenty-three seconds.

"Twenty-three seconds?" said Fadlan.

"Twenty-three. Piercing, a raid on chaos, then peace and

serenity. Sunlight falling through the storm clouds."

Fadlan pumped his lithe brown arms. "Who are you? Benne Anderson? Ingwe Malmqvist?"

Egil stuck his tongue in the gap in his grin once tenanted by a tooth. "I don't see a Viking theme."

Fadlan occupied himself with a minute abrasion on a tuning post. He was visibly holding out. "The quickest way to a cool guitar riff is a nasty, brutish distortion. It's all in the timbre."

I resumed my finger-dance on the keyboard.

Gudrid sighed. "I still don't know, Grammaticus."

"There's lots of Viking in this song; I'll work on it," I assured them.

"It isn't just songwriting. We need to get a better crowd than a tavern full of farmhands screaming 'play Dancing Queen.' Remember our last gig, in front of six Belgian people who nodded their heads in silence and drank sparkling water?"

"Every band starts somewhere."

"Somewhere for too long becomes nowhere. Is RangaRock still the prize? What do you want from this band, Grammaticus, and our music?"

My mates waited for a reply; I felt a heavy torpor building.

I said, "Viking metal is a constantly shimmering landscape. Tricks, alluring sound. The audience wants to be led to a magical place. A loud, raucous, magical place."

I wondered if I had made them a little too hungry for the win, but my reply seemed to hold them at bay. Egil swung his slaty voice into my lyrics with touchy compliance, a honeyed syncopation against our instruments' velocity. The music burst into life, bizarre and beautiful, but oddness lingered about the practice, a vibe. Something ugly was drifting close.

Then, with absolutely no warning, the image of the dead girl intruded on my thoughts again, further disrupting the song, the fluttering feathers, and the ripe ruined lips. As if in a dream, I saw her rise from the lake ice and glide overhead, drifting toward the blue line of the far mountains.

6: The Wolf Gallery of Abbe Laurent

The next morning, I anticipated a hounding from the Constable as I entered the precinct house. His face was lusterless under the lights, yet I was drawn into the labyrinth of his gaze. I braced myself. Then, Jerker thumped me on my back with an open hand.

"Hello, buddy. You're just in time. We've got a great big day ahead. We begin the research today."

My voice rose a quarter-tone, "The research?"

"Footwork, digging, boy." The Constable swept between us with a deep, tragic grunt. He turned to the patrolman. The patrolman's lower lip jutted out.

"You will oversee the clerk."

"With an eagle eye," said Jerker.

I cringed, making a faint attempt to retreat toward my post at the records window. Almost as in a dance-like movement, the Constable pulled me back and pressed something into my shirt pocket. I reached to see what it was, but he stayed my gesture. The Constable said, "You have two objectives while you are in Grimke. First, see the magistrate and grovel. Second, go to the Fashion Institute."

Jerker's face darkened. "I do understand groveling," he replied, "but I do not understand the visit to the Fashion Institute."

"You will when you get there, or I hope you will. I have given a relevant artifact to the records clerk. The initial address you are seeking is 94 Linköping."

"Ja, 94 Linköping," Jerker echoed back.

The Constable followed with another item immediately, thrusting a moleskin notebook beneath my arm, his good eye fixed on me. "Kolbitter, this is for your research. Show the librarian the article in your pocket as well. Take notes."

He flushed with an air of mild exultation. "Perhaps this way, you can even redeem yourself, boy."

Jerker bounced down the precinct steps ahead of me. I was glad to be out of Fulaflugahål. The gray iron columns of the train station fell away, and the rails clapped beneath us. Jerker clung to a folio of images he had prepared when Snorri found the victim in the ice. Meanwhile, I peeked in my shirt pocket. The same tuft of wolf fur the Constable had dropped in my palm so long ago was snuggly tucked inside.

þ

As we negotiated our way on the Interregional Express to coach seats, Jerker said, "Why don't you want to help the investigation, Grammaticus?"

"And be the Constable's whipping boy?"

Jerker settled on a bench, conspicuous in his azure uniform. "The girl in the ice, no one deserves to die like that."

"No, never."

"It is like a duty to help."

"The Constable can appeal to other districts for backup."

Jerker snorted in a tone that hinted of a melancholy he did not himself possess. I wondered if he was merely trying the words on for size when he said, "Nordic bureaucracy is the only thing slower than a Nordic winter."

"You have been listening to Bergthora too much," I said.

We occupied the compartment with a dozen other passengers, yet no one troubled us until the ticket agent approached. I looked up at the agent's stiff cylindrical cap trimmed with silver piping and a mustache that might well have been stenciled upon his lip. "Ticket."

I slipped my fingers in my pockets. The agent stared down at me gravely. I continued to rifle through my clothes, jacket, shirt, trousers, all of it, before offering a plaintive smile. My pockets were unaccountably empty.

Jerker, who was not asked for a ticket, made no effort to assist me. He stared out the window as if engrossed in the scenery.

Two elderly female passengers on the bench whose headrest I had been tapping joined in the scrutiny. "Rather shaggy, he looks," said one, laying her spotted wrists upon the head of her standing cane. She gave the cane a little flick and let it clatter in the aisle. "Officer, please get that cane for me."

Jerker retrieved it with a smile.

"Officer, is that boy with the skinny arms on the police force?"

"He is a clerk, madam, an administrator, not an officer," Jerker said. Seemingly as an afterthought, he added, "He is also not trained for forensic duties."

"He looks like a delinquent who jumps the station turnstile to avoid a fare."

Her companion redoubled her frown. "He is, I scarcely know how to say it, he is…"

"Frightful."

"At least."

"Ghastly."

"That term gets closer to the mark."

"Pathetic."

"You've nailed it."

Jerker leaned back on his bench seat. He leveled his gaze, "Is that true that you jump the rail to avoid paying the fare, Grammaticus? That is illegal, you know." Jerker turned and shrugged to the ladies as if to say, "Do you see what I have to work with?"

The woman pointed the tip of her cane at my ankle. "There it is, you fool."

I saw the curl of paper lodged between the top of my canvas shoe and sock where it had fallen and become stuck sometime after I had laid down my coins. The ticketing agent studied the printed stub, produced a penlight, and shone a purple beam on the paper. Finally, he held the ticket aloft, and scratched it with his nail.

"I can buy a new one," I offered.

"Why?" he asked sharply, punched my ticket, and passed into the snaking body of the vehicle.

Jerker nodded to me in a way that suggested I had passed a grave trial. Then, he added, "Grammaticus, perhaps you should stay away from this investigation. You are, after all, not a police officer."

I curled to my end of the bench. The track rhythm was muffled and pleasant, and I fell under its trance. The train never seemed to alter speed or jar. The juniper along the shores of Lake Munch gave way to birch and elms as we ascended into the hills, my narrow face and black hair reflected in the glass. I saw in the reflection Jerker had turned to peek into his binder of photographs. When he rummaged through the last few images of the girl—her bloodless face, the swelling wings—he squashed his fists down to flatten the cover closed.

As we journeyed on, the patrolman drank cup after cup of strong black coffee. I purchased vending machine icing buns whose paper wrappers Jerker read meticulously before discarding. About halfway to our destination, the train slowed, maneuvering through a set of municipal junctions.

"What is that?" I asked.

To the west of the tracks emerged a high-barred fence that enclosed a ferroconcrete mass of many barriers and parapets and a lawn of asphalt, lined with guards in black uniforms, black weapons at their sides. The blades of a helicopter bowed over the tarmac like the wings of a dragonfly. A nebulous tension began to consume me as we rounded the embankment, our rail car creeping by the fearsome building. I felt as if we were in a small trawler peering up the bow of an icebreaker, bearing down upon us.

"The Grimke penal facility." Jerker circled the pad of his thumb upon the portfolio cover, nervous.

To my relief, we sped on. In another ninety minutes, the sound of the tracks changed. Metal wheels began whirring as they adjusted speed. The rail cars clip-clopped over bridges along the estuaries and canals surrounding the great metropolis of Grimke. Mist over the estuaries thinned in the sun, and the passengers of our compartment shook off the drowsy sheath of the morning.

"What a handsome city, there's no place like Grimke," Jerker crowed.

As I stepped from the car into the central city station's bright mall, the elderly woman with the witchy fingers hobbled to my side. "You're lucky that agent did not have this patrolman arrest you and toss you out to the dogs at Grimke. Hiding your ticket in your shoe."

Her cloudy eyes searched my face for yet more damning truths.

þ

Nearly half an hour passed as we meandered away on foot from the station. Our destination, a crumbling old edifice, always loomed within our sight though we could not seem to locate the road that would take us directly to it. Finally, we stumbled into a small open square. Marveling at the ornate pediments and prim black spire, Jerker mounted the steps of a nearby building.

"Look," he cried, pointing to the carven lettering of the stone.

We had arrived at the Ministry of the Chancellor of Justice to report for the inquiry.

The visitors' booth guard was a young woman with cropped pink hair and bulging muscles in her jaw. Jerker explained that we were reporting for a hearing. The agent stared at Jerker's hands on the sill; the patrolman removed them. She then requested the summons. Jerker surrendered the envelope the Constable had sealed at our departure, and the agent instantly broke the seal. She worked the ribbon of muscle in her jaw. Flashing an ultraviolet light on the pages, the agent ticked various places on the paper with a pen and then asked for Jerker's identification. Finally, she asked for mine, which underwent even greater scrutiny. Next, the guard returned to the forms and ran the purple beam over them before flipping to see the papers' blank backsides. She reviewed the blank sides with as much care as the printed.

Seven minutes passed; the agent's examination wore on. She let her shoulders slump, suggestive of disappointment until, at last, she looked up.

"Is this a joke?"

Jerker leaned forward, puzzled.

"No joke at all," he insisted and explained the envelope contained a summons from the Ministry of the Chancellor of Justice. "We have a hearing inside."

After a frozen moment, the attendant said, "No, you don't."

"Why not?"

"You have the wrong 94 Linköping; the forms say you were to report to 94 Linköping Gate. This location is 94 Linköping Avenue."

Jerker examined the clutch of forms and murmured, "Perhaps there is that little bit of a difference."

"No *perhaps*."

The guard drew from beneath her window a directory disclosing a government building in another neighborhood far to the north. Jerker frowned. "Must be a typographical error, ma'am. But we must accept it, the halls of justice at Grimke are great indeed."

"You must go to the designated 94 Linköping, typographical error or not."

The attendant next produced a paper map and showed the destination. She advised us to hurry. Jerker was unable to reach the Constable at his mobile or landline; neither could he get hold of Bergthora. We rushed back to the depot to catch the departing connection. Our rail car jockeyed north over ash-stained tracks past grey box buildings.

Fortunately, our humiliation had evoked the pity of the pink-haired guard, and a squad car from the local precinct met us at the platform. The officer at the wheel gave a moue of discomfort at our strange accents.

"Strangers, eh?" He asked if we meant 94 Linköping Road. Jerker repeated the address and frowned: we would miss the appointment if we dallied. The location at which the squad car let us off was a small municipal park building on the furthest outskirts of the city. Cakes of mud flipped from the tires of the departing vehicle.

Jerker assessed the empty building, arms folded over his chest. The hills behind the structure were shaped like haystacks and rose to the height of seven or eight men. Jerker read aloud the sign on the door to confirm the address. In the bland perkiness of Scandinavian tourism prose, the sign informed inquirers that the knolls in the back were once not only the sacred burial ground of an ancient Norse tribe; the site was also used for human sacrifice.

"I don't think this is the place either," said Jerker

The sign also indicated the building would not be open for several weeks.

Jerker kicked rocks at the building. Without a ride, we took to our heels, and the hillocks of 94 Linköping Road receded behind us. We trudged the mile back to the platform and boarded the return train to Grimke.

I fingered the torn seal on the envelope as a band of vermillion light crept across the sky. "What will happen to us now that we have missed the inquiry, Jerker?"

Jerker smiled at the trees sweeping by. "Ja, my friend. It's probably another nail in the coffin of our backward little outpost."

Ahead lay the second part of our assignment, the visit to the Fashion Institute.

þ

The Institute was wearily far from the central depot. Our footfalls echoed through the marble entry of an edifice that housed a library, as evident from the stacks and high ceiling. A Librarian wound from behind a tall oval bookshelf to greet us. Jerker laid out to her the Constable's instructions and the significance of identifying the fur's meaning, rounding up with a doleful rumination of the un-Scandinavian-ness of incorrect paperwork.

The Librarian's cheeks pinked at the mention of the Constable, seemingly recalling an old fondness. "I have provided him intelligence on several cases. His list of exploits is grand indeed. And his ravens, Minsk and Tannin."

"Minne and Tanke," said Jerker.

"Delightful names," affirmed the Librarian.

I fished the scrap of wolf pelt from my pocket. "The victim is a woman of undetermined, perhaps foreign origin. Dead, buried in the winter ice."

"This sample came from what she was wearing?"

"The Constable found it nearby on the ice."

"He assumes it has to do with the dead woman?"

"Evidently."

The Librarian donned a pair of white examination gloves and pressed a jeweler's loupe to her eye. She inspected the remnant of wolf fur from every angle. "There is glue on one side, cheap as flour paste, might as well hang wallpaper with it." Her attention was now drawn to the portfolio Jerker was holding.

"And what is in that binder?"

"Pictures of the victim," said the patrolman.

"Dreadful. Not for me," the Librarian replied, then whirled on her heels and clicked into a vault beyond the ring of books.

Setting the portfolio of photos on the counter, Jerker stuck his thumbs into his belt and waited. "Such complexity," he said.

The Librarian returned, gripping a cart she wheeled to the center of the room. Atop the cart rested a colossal book, three feet tall and nearly as wide, its water-warped binding exposing ribs of cloth and vellum. The pages' edges were ripe with flocking, blistered with age, yet the miraculous prints within were unharmed. Jerker's mouth gaped. "I have never seen a book so big."

"A double-elephant," she said. "The printer's term. Perhaps it will yield clues the Constable is seeking."

On its cover, the title: *The Wolf Gallery of Abbe Laurent*. The Librarian swung the binding open. The volume was filled with delicate stippled watercolors so artful they might have passed for botanical or ornithological prints. They were neither. The theme of the collection, she explained, was wolf fur in Scandinavian clothing. Image after image swept by, casting back through time, from Greta Garbo in stoles to nineteenth-century industrial moguls in fur-collared greatcoats. Next came the silk court suits of the seventh-century lords trimmed in canine pelts, back finally to hide-wrapped peasants in turf huts. The fabulous prints formed a delicate archipelago to a lost world.

The Librarian's eyes gleamed. "Hand-colored engravings majestic in artistry and dedication. This massive folio is by an obscure figure, the Abbe Laurent, a theatrical costume designer by trade. He was a negligible man who had apprenticed himself to the great dramatist Strindberg." The Librarian inhaled, a swelling pause, then she released her breath. "Negligible, that is until the master grew too autocratic."

Jerker drank in her words. "I have just heard such a thing about this Strindberg fellow. Too depressing. I like comedies."

"Perfect," said the Librarian. Her voice shifted timbres. "Onward with the tale, gentlemen. Laurent, the sad acolyte, humiliated by one browbeating too many, dedicated himself to the existence of a monk. In a paroxysm of rebellion, he secluded himself in a monastery on a distant hill, ate porridge, and chanted matins."

"What a star-crossed soul," said the patrolman.

"A decade of exile could not assuage the man's yearning. One night, he snuck back to the hall of the Royal Dramatic Company. Among the pews, he chanced upon a young actress in prayer over her lines. She said her name was Miss Gustafson. The young actress schooled the fugitive monk in the natural dramaturgy of life. Forget the diatribes of Strindberg, she counseled; a great actor must watch as much for the unspoken as the spoken. Silence is expressive."

The Librarian's voice rose and fell in lulling cadences as she told of how Abbe Laurent plunged madly in love with the girl. Yet he was an ugly and poor monk forbidden carnal wisdom. His eyes drank in her stage costume. He studied her supple bare shoulders, the dimple of her collarbone, the urgent pulse of her décolletage beneath a plush fur stole. Shame ushered the broken man back to the monastery, where he spent the following year sequestering with his dark icons, turning every mote of his will, his discerning eye, his precise hand, his lust, and his abandoned hope, to his engravings. In them, he was able to trace the history of the wolf pelt through the centuries of wild habiliments, simple, brutal, elegant, commencing with the soaring portraits of Miss Gustafson. The prints swept back from the sophisticated beauty of contemporary outerwear to the prison-less incarceration of the village serf, telling the story of the epic cloak of the Norse people. When the Abbe emerged again from his seclusion, willing to offer his gifts at beauty's feet, he faced a craven horror he could not fathom—modernity.

Posted on the side of the Royal Dramatic Company theater wall, he saw a lurid poster for a film featuring the young actress with whom he was in love. Appalled, he shrunk back. She had changed her name to Greta Garbo.

Pained beyond measure, Abbe Laurent threw himself in the icy river, his corpse never to surface.

"Garbo drove many a man crazy with desire," the Librarian chuckled.

Jerker sighed, "What an ordeal, so melancholic and exquisite."

The Librarian smiled wanly. "That was the melodrama, now for the science." She showed the spine of an accompanying monograph, tiny by comparison and slim as a book of poetry. Pewter letters were printed on it: *Appendix to the Wolf Gallery of Abbe Laurent*, by (name unreadable). Her gaze grew pinched. "We are unaware of who wrote the Appendix, penned in the nineteen twenties as an adjunct to Abbe Laurent's classic posthumous publication. The Appendix is a masterpiece, too, falling somewhere between criminal forensics and dramaturgy. The author was likely a high-level investigator, one who had turned against the ministry's bureaucrats."

The Librarian swept her hair off her face, head bowed into the semicircle of light seeming to pour from the book. She read from the text, the words a liturgy:

> *Con men and hucksters use fashion to deceive, firefighters and doctors, to demarcate refuge and healing. Fashion signifies. Hence, our fascinations with the wolf pelt. The beast evokes the essence of our nation. Familiar, strange, stealthy, loudly baying. A wolf is a friend who frightens, a dog before it was a dog. Theatrical costumes that feature wolf pelts always have an enormous influence on the audience, clothing to adore, and to fear.*

The Librarian turned the massive illustrations. While each print held its beauties and terrors, the last image was of a savage man bound in the hide of a wolf, thrashing with rage. Carrying a bronze sword, he was ready for battle, poised to cast himself upon his foe, his teeth clenching the edge of his wooden shield.

"This last image is remarkable," the Librarian interpreted in a low voice. "He is a berskerker, a Viking warrior who put himself into a frenzied trance when entering battle. Scholars say the sacred state gave him superhuman strength."

"Battle fury, a kind of spiritual transportation," I said.

"Ah, you know something about the subject."

I put my hand close to the velum, careful not to touch it, and whispered, "I'm in a band called The Berserkers because, you know, our music is crazy fun."

Her reply was loud, "Oh, my."

I cringed. "There are good berserkers and bad berserkers. We are the good kind."

"The good kind?"

I stiffened and raised my voice, before Jerker became suspicious, "Perhaps this image gave the Abbe courage to cast himself into the river."

A dark looked crossed the Librarian's face though she continued to fan the pages without a break in her movements. And then, the woman uttered the last phrases of the volume: "*Is it release from the intoxication of violence and the flight toward redemption that characterizes our souls? Or an eternal return to thickening rage in a twilight of fear?*"

The Librarian lowered the cover shut. "The good kind is exceedingly rare," she concluded.

Exhausted, apparently, by the ardor reading had spurred in her, she sank into a tall chair beside the cart. She admonished Jerker that fashion indeed signifies, a scrap of wolf pelt was profoundly significant to the case—but, unfortunately, her resources were exhausted, and she could be of no further help. She wished the gentlemen of the Fulaflugahål precinct good luck.

Jerker inquired whether the Librarian could share more

details about flour paste, but the woman merely tossed her cotton gloves on the cart and gave no further on the point.

þ

Jerker rounded the cobbled streets of the old medieval section of Grimke on our way back to the train platform, black spidery waterspouts leaping down high walls, iron lamps thrust over the alleys. I thought nothing could have been stranger than our trip today. Was it even worth it for me to return to the precinct? Could I not make money another way to fund the band?

And what of the victim? How could I refuse to help find justice for her?

Jerker seemed to give partial voice to my thoughts. The patrolman confided he dreaded reporting that we had failed to make the inquiry. "Hours wasted; public funds chucked into the gutter."

I said, "Everything just gets stranger and stranger with this case."

"So unfortunate, Grammaticus. It would be much better if you could just find the killers and get into a knife fight with them or something. Frontier justice, like the movies."

"A knife fight?"

"Idle thoughts." His eyes lit up. "We could test the theory of the three pokes with a long skinny knife."

"Fact gathering?" I asked, and plunged my hands deep in my pockets and commenced a chord sequence.

The Interregional Express departed the depot once more, smoothly overcoming its inertia and advancing at a liquid pace. We sat staring at the threshing darkness. Jerker observed that Grimke was an old and complex city; the mix up was both understandable and, likely, unavoidable. Nordic cities were encrusted with strange grottoes and blind alleys where anyone might get lost.

"What the devil," Jerker exhaled at length. "Life is full of oddities."

7: Kvasir's Mead

Two days after that turbulent visit to Grimke, we ventured out again on assignment. Time seemed to move according to the Constable's inner clock's fickle mechanism, inscrutable to everyone but him.

Bergthora, Snorri, and I had arrived at the *Kvasir Mead Company*—the establishment indicated by the Constable—a few kilometers outside Fulaflugahål. Bergthora and Snorri sat in the front seat of our brand-new precinct sedan. I occupied the unlocked cage in the back. The noonday sun peeked around the company billboard's edges, a ten-meter-tall female figure towered over the car park. She was a majestic logo. Wings sprang from her helmet, leather guards covered her wrists, and a steel corset curved downward from cleavage to hips. She gleefully offered mead in a ram's horn to the sparse traffic.

Snorri clucked his approval. "Now, there's a lady to work up your thirst."

I noted the billboard in my moleskin notebook. Then I said to my companions, "A Valkyrie, like the victim in the lake."

Bergthora twisted around from the wheel to glower at me. "You're here to take notes. No opinions, no interpretations. Notes only." She parted her mouth as if to smile, a somewhat disquieting look for her, before slipping her fingers through the wire mesh separating us. "At some point, I'm going to report this to Grimke. Him, you, all of it."

I avoided looking into Bergthora's eyes. Through the sealed doors of the vehicle, I could smell the thawing springtime soil and hear birds chirping new tunes. Snorri turned toward me. "You know what I'd have done if Bergthora poked her digits at me through the wire, Grammaticus?"

I thumbed the seat strap.

"A broken finger would make it more difficult for a sergeant detective to pick her nose on the job," said Snorri.

Bergthora retracted her hands from the mesh. "Grimke will want to know about a physical threat to a senior officer as well."

The sedan doors clopped closed behind us. Snorri squinted up at the thighs of the soaring Valkyrie again. "There's certainly some fine artistry in that thing."

"A miracle of marketing," Bergthora snapped.

The Kvasir Mead Company was a flat industrial blockhouse, its entrance door wedged between the Valkyrie's ankles. Snorri plunged through first. Bergthora shouldered past me, the sleeves of her jacket flashing like the pelt of a seal slipping beneath an ice floe.

We descended to a bunker with no windows or natural light. The air was a fug with odors that blended the familiar and the strange—pipe tobacco and wormwood, dried fish, and bog myrtle—scents of long seclusion. Stacks of cardboard boxes cluttered the floor, with empty drinking bottles here and there crowning a slapdash column. My heart leaped as something small and hard zipped past my ear. Snorri swatted at it but caught nothing. The furious unseen bug simply circled back to menace us again.

Another voice cut the darkness. "It's a bee. Stop swatting at it, or you'll invite a sting."

"Well, well, well," said Bergthora on a descending scale. "Sending the attack bees when we haven't been introduced?"

The sergeant detective had spotted the older woman first seated at a counter among the bottles and crates. Her skin was coppery and burnished, while her nose and brow formed a ridge over which her tall red cap dangled like the runner of an overturned sleigh. Despite being old, her hair was still black with thick side-braids, bangs cut straight across. She was seated on a stool at a glass counter, the wall behind her covered with animal hides. A rope of smoke looped up from her bone-stemmed pipe.

The woman said, "What do you want, Boss?"

Bergthora rocked back and forth on the balls of her feet. "The sign outside says Kvasir Mead Company."

"It sure does, Boss." The little woman popped a ring of smoke from her mouth.

The sergeant detective waved at the pipe smoke that seemed to want to worm up her nose. She cleared her throat. "We are here on behalf of the Fulaflugahål police. I certainly am anyway. The name of this establishment appeared on an article of clothing found at a crime scene. We are looking for a proprietor. Are you the proprietor, Mrs. Kvasir?"

The little witch cackled. "Mrs. Kvasir. Really? Don't you read no books?" Her eyelids hinted at an interior fold, like the girl in the lake. A pique of amusement shook her frame. She turned to me and stuck her left thumb across at Bergthora. "Boss is really a sergeant detective? Let me clear this up."

The little woman handed me a bottle, rolling it to expose the back label before instructing me to read the print aloud. I complied:

> *The wisest man that ever lived was Kvasir. No one could pose a question to him for which he did not have an excellent response. His reputation grew as he travelled the world, dispensing wisdom. One day, a pair of grudging dwarves coaxed Kvasir into their home. They slew Kvasir and used his blood to make mead and distilled into it all of Kvasir's wisdom. Anyone who drank of it would become either a sage or a poet.*

The woman was rocking on her stool, savoring her moment. A bee landed on her cheek and traipsed in figure eights, undisturbed by the woman. "That's a Viking legend about the origin of poetry. Marvelous, don't you think?"

Bergthora's mouth had fallen partially open, and I saw her press the tip of her tongue against her incisors. "You're telling me you make mead with human blood? I'm not here for fairy tales."

"Lordy, no. My daughter chose that story from a Viking book called…hum. What was it called?"

I pointed to the bottom of the label where the source of the tale was identified. I began to feel secret respect for the tiny woman. She read the words at my fingertip. "That bit is from a book called *The Edda*. Mead brings wisdom. Mead warms the heart and tongue; it is for telling stories. And blood is in the recipe of any good story.*"

Fetching a pouch from a pocket in her skirt, the crone packed a fresh wad of tobacco into her pipe, pursed her mouth around the stem, and lit, drawing fully. "Figuratively speaking, of course. That's just a roundabout way for me to say I ain't Mrs. Kvasir. Surely, no such person ever existed."

Bergthora slapped a loose strip of hair back in place on her scalp. "Obstruction of justice is a crime in this country. Are you familiar with the laws of our country?"

Possibly Berthora's threat pushed the woman over an edge. Possibly the interrogation was more fraught for the crone than she let on. Or possibly, the tactic was merely an excuse, a prelude to greater upheaval, but what came next was a blur to me. The old woman tilted her head to the side, and a look of anguish overcame her. The bee on her cheek suddenly flew off. Her pipe clattered to the floor and tobacco sparks lit the gloom

"Aud! Aud!" the little witch shrieked.

There came a tormented bellowing from some hall or room beyond the one I was in, footsteps pounding like a beast dashing toward us, summoned by the call. The wood door behind the counter burst open. Bergthora jumped behind a stack of crates, crouching for protection. Snorri dove into the shadows, too, lost from my sight.

Into the gap stepped the largest person I had ever seen,

over seven feet tall, dressed in the canvas suit and netted helmet of a beekeeper, laboring to pass under the jam. In a considerable fluting contralto, the creature roared, "I will save you, Mother!"

I could tell it was a girl by the voice, although I'd never heard the voice of a giant. The top of her helmet touched the ceiling. The fine cross-hatching of the veil obscured her face. Bees began to pour through the shattered door opening, too, dozens of them circling near the ceiling. She grabbed a cardboard box from a tilting pile and flung it against the wall, where it burst into a shower of brewing spices.

The sergeant detective stiffened for the impending assault. However, no drubbing came. In a whoosh of crumpling canvas, the huge young woman clutched at her chest, reeled, and toppled to the floor. Her colossal voice diminished to a squeak.

"My heart," she whimpered.

I gawped at the strange theater. Bergthora stepped from behind the bottle crates. With a snatch, she swept the netting from the helmet. Now, it was as if this sergeant detective were the curator of a waxworks unveiling a melting disaster: the face behind the mesh was that of a teenager, exaggerated by the long jaw and high-arched cheeks of gigantism, skin flecked with flushed red spots.

As I edged nearer to her, my toe bumped against something soft on the floor. Snorri was lying on the concrete, an arms-length from the would-be assailant.

"The big girl is, okay?" he asked.

"It seems so," I said.

The little woman knelt beside the girl, patting her immense arm. The giantess's smile was cadaverous. The broad flesh of her lips and dark, sad eyes made me think of the eyes of a horse. Staring at the prone giantess but addressing Snorri, the crone said, "This is my daughter, Aud."

Aud's mother had recovered her pipe and was turning it

over to look for fractures. "My girl has a curse," she stage-whispered to me. "A giantess's bones don't know when to stop growing, and her internal organs don't like it. In the legends, giants live forever. In this world, however, they depart too soon."

A new match flared. The old woman sucked in the smoke and grew calm. Aud rolled to her back on the concrete, wrists falling to her chest. Her mother's lament, it seemed, was all too familiar.

Snorri, now lying on his left side, propped his head in his palm. He seemed to take the lead now, without Bergthora objecting. With his right hand, Snorri retrieved photos from his pocket; images Jerker had captured.

Aud's cheeks grew blotchy as she began to cry. She pointed to the feathered harness and confirmed the costume was of a Valkyrie, "Her name was Misty."

"Did she have a last name?"

"She never told me. I knew her only as Misty."

"Where was she from?"

"Some days she was from the north, some days from the south. Once she was from the east. The story always changed, but friendship requires no origin papers. I liked to think she was from Elfland." Aud ran her finger along the edges of the photos. "Misty wore that costume when giving out samples of mead at the Fulaflugahål bars."

The crone interjected, "The costume was ours, a gimmick, you see, for attention."

One corner of Bergthora's mouth flattened, and she interjected, "Miserable Viking kitsch. You can thank Wagner for those horned helmets and tin braziers. You're saying you knew the victim and didn't report the relationship?"

The little crone cradled the pipe in her hand. "Saw the headline in the paper. Said to my girl, trouble there, let the law come to us." She sat back on her stool, listening to her daughter and blowing out occasional plumes of smoke.

Aud continued, "She was a waif who had strayed far

from her homeland, and my heart went out. She was intensely shy and nervous, a person to whom self-confidence does not come easily. She seemed fearful of saying too much. It seemed her mother was from some distant seaside district, and her father had been a deckhand who vanished into a gale."

Here the interview seemed to drift in a mystical direction. The giantess said, "I will try to give you a sense of what I mean. I am deformed; I am grotesque. She befriended me immediately. There are few people other than my dear mother who show affection toward me without expectations. She was the rare type whose outer beauty reflects vast inner beauty. She hardly talked and wore no makeup that I could detect. Freckles. In the sunshine, her skin dazzled. Her lips were full. Her eyes shone like silver shadows, always glancing sideways at me over a timid smile. I had the impression of a carving or an abstraction. And like a great work of art, the first layer revealed another and then yet another. In her, I saw a million-billion people, multitude upon multitude of other souls. Imagine a point that contains all points. In her, her glory, I saw everything, all space, all time, all splendors."

"You got all that from a face?" asked Bergthora.

"More or less."

Snorri and I held each other's gaze. Snorri said, "A universe in a grain of sand."

"She has a deep spirit," I agreed.

Aud swept her hand from her head to her feet as if she were an aristocrat reclining on a divan. "I am vulnerable to the natural cruelties of the flesh. I am acutely aware of the human form. I am a monster."

Her mother said, "The flesh; this is what makes you forlorn."

"I spend my time in the shadow of this truth: I must love my friends now or never, for I shall not be on this earth as long as others. Invariably, every human soul grows dearer to me and more beautiful every day."

Snorri said, "Your friend was killed brutally. She was stabbed and frozen in the ice. What or whom was she running from?"

"The poor girl never quite fit in at home, yet fared little better in Fulaflugahål. She fell in with a bad crowd."

"Who?"

"The Thorstein brothers."

"Who are they?"

"Men who frequent a local disco. Men who pimp for a nearby brothel," Aud snorted. "They came looking for her not a week after she started with us. One of them was bald with a wild black beard cut straight at the bottom. The other was spiky-haired and wore a two-toned suit."

"And how did they know to come here?"

"They must have gotten our name from our drink samples, the samples she dispensed at bars, and our location from her costume."

"Now for the costume," said Snorri. "The harness was made of some kind of special woven leather?"

Aud said, "Leather from the boiled skins of unborn reindeer, tanned with spruce bark."

The mother interjected, "It's one of the fine arts of my tribe, love."

My eyes traveled to the hides on the wall. Bergthora frowned as if her darkest suspicions had been confirmed. "Horrible tradition."

Aud said she'd heard stories about the Thorsteins. There had been a fight in a pub and they had beaten a man and crushed his larynx with a beer stein. "They are obsessed with violence," said Aud.

"Anything else? Anything distinctive about them?"

"I've heard they are fond of wolf fur. The black-bearded one lined his boots with the stuff. The two-tone trimmed the lapel of his suit with a downy black pelt."

"A bit flashy for hooligans," said Bergthora.

"Wolf fur in garments goes back centuries," I remarked. Bergthora's eyes went icy. "No one asked for your opinion."

Aud contemplated the blue smoke from her mother's pipe as if she was reading fate in its whorls. "The brothel. The building of flats on the other side of the river near the train station."

Bergthora shared a knowing nod with Snorri. "That place doesn't fool anyone, although I recognize, of course, it's not meant to fool the paying clientele."

Snorri said to the giantess, "Why would she go there?"

Bergthora said, "No documents, no questions. A girl can make money fast."

Long silver drops slid down Aud's cheeks, with mucus pooling on her upper lip. Snorri sprung from the floor and offered his hand to the giantess. After several attempts, Aud was standing again.

Once on his feet, too, Snorri took to sharing puffs on her mother's pipe. The sergeant detective grimaced irritably. Aud continued, "In January, Misty stopped showing up to get her bottles and her pay. She disappeared along with the wings."

"What did you do when you didn't see her at the designated hour?"

The mother answered, shivering slightly. "I figured she had moved on. People do that, especially if you pay cash wages. Nothing I could do." Then, she wailed and swung an octave above her speaking voice, full of regret. "Ooooohhhh! I put the waif in a girly costume to boost sales. So now I have become an accomplice to those pimps, no better than a whoremonger."

Bergthora drew back her lips. She said, "Dispensing mead samples was surely better for this girl than her starving in the ice fields of her home."

Aud's tiny mother ignored the sergeant detective and leaned her head against her daughter's high hip.

I realized now that when we stopped talking, there was a silence that had not been there earlier. The bees drifted up into the pipe haze, shell-like bodies clacking.

To relieve the pressure, I said, "I didn't know it was possible to raise bees indoors."

The giantess stroked her mother's hair. "Mead requires honey. The environment of a building is not very different from a cave, and bees are okay with it."

"We were instructed to get essential information. This chatter is not *that*," Bergthora reproached.

I said, "It was a riddle to me. I was just…"

"The law doesn't like riddles. The law likes facts," Bergthora shot back.

Aud tapped the top of my scalp to get my attention. I gazed up the pillar of her flesh. "Your Boss does not understand that riddles contain their solutions. That is old wisdom. Riddles are good for the soul."

The pompom on the little crone's cap shivered. She turned her back to us, raised her hands to the ceiling, and dashed her pipe this way and that as if it was a magic wand. She seemed to address the bees. Her voice rose in a rhythmic chant, muttering words indistinct to my ears. I could not say whether her flying arms and theatrics excited the swarm or if there was real sorcery in her charm. The insects were roused and made such a din that the sergeant detective could not speak over them. They began to swoop and strike. Bergthora threw her jacket over her head like a cape and raced out the door. Snorri followed behind her. Meanwhile, compelled by what manners I do not know, I touched my hands together and bowed.

"Goodbye!" I called, chased by the swarm.

Behind me in the door between the ankles of the Valkyrie, the giantess emerged, her face veiled in bees.

"Farewell, brave thane," echoed her contralto.

Back in the car, Snorri said, "The big girl is impressive but why does she speak in that peculiar way?"

I pressed my fingertips through the separating cage. Bergthora bit the end of a cigarillo. "Reading too many graphic novels, I'd say."

8: Nils the Fat Boy

The warmth was beginning to stir the air with the promise of spring even as we continued to herd case details for the Constable. A week after the mead brewery, my next assignment from him was to accompany Bergthora to certain haunts on an industrial stretch of lakefront. It was the first time I had seen the sergeant detective since we fled the mead hall.

I asked, "What did you make of the bees attacking us? Was her incantation magic, or was it just her flaying arms and shouting that excited the swarm?"

Bergthora's gaze remained fixed on our destination. "Doesn't matter. I'm just glad that dwarf Snorri Sturlusson is not tagging along today."

We had come to the last grey tenement wedged among the concrete marshes and stood beneath a weathered entrance awning. The sergeant detective made an expression that conveyed she was unsurprised when the door to the flat opened at a touch.

"These places are never locked," Bergthora explained. Then she probed her jacket as if searching for something. She swung about and started off. I panicked, eyes widening.

"Bergthora, where are you going?"

"Forgot something in my car."

I had arrived separately and parked at a distance, as the sergeant detective instructed. Oddly, she departed toward where I had left my vehicle rather than the direction she had come from, disappearing amid the shabby edifices. I stood under the canopy staring at the unmoving door, not attempting to open it further or to close it, my nervous fingers thrumming my abdomen.

The sergeant detective patted her breast pocket upon her return. "Got it." She scowled at my racing fingers.

The interior hall was high, with stippled yellowing wallpaper, the rail of the stairs thick with a batter of green paint. An obese boy stood at the top of the landing. He wore faded jeans with suspenders parting over his belly. His blond hair was cropped short, and his face gleamed ruddy pink. We trudged up the steps. At the top, we stopped and waited. The fat boy held an open tabloid newspaper in his hands, head tilted back as if reading with punctilious care.

He lowered the pages enough for me to see his pupils. "Oh, you're back."

Bergthora turned to me. A ray of light from the window above the landing illuminated the capillaries on the sergeant detective's nose.

"Is this lout a friend of yours?"

I was baffled. "I have never been here before," I stammered.

The fat boy snapped his paper closed. "Just goes to show, you johns all look alike."

"I'm not a john."

"Whatever." The boy announced it was three hundred kroner to go beyond the door. For eight hundred kroner, a variety of entertainment was available. "But a woman, if she likes girls, plenty are game."

After a thick-lidded appraisal, Bergthora said, "What is your name?"

The fat boy tipped his head back. Finally, he said, "My name is Nils."

"What's your story, Nils? You look too shrewd to be lurking around here."

Nils shrugged. "Kicked out studying to be a sous chef."

"Terrible to hear."

"Tragic. Swung a cleaver down in the wrong direction."

"And?"

"And took off the Nutrition tutor's pinky." Nils ran his thumb along the crease of his tabloid. "I never did like Nutrition."

"Did the tutor press criminal charges?" said Bergthora.

Nils squinted. "Lady, if you aren't going inside, then be off."

Bergthora made no effort to leave. "Listen, Nils. Two blokes. Tall. Thin. We're looking for them. One is bald; the other wears two-toned suits."

Nils shook his head. "Perhaps if you could paint them in more detail. Their tone of voice. Teeth. Hair. Mannerisms. Odor is extremely useful for painting mental pictures. And more about their peccadillos."

"Peccadillos?"

"And mannerisms."

Bergthora rocked on her heels, "Hmm."

"Think."

"Whiney voices."

"Good, good."

"No missing teeth."

"Now we're getting somewhere. And?"

"Let's see, both affix fur to their collars."

Nils scratched the white expanse of belly bulging from the bottom of his stained T-shirt. He put his thumbs in his suspenders and issued a *put-put-put* sound from his lips. Nils' gaze drifted away, creeping along the cracks in the wall, up to the ceiling, and then across the ceiling, as if he could tease an answer from the grand mystery of the plaster. Finally, his gaze settled again on the sergeant detective.

"Ransacked the old memory banks, lady. Nothing. Sorry."

The sergeant detective presented her badge. "Listen here, Nils, it is not illegal to sell sexual services in our country, but it is illegal to pay for them. A paradox, of sorts, but this *is* our national law. It's better for the women. Do you know our country's laws?" Bergthora advised the boy she was there to review the premises for legal compliance.

"Shit on my boot," the fat boy muttered and swung the door open.

þ

Girls with almond skin, salmon skin, dun skin sat in a small room on a bench waiting. Their weary chatter stopped, and they looked at us. The large room was subdivided by plasterboard walls thin enough to hear through, with an open shower stall at the end of the expanse. The showerhead dripped syrupy yellow.

A mix of feelings eddied through me as I crossed into the room, a welter of fear and outrage, pity and lust. I had begun to finger chords the moment I entered. A tall woman with skin the hue of raw umber lifted herself from the bench. Her narcotic-dilated eyes shone like the rims of an eclipse.

She pointed to my hands. "What is that?"

I became aware of my movements. "A rather vexing C-G transition."

She swayed, losing focus, smiling.

"Music," I clarified.

"You make songs?"

I desperately wanted to say yes for her sake as well as mine, but the tall lady shushed me, her posture at ease as she took my hand and gently pulled me down the hall. We entered one of the plasterboard rooms where she embraced me, softly weaving her long fingers into the locks on the back of my head. A mix of perfume and sweat cloyed the air.

"I'm not here for…" I stammered. "What is your name?"

"Zuwena."

"That's lovely. We're here looking for crime stuff, evidence."

"Evidence?"

"Yes."

"Who is she you came with?"

"Fulaflugahål police."

Her large pupils scouted the darkness, fixing on

nothing. "You are the police?"

"She is. I'm not."

A small tide of emptiness washed over me as the tall woman slipped her fingers from my hair. I handed her a towel from the cot to cover her nakedness, explaining that a girl had been found dead back in wintertime, frozen in the ice of Lake Munch. A woman with freckles and pinched eyes and dyed yellow hair.

Zuwena balled her fist in anger.

I said, "You knew her, then?"

"I knew her."

"What was her name?"

My companion considered the question as if it had never arisen before. "She said her name was Misty. She was here and then gone. They promise you a job, and you pay them to bring you to this country, only to find there is no job. Only this. Twelve customer quota daily."

"Who promised you a job?"

"Two guys."

"Two guys?"

"Tall guys. Wolf guys."

"Tall wolf guys? Guys named Thorstein?"

Instead of directly responding to my question, the tall woman started to sing, a breathy rippling sound that could have paired up well with the tempo of my anxious hand. She was drifting, drifting. Yes, I had lost her.

"Kwa-heri," she murmured, and her eyes lifted toward someplace far beyond the shadows of the room.

þ

I returned to the hall where the women were still sitting on the bench. Bergthora approached. "Special reconnaissance?" she asked. I expected a smirk, yet her gaze was sunken in the bleak haze of the front room. I was startled by the plaintiveness of her expression; I considered Bergthora far fiercer than me. The sergeant detective spoke loudly enough for Nils to hear out on the landing. "My daughter went on holiday to Riga in her last year of school. It was supposed to be fun, an exploration for young minds. It turned into a nightmare. She was abducted."

I searched her grey, welling eyes. The tale was utterly new to me, and I was arrested in my steps. Her voice fell to a rasp. "For years, I searched, mad with terror until . . . she was found in a place like this . . ."

Nils lounged in the doorframe with a gaping look like someone had dropped a coin on his head. He squinted one eye, wary.

I reached out to Bergthora in consolation and shock, but the sergeant detective had turned away. She strode down into the warren of rooms, picked a dreary door, and kicked it open. I saw through the crack. A girl, crouching, strings of saliva running from her mouth, pink as if mixed with blood. The man over her struck the girl with the back of his hand. Then, he saw Bergthora.

The sergeant detective moved quickly.

"Bergthora," I cried, but it was as if I had said nothing. With a diagonal strike, she planted her fist in his throat; the john reeled. A swift blow with her fist to his paunch and the man collapsed. Meanwhile, the girl scrambled behind the protection of the door. The man staggered out of the room and down the stairway.

Bergthora rubbed soft tissue on her shoulder, then continued to kick the doors wide on either side of the aisle. "Out," she shouted, "Out."

Men fled; girls crouched.

Nils the Fat Boy muscled his way into the hall against the tide of fleeing clients. He held a weapon he had fashioned from the tabloid, an old paper-folding trick from the soccer terraces, which became a blackjack of considerable effectiveness when the paper was twisted tight and wetted.

"Hit an officer, and you'll go down hard, Fat Boy Nils," the sergeant detective said.

A mask of woe settled over Nils' face. "I don't get paid enough to be dead."

Bergthora rubbed the knuckle of her right thumb, the hand she had used to bash the john. "Nils, as I said, we're looking for two specific individuals. We received a tip they hung about this place."

"Customers all look the same to me."

"Not customers. Two guys, quite distinct. Tall, lean. One had a beard, the other wears suits."

"Faces lost in a sea of other faces, lady."

"Wolf fur on the clothing. Brothers. Sound familiar yet?"

Nils let out a long rumbling belch.

Bergthora stepped back, waving her hand before her nose, "We were also tipped off that they frequent a local disco. Obstruction of justice carries a long sentence, Nils, accomplice to murder a much longer one."

"I ain't saying nothing," Nils kneaded the soggy blackjack as if he was mulling an anxious thought.

Bergthora trekked back down the steps. "You don't know a thing about us, Nils. We were never here, Nils the Fat Boy. Better for a girl to put a bullet in her head than end up in one of these places."

As we descended, the sergeant detective turned to me. "You like the dark one? A fine-looking gal."

"She, I mean, she..." My attempt to explain myself failed miserably. "She was telling me about the murdered girl and things for the case. She might be a kind of witness."

I observed Bergthora's sneer from the side. "Witness interviews are beyond your pay grade, Kolbitter. You should have called me."

þ

We crossed the street, out of the block of flats. No sooner were we at the curb and in the trenchant light of afternoon than Bergthora stiffened. I initially thought she might have been wounded in the fight, that maybe Nils had injured her as we withdrew. But there was neither blood nor gaping wounds nor blanching flesh.

The sergeant detective lit a cigarillo, waiting, thinking to herself.

My fingers began to choke out notes. "That fat boy, Nils, he said he went to cooking school." Bergthora pinched her cigarillo with an almost predatory grip, head bowed. I continued, "Snorri thinks the killer used a culinary torch, remember?"

The sergeant detective looked up. "Right. And Jack the Ripper was an interior decorator."

Silence languished between us. As Bergthora neared the end of her smoke, I spoke again, softly, "I never knew about your daughter, Bergthora. I'm so sorry."

Her blotchy skin slackened. A terrible grin overtook her face. "I don't have a daughter or a son. Never wanted children, Grammaticus."

The sergeant detective abruptly turned and walked in the direction of her vehicle.

As I looked up, raw with confusion, I saw beyond the tattered awning of the entrance, the tall woman in the window overlooking the street, pupils still wide. She called out, just as Nils' pudgy hands yanked her back into darkness, "Farewell, my friend. *Hup*."

Unsettled, I crushed the pedal, wrenching my mini from the curb. There was a hollow indistinct roar, and the mini lurched into the turn and banged downward, a ship plowing into a reef. I got out to inspect the damage. On the street, I discovered two wheels wedged at angles under the car. The lugs nuts were missing.

9: A Secret History

The shock of the brothel, the vandalized mini—I bolted, moving in galloping strides, my heart pounding frantically. It took me a while to gather my senses. I must take this to the Constable. By the time I reached his estate, my skin was raw with thorn scratches, and my jacket smelled of the scrub juniper I had crushed stumbling through the trees. I thumped on the door with the heel of my fist. After countless minutes, a bolt scraped, a latch lifted, and the door crept open. A pale crescent of the Constable's face filled the crack.

"Sir," I began.

The angled light behind the door widened. Harsh furrows formed across his forehead, cravat askew and clumsily folded. Without providing any further information, the Constable pointed to the library and turned on his heel into an unlit corridor. The fingertips of his right hand touched the wall as he disappeared.

The yellow light of the library glowed. Within, Minne and Tanke shared a bar stand and were looking around actively. I edged toward the birds and tapped my chest. Minne gave a deep rasping noise. Tanke took three claw-steps away on the bar.

The Constable was long returning. The shelves of the library ran to the ceiling, containing hundreds, if not thousands of titles. He had books I knew well: classics and the old sagas, lots of volumes on specialized police topics, and, oddly, an entire section devoted to beekeeping. I immediately recognized the blue binding and flaking silver print as the antiquated manual from that day on the ice.

When I pulled the volume from the Constable's shelf, a sheaf of unbound pages fell out. Panicking, I hurried to gather them up before my host returned. But the temptation of a look into a private trove was too great. I scanned the first sentences:

> *Shall I venture a brief yet grand portrait of the man? When I look at his face, what do I see? His face, in a mirror, a shop window, a pond? Volutes of hair, their mercury sheen. Epidermal crevasses. A black lens. Although this blemish has traveled with him, or me, many years, it is in this scar, I recognize the creature most fully—him, myself—and oblivion. Attributes of a sorcerer, indeed.*
> *So begins my authentic autobiography.*

Maybe I had discovered the memoir of a hidden life or an incriminating confession. But I slowed myself. With the Constable, contrary truths were always at play. It might, just as likely, be a subterfuge and merely another tattered mantle. I spoke aloud to myself and to the birds, "I believe the Constable is an aristocrat with time on his hands."

Tanke let out a soft *korrrr*.

I heard the Constable returning, stopping in the dark corridor to polish the frame of a portrait. Perhaps a spiteful mood took over me as I shoved the loose pages into my shirt, replacing the blue volume just as my host appeared at the doorway. I saw now he had kindled a fire in the hearth in the dinner hall, where we'd had the rare cognac. Flames leaped among the stones.

"Sir, I am here because I need to tell you about what I saw."

"Must you? You are an inelegant and luckless fellow."

"Of course, sir, and I hardly know where to start. I noticed you have books on beekeeping. Let me begin there. At the mead brewery are a mother and a daughter who keep bees for—"

He interrupted me. "Have a seat, boy."

I sat in an old, spindly chair. It creaked under me.

The Constable said, "That chair belonged to a great Scandinavian composer."

"Oh, sir. Who?" I began to rise.

"Henning Mankell."

"The crime novelist? He writes music too?"

The Constable pressed me back down. "Certainly not. His grandfather, who is the actual talent in the family."

"Constable, you told me to keep notes. I have to tell you what I saw. Crazy things, and terrible violence."

I still expected a vigorous dressing down for arriving without notice. Instead, the Constable simply grunted and nodded. I proceeded. First, I recollected the visit with Bergthora and Snorri at the mead house; its proprietors, the giantess and her mother; and the details of the victim's work dispensing mead samples.

"Go on, boy."

Next, I moved to the trip to Grimke and the muddle with the inquest, followed by the memorable encounter with the Librarian, the fabulous book, and the tale of Abbe Laurent.

"The librarian has a great deal of regard for you, sir."

The Constable let his good eye dart out to the hearth, then back to me. A smile played at the corners of his mouth, then disappeared.

"I confess, sir, in some mysterious way, that book redeemed the fiasco."

"A good book will do that."

His hair looked like stirred cinders in the reflected light of the hearth. Finally, I recounted the visit to the brothel, the obese bouncer Nils and the women, as well as Bergthora's violent march down the miserable passage. "The victim seemed to have found work at the mead house, under the protection of the giant girl. Sometime during that period, she began to work at the brothel to get more money. And she may have been coerced."

The Constable's good eye glittered, flicking like the tongue of a snake. I had a wild notion of torches, flaming cressets, the rattle of iron-bound wheels and the snort of dray horses. A shapeless army with the Constable at its head, cracking a lash.

"Madness," I said.

"Madness?"

"Complete anarchy."

"Distressing."

"Yes, sir. Worse. Lunatic farce, every moment of it."

The Constable was now clasping the bookshelf. The fire popped and reported like a rifle going off. With a cast of disappointment seeping into his tone, he said, "All that is well enough, boy, but you haven't done the hard work. The work you were born to do."

I narrowed my eyes, incensed. I felt like a toy balloon blown in a storm. Looking to the right of the Constable's right ear, I saw a space on the shelf where the blue volume should have sat. My eyes darted about, then down. There rested the blue book, fallen on the floor. Minne sat on its open pages, head down, as if studying the folio in mischief. She pecked at it. My blood ran cold, and I clutched my knees.

The Constable's gaze had not followed mine, and he continued his previous thread. "What are you, Kolbitter?"

"I'm a records clerk. I have worked several years in records, sir."

"You embrace your disappointment, do you?"

The Constable promptly transferred his attention elsewhere, searching for the blue volume until he spotted Minne on the floor atop the pages. He shooed her off, saying, "Studying again, are you, Minne?" He picked up the blue volume. He paused, searching for something before quickly dismissing it, evidently distracted by other thoughts. He cradled the book in one palm and let his fingers unfold, the leaves falling open at the point of most fatigue.

He chuckled softly then recited what appeared on the page:

Section Y, Certain Characteristics Essential to the Inquiring Officer: It goes practically without

saying that an Inquiring Officer should possess—
of all those qualities a man in his position should
desire to possess—unbounded zeal and
concentration, self-sacrifice, stamina, a quick
study of human behavior and the character of
men, education and agreeable manner, sublime
commitment, and comprehensive knowledge.
These are qualities whose importance is
habitually disregarded. Certainly, and above all,
nothing is more deplorable than a drawling,
sleepy, scrofulous inspector.

The Constable clapped the book shut as though shutting a casket. "We shall not pretend you are an inquiring officer, certainly not by this definition. Do we agree?"

I felt my Adam's apple bob as I swallowed. "I'm not scrofulous."

He spoke more gently now, though hurriedly. "I believe in precision, boy: rigor and swift insight. Again, I ask: What are you? What are you in your heart, Kolbitter?"

"Please, I don't know what you are asking. *You* summoned *me* ages ago."

"You are a musician."

His blunt statement seared my ears. Was this an observation or, I feared, an accusation? I pursed my lips. My eyes leaped to the door, then the hallway, desperately seeking some way to escape the ignominy.

The Constable pressed on. "A musician. It's easy for me to make the inference from the data. First, the tendons on the backs of your hands are very blue from heavy use. Second, the pattern of behaviors. I have seen it repeatedly: you race your hands on the edge of the desk after you retrieve a record folder or answer an inquiry. You'd spoken of this reflex to the Grimke officer, regarding the key fob."

I sunk back onto the rickety chair. It was as though he had flung me like a naked beggar into the town square. I stared at the backs of my hands and the tendons that had betrayed me.

I said, amazed, "You got that all from inference?'

"No," he said. "There was more obvious evidence. Recall, Kolbitter, what you scribbled on the scrap at the end of your notes that day on the ice, the fragment I tore off, and gave to you."

"The music. You're a musician too, sir?"

"No."

For reasons I did not myself fathom, I said, "I should never have noted to hold an F# that long."

The Constable turned his whole torso to look at me. "You and I are prisoners of a similar fate. Like any art, like music, an investigation is a juggernaut. Once it is underway, it cannot pause. It cannot undo anything. It cannot stop to explain itself."

The plumage of the ravens shone green and blue in the dark light. The walls of books loomed over me, oppressive. Consumed by a crushing sense of resignation, I cast myself under the wheels of the grinding cart that was his inquisitive good eye. In a burst, I cried, "This case is utterly backward. This girl, Misty she was called, she was an immigrant from far away and had no labor permit. She handed out drink samples at taverns, then was forced into a brothel. The cape of feathers was a Valkyrie's costume, intended to evoke a great mythic past, but it only attracted the worst type. Thugs. There you go, I have solved the murder. Ha!"

The Constable strode past me to the wooden chair and gave it a violent kick. It clattered across the room and came to rest near the wall. We both looked at the unbroken chair.

"You have not." His tone had gone shrill. "You are just beginning and are seeking to escape. Imagination, boy, that is what this sort of investigation demands. You know the burden of vision."

"Music is not police work."

"Music is recognition: patterns, and the breaking of patterns. Psychology, discovery. Such is the faculty of reason at work."

I yearned to cry out as if, finally, in some way, the Constable and I had reached a consensus. I wanted to exclaim, "Yes, that is what happens when I write a song, especially when performing for an audience. Connection occurs."

Yet words stuck on my tongue. The Constable's declaration could not truly capture every hour of every day crouching over the keyboard, the sorting of pages, fleshing out musings from usable bars under the summons of a new tune. Could this be called rationality? Or some sad, complex irrationality? What did my labor deliver but a few minutes of head-banging fun?

Minne leaped up from the floor to the bar and joined the conversation, chirping in a soft singsong for what seemed an infinitely long moment. After the performance, the Constable chucked her under the bill and cooed, "Far more important, music expresses what is hidden and cannot be said; music hints at the inmost nature of things. Music is enlightenment. Melody is intelligence."

"But my melodies are—I write chaos, too, sir, dissonance."

Then it occurred to me: the half-baked swindler hoped to see what stunts I would do to make him laugh. He didn't need my collaboration. He needed stimulation and empathy. Yes, the Constable needed admirers.

"Nobody cares about this dead woman," I shouted, rising from my chair and stalking into the foyer. I threw the door open, and my words rang out, a hammer upon the anvil of darkness. "I am done fact gathering, done with wheel spinning."

My host stood gaping. The blue volume had fallen from his hand. I swept my fists from my face, where I had clenched them, and down before my chest. With all the wounded grandeur of an opera buffa character, I bumbled out the door into the black night.

10: Battle-Ready Tune Mongers

The door on Fadlan's flat was open. Fadlan and Gudrid and
Egil continued to speak in low tones that changed when
they saw me. Gudrid fiddled with the velvet rose on the
band of her cloche. "Fadlan, is that a real Ogleworthy
Flying V?"

Fadlan thumped the body of his bass. His voice bounced
up at the end of his words, artificial. "Circa nineteen
seventy-two. Found it at a jumble sale in Grimke."

I stepped toward my keyboard, still by the window
where I had left it.

"We weren't sure you were going to make practice,"
Egil said.

"My boss, the Constable, utterly impossible," I
continued. "Talking with him is like a dialogue with a
drunkard."

Egil pressed his tongue into the gap in his front teeth,
the flesh bulging like a piece of pink chewing gum, then
drew it back. "Cool."

I faced Fadlan again, "It's like everything is sort of half
black magic with the Constable."

"Maybe your boss is one of the Illuminati," Fadlan
smirked.

"Every day he inches closer to madness."

"Shake it, dude," Grudrid interposed. "Where's the
golden boy Grammaticus we know, the brilliant Norse
metal composer? We need a single great song, an anthem,
a block buster. Stop letting this investigation silence you,
and start letting it galvanize you."

"Every note a diamond," Fadlan agreed.

Gudrid swiped up her drumsticks from the corner where
she had cast them. "A finale, a magnum opus, an epic tale."

"I'm a records clerk. I don't have epic tales."

"Are you so sure?" Fadlan blinked his coal-black lashes

and turned to Gudrid as if to start another conversation. "How long were you in jail, drummer girl?"

"Months."

"Did you play any music in jail?"

"Drumming things with my bare hands, and sometimes brushing my fingernails together like some kind of Cuban gourd scraper."

Fadlan turned his deep brown eyes on me with mordant patience. "Write about that, about jail and confinement, Grammaticus, and bearing on despite all."

Gudrid said, "No one is allowed to plunder my personal history. Besides, Vikings didn't have jails."

"They had outlawing," Fadlan said, "and people getting kicked out of the clan, shunned forever. They had exile."

I pinched the bridge of my nose. "I'll write about exile."

"Don't fritter over the introspection, Grammaticus. Exile has been done before."

"Sorry, Gudrid, sorry, Fadlan, I don't have any heroism to tap."

"Then go get some!" Gudrid pointed a stick at me like a weapon.

"Like what? Like slaying a dragon?"

"Nothing is useless to an artist, as you said. Embrace your fate, and be ready for anything. I don't care if you get washed out to sea or are swarmed by a coven of witches or take a magic carpet ride. Step out of reality for a bit. Find providence in the fall of a sparrow. We need something epic." Gudrid's cloche had slipped back on her head, a helmet now framing her round face. She muttered as if to herself, "Somebody needs to nudge our sword-lord smack into the lair of a fiery dragon."

Fadlan laughed, almost cruelly. Slowly, I laughed, too. It was true, as I had thought before: I had made them too hungry for winning RagnaRock.

"Dragons!" Egil cheered, "We, The Berserkers, are nonpareil battle-ready tune-mongers. Let's murder the beastie!"

Then he let loose a commanding howl in B flat, right at bar twelve where we had left off. It was past midnight, yet I lowered my head to the keys and grinned at the backs of my hands. Fadlan and Gudrid settled into the flow of their instruments. Egil was not just singing; he was a persona now, a down-at-heel Pavarotti.

Fadlan then began doing vigorous physical contortions to wrest the proper sound from his instrument. I smiled with my lips crooked. "Stop noodling, Fadlan."

"We are supposed to be revolutionizing Viking heavy metal," Fadlan retorted. "That's why I favor alternative turnings."

Egil commanded, "Pluck it like a koto, Fadlan."

Fadlan laid the base flat on its back, studying at it. He adjusted the reverb, then stretched his arms over the instrument from the bridge to the headstock and, feathering his limbs this way and that, pinched out a vibrato.

Egil circled his left wrist with the forefinger and thumb of his right hand. "Sounds like a koto being played in a cathedral. I can let loose to that."

"What about the song structure?" asked Gudrid.

Something was afoot, maybe more than just me being late. Gudrid knew what kind of guitar Fadlan played, and nobody had ever raised song structure before. I paced about the room with my fingers steepled before my chin and fell into song writer mode, lecturing. "I want melody emerging from mood and texture. I don't want to write three-minute tone poems. I want an eight-minute wonder-wall of sound; then the song will end with the keyboard droning like killer bees."

Fadlan's eyes narrowed. "First you are late. Now you are asking for death-metal cliches?"

"The killer bee sound is symbolic."

"Screw symbols."

"Whoa."

Gudrid swooped in. "You've said it yourself, Grammaticus, Viking metal is more about attitude than—"

Egil interrupted her, "Get into it, mate, or you're out of the band."

I reeled back from the keyboard. "What's wrong with you guys?"

Fadlan slammed his hand on his base. "You made us believe in the dream, in Viking metal and RagnaRock, and now you don't. Well, the dream is stronger than you."

Gudrid said, "Songwriters write songs. If you can't, don't bother showing up."

As I hit the door, I fired back, "Creativity is not a spigot—you don't have an inkling what this takes, the rigor amid bedlam. As a composer, I am a camera. I pause, I observe, I record. Nothing is valueless to an artist. Someday, it will all be fixed in a bath of chemicals and emerge as a magnificent, arresting image."

"Oh, and also," I snorted, "Don't forget the show coming soon, a paying gig."

11: Metal and Bone

With my mini still in for repairs from the missing nuts, I found myself again wandering on foot. I hurried, as if speed could overcome failing to pinpoint the exact reason for my misery. My course downhill was certain only when the light of the shoreline flickered among the leaves. The branches thinned into a series of clearings, which joined an old footpath. I was delivered bramble-stung and exhausted to the Fulaflugahål train terminal, the fateful origin of my failed assignment with Patrolman Jerker. I collapsed on my knees to the rail cinders.

I heard the scuff of shoes approaching and raised my head to see two figures gesticulating in what seemed to be a mild argument. They were unaware of my presence until I spoke.

"Oh, hello," I said.

Snorri said, "Grammaticus, you're as pale as a corpse."

Bergthora hitched her thumbs in her belt. "Looking for your dark lady from the cathouse, Grammaticus?"

I pressed up onto my knees. "Why are you walking way out here on the tracks? And why together? I thought you were enemies."

"We are," said Snorri.

"Absolutely," agreed the sergeant detective.

Bergthora stepped carefully between the rail ties. "Why are *you* here? It's illegal to pay for sex in this country."

I brushed cinders from my skin and the juniper-berries from my jacket before tugging the hair from my eyes. Everything spilled out of me. I was expansive about my encounter with the Constable. As my eyes flared, I piled injustice upon injustice, relishing my outrage and basting myself in juices of self-pity.

Bergthora made a sideways movement of her head, a signal to Snorri. "Well, goodnight, Grammaticus."

I stopped mid-gesture. "Where are you going?"

The two stared at each other as if contemplating whether to answer.

Snorri said, finally, "To the disco. The sergeant detective wants to check out the lead from the fat boy you guys met. What was his name?"

"Nils."

Snorri said, "I'm going along to get snaps. Will you accompany us, Grammaticus? Snaps cure any malady."

I shook my head vigorously, an emphatic no.

þ

Snorri ordered snaps and I, one small beer. Bergthora requested cognac.

"We serve no such drink," said the publican.

Bergthora studied the seedy bar. "Vodka, any kind. Neat."

"You think this is the disco Nils said the brothers came to?" I asked Bergthora.

"We'll see. There are others nearby, too," the sergeant detective replied.

The disco was little more than a pub with a brown glow, dance floor, and stucco arches. The late-night crowd had begun to gather. Men in leather blazers, dark shirts, and glistening hair lingered at the bar while women danced in troupes on the scuffed floor. All seemed to have a gaze of vacant longing.

As we settled into our drinks, I unfolded the tale of my sabotaged mini.

"Bad neighborhood where that cathouse is," Bergthora said.

I turned my beer glass, "Petty theft? Mischief?"

"A warning, Kolbitter." Bergthora downed her vodka shot in one go and waived for another.

Snorri swung his gaze around the room. "Maybe attempted murder."

"W-what?" I choked.

Eager now to change the subject, Snorri said, "I have an aspiration, a goal if you will. I shall spend my later years drifting upon the shoals of Mediterranean ease—permanent holiday. Depart with chums from the Fulaflugahål train platform, sated with beer and potatoes and herring, borne on a desperate wish. Headed for a reckoning."

Bergthora received her second shot and downed that too, before placing a cigarillo between her lips and leaving it unlit. "I have no desire to hear of your aspirations."

"It is a beautiful dream." Snorri rolled his snaps glass between his fingers. He seemed to anticipate another quip from Bergthora. "Do you think I joined the Fulaflugahål police force to grow stupid handing out parking tickets?"

"And yet you achieved that," said Bergthora.

I said, "Why *did* you join the force, Snorri?"

The little man smiled dreamily. "Lucia."

Bergthora fixed her teeth around the filter. "Magnificent. A love-interest."

"Soccer, soccer. At twenty, I aimed to be the gentle outlaw; I hopped on a train and wound up in Milan, which was so unlike home. Perhaps it was the weather or the bright sun."

"Italians will never learn the meaning of work," said Bergthora.

"Perhaps it was the lilting singsong phrases of the locals. Perhaps it was the eye-bulging roar of the Milan supporters that ignited me. Right here." He tapped his sternum. "I didn't go back home for five years."

Bergthora said, "So you were a soccer hooligan."

"My mates and I ran about in packs."

"You jumped the turnstile, a fare thief."

I cringed, remembering the Interregional Express.

Said Snorri, "A terrace gypsy. Not a thug, a pacifist."

Bergthora snorted, "A pacifist on the police force."

"I welcomed anything that came my way. I dug through

skips for food, drank from any running pipe. I let go of any concern other than where to bed myself for the night. I turned to busking, spinning in my head and whirling goblets of fire before crowds. I sold cheap whirling toys and stole matchbooks from restaurants: more coins, ever more coins. One evening in my third year of panhandling, standing on the upper tier at a match, crushed against the restraining mesh yet still able to urinate on a tight-lipped, shy group from Finland below, I noticed the dark-haired girl. Her skin glowed like polished cypress: Lucia, who I treated to a beer. In time, we married, and I took her back to Fulaflugahål. It was she who convinced me to join the police."

"God help us," said Bergthora.

Snorri circled a fingertip around his narrow, bell-shaped glass. "Forty-two years I was married. Lucia pulled me up by the short hairs. Everything was for Lucia, for I loved her. Lucia, Lucia, my life."

Bergthora covered her mouth with her fist and belched discretely. "And she convinced you to lie about your height, too?"

"The bent keel must be fared straight."

"You're bent, that's for sure."

"It was a good plan until a forgotten document showed up decades later."

I lowered my head upon hearing Snorri's comment. Bergthora produced the fur clip and tested its texture with her thumb, the bristles bouncing smartly back.

"I don't remember you checking that out from records," I objected.

The sergeant detective flipped the sample over to look at the crackled glue and then slipped it back in her jacket, patting the pocket. "I have my own records department right here." Next, she removed prints of images from an inner breast pocket and handed one to Snorri, who made the rounds, flashing the photograph at nearby patrons. He inquired among the patrons whether the girl looked familiar. Their responses were minimal; a few praised the artistic quality of Jerker's work. No one, however, acknowledged knowing the girl.

Snorri offered a photo to me. "Perhaps Grammaticus will assist with the data gathering?"

I sipped my beer in silence.

A man with skin scaly as a dried fish and abnormally short arms hovered around the patch of floor where the women danced. As Snorri walked by, he put his face close to the photo and then drew back, disquieted. "Back in the early nineties, I was driving a truck on a Czech highway near the German border. There were three hundred women lined up on the side of the road ready for a go, a go for the cash, you understand. Easterners."

Bergthora arched a brow. The man continued. "That girl in your picture looks like one of them, any one of the whores on that long Czech highway." He stretched his stubby arms to mimic the great trail of women.

Snorri searched his photograph again. "He thinks she is Eastern European?"

The short-armed man overheard the words. "Alien, with those eyes and that skin. Maybe one of those strange northern clans with ice forever forming on their eyelashes, people who make fences of reindeer antlers on their graveyards."

"Bedouins of the Arctic," the sergeant detective downed her vodka and stood. "I don't see the targets. Nothing of use here."

"Targets? What targets?" demanded the truck driver.

Bergthora's speckled jowls slowly relaxed. She repeated the now familiar look and dress of the Thorstein brothers.

"Maybe, maybe. A drink would prime the memory pump, officer," he said.

I recognized the lavender geese of a twenty kroner bill as it passed from the sergeant-detectives hand to the hand of the thirsty driver. The man with the too-short arms put his hand gently around the back of Bergthora's neck and brought the sergeant-detective's ear near his puckered face, a curious gesture for him to give and Bergthora to tolerate.

"Check the lakefront southeast of the city. There's a cove some dubious types use."

"A cove they use for what?"

"Comings and goings."

"Comings and goings," the sergeant detective echoed.

"Darting about on a rubber raft appropriated from some witless harbor patrol."

The driver opened his right palm, apparently expecting more kroners. Bergthora gave a faint, ghastly smile and turned away. "Let's go to the next disco, Sturlusson."

"There is another disco in Fulaflugahål?" I asked.

Snorri bowed slightly to the short-armed trucker. "Tak, mate. We will get another drink elsewhere."

Bergthora laid her hand on my shoulder again, a signal for me to follow.

"But I haven't finished my beer," I lamented.

"Suit yourself," the sergeant detective raided her side pocket and cast some heavy coins on the table, then made for the door. The short-armed man picked up a coin and rotated it as though valuing a rare find. He swung to watch the two depart. I escaped with my drink to another table in the shadows. He shouted to the exiting pair, "The Berlin Wall fell, and then the women's knickers fell. That's capitalism for you."

His laughter swelled out onto the darkened street.

þ

Shortly after Snorri and Bergthora had departed, I saw two tall, gangly men emerging from the bathroom.

"After you, Thorkill," one said.

"Tak, Thorvald, my brother," said the other.

Despite sitting a few tables away from me, they were close enough to overhear their talk. Their pale bony fingers spread around their drink tumblers. Thorkill leered at a bulbous girl circling on the dance floor.

"Ja ja, that's how it is," he encouraged.

Thorvald seemed to weigh merits and demerits in response to an implicit question. "Swelling tits, swelling bum. I would do her."

Thorkill replied, "I should think. Ankles up at the ears."

The dancer circled toward them, nearing closer and closer. I could not say whether she had heard their chatter, but I did see Thorkill's outstretching hand wander through space until it touched the band around her upper arm, a strap of woven metal. Meanwhile, his skin shown fair almost to translucence in the gaudy light, his eyes an unnerving blue. He swept his hair in a wedge from his temples back over his ears to the nape of his neck. He seemed the type born into a two-toned suit and loafers, ready for dub. I thought the fur lap was the strangest aspect of his apparel. Grey and ragged, it curved from his ribs to his neck. It seemed to belong to a more decadent kind of clothing.

Thorkill corrected the links on his shirt cuffs.

"This is my brother, Thorvald," he announced, pointing to his brother like he was displaying a prize stud in a farm show.

The girl smiled, apparently registering Thorvald as the brother with the more robust physical endowment and the lesser intellectual prowess. Thorvald was primitive with skinny-hipped jeans and cherry-red twenty-eye mosh pits paired with a tee that hugged tight to his pectoral-heavy torso, framed in an open plaid lumberjack coat. Despite his hairless scalp, he wore a long beard cut straight across the bottom, as if sheared with a knife.

As with his brother, Thorvald trimmed his coat with a shaggy wolf pelt.

"Magnificent clientele, this place," said Thorkill.

"Fetching," agreed Thorvald.

The brothers smiled so that their teeth showed. The girl

tentatively glanced from one man to the other. When she spoke, it was with a thick foreign accent.

"You from around here, darling?" Thorvald asked her.

"No, I not from Fulaflugahål."

"The language is a barrier, eh, just visiting surely."

"I not visit. Work."

"Where do you work?"

"Not work yet."

Thorkill plied the wolf pelt at his collar. "A puzzle. You work, yet you don't work. Are you from one of those godforsaken Baltic pigs' wallows?"

Thorvald interjected, "She sounds more like the chick from Belarus."

The girl brightened at the name of the city.

"What is your name, my sweet?"

She was silent.

"No name. A cipher washed up on these shores. Hard to get along, not knowing up from down, Love?" Thorkill was smilling. "But everyone needs employment. Without employment, you can't stay in Fulaflugahål long."

The woman seemed weirdly mesmerized by Thorvald's rectangular beard. Complete silence ensued for a moment.

Thorkill placed his hands on his knees. "If you need work papers, we can help."

"It's easy," Thorvald encouraged.

His brother provided the clarification. "Very leisurely, except, perhaps, for special requests. Those can be demanding."

Thorvald added, "No labor permit means you could get reported even by a perfect stranger."

The girl backed up, taking in the spectacle of insolence. Her eyes flitted over me, almost unseeing. I dropped my gaze to the floor as she passed. At this time, a short-armed man in the standard brown utility coveralls of a truck driver leaned uninvited into the interaction. He tapped a malformed forefinger on the tabletop.

"Heard all that, boys. Settle down. The ladies like to

dance and be social. We're here to relax, not fight. Do you want me to call the police back?"

"For me, fighting *is* relaxation. What about you, Thorvald?"

"You suppose I know my mind. Brother, I shall follow you."

Thorkill sat quietly for a moment after this remark. Then he said, "You are a piece of work, Thorvald. Such promise, yet so malleable. It makes me melancholy, but in a happy way."

Thorvald replied, "And I, happy in a melancholy way."

"Very well."

The two thugs clasped each other and were soon laughing, apparently beyond their control, for they became loud.

The brow of the short-armed man puckered. Thorvald ran his eyes over the man's brown one-piece rolled high at the sleeves. "Sharp duds. You can drive a truck with those arms?" He shifted his cherry-red boots beneath the table.

The trucker balled his hands into fists.

Thorkill shifted on his stool around to his brother. "Tonight, I am happy, but I distrust such utter and complete happiness. After all, it cannot last. What is my life lacking this moment?"

Thorvald combed his hand down his whiskers then touched his thumb to his fur collar. "You have such good color, and your face is shining. You lack nothing. Your life is fulfilled."

"One item is deficient. So, let's do the trick."

Although Thorvald's next words came out in a measured way, his eyes flashed with a distinct recklessness. He focused on the trucker. "Do you know when you have struck well? I know it from the pressure of the handle on my thumb and the way it turns. When the handle turns, metal has touched bone."

The look on the short-armed man's face was one of bafflement. "Struck well?"

Thorvald's pupils dilated. He quickly pulled out a tactical blade and unfolded it in one action. I shrunk against the back of my chair and heard the gasps of nearby females. In a swift second move, he pierced the knife into the truck driver's thigh. When Thorvald pulled back, I saw teeth on the red blade as it slashed up and out.

Just as the driver's eyes widened enough to grasp the micro-horror of his splayed flesh, Thorkill and Thorvald Thorstein were out of their seats. His shrieking was louder than the motorcycle tires squealing in the street.

Interlude One: Quant

Sirens whirled to a stop at the door. The trucker had refused medical help and blanched further at lodging a criminal charge. Men hunched over their drinks and women screamed when he fainted. The evening crew from the precinct house arrived, beat officers I recognized from other shifts but did not know. These officers did not include the Constable.

"It's the clerk from records."

"Don't trust him."

"I heard from Jerker he hides from ticket takers."

The other officer agreed, "Predictable, guys like him."

"That's not me," I protested.

Spending the three hours in police custody, I recounted what had happened, all I had seen, including the wolf collars. By the time the officers had finished with me, the other patrons were gone, long since dismissed. They released me mumbling under their breath, "This one attracts trouble."

Arriving at my bedsit, I fell back upon the mattress. But I was too exhausted and restless to sleep. When I rolled over, the sheaf of pages I had stolen from the Constable fell from my shirt. They were composed on the Icelandic bank Glitnir's stationery in the manner I was accustomed to from the Constable's records requests, swirling longhand with backward tilting capitals.

The Constable's First Autobiography

Shall I venture a brief yet grand portrait of the man? When I look at his face, what do I see? His face, in a mirror, a shop window, a pond? Volutes of hair, their mercury sheen. Epidermal crevasses. A black lens. Although this blemish has traveled with him, or me, many years, it is in this scar I recognize the creature most fully—him, myself—and oblivion. Attributes of a sorcerer, indeed.

So begins my authentic autobiography.

Facets of a hidden clockwork. His humors play out in planetary swings. His relationships are secretive, reckless, trusting, and gravid with both admiration and disappointment. Harsh. One might suppose this man hewn with a mallet and chisel, like a woodcut. I have observed him in private moments, when he thought himself least on display, surprisingly happy, voice strong, engaged among police cadets, those earnest youths with muscular forearms and razor burn and shower-wet hair.

~

I once heard my ancient colleague boasting, "How much do we pay for our obsessions. Be prepared."

Chuckling, I did not reply.

~

The Constable was the son of a hipster couple who lived in an avant-garde circus, street buskers borne on stilts and trapezes, with lefty and lofty political intentions. Of course, a sublime preparation for youth. On stage, his father interwove the roles of clown and human cannonball. Offstage, he sported a soft-brimmed hat, wisecracked allusions to Bertolt Brecht, drank heroically, lost sure bets, and patted girls' bottoms.

The Constable, of his mother, mainly recalled her narrow teeth, dry blonde hair, and her Jenny Lind figure, buxom and maternal. She worried excessively about the well-being of her only child. Her ideals were immense, her worry guileless. She dispensed tinctures and ointments, spoiled her son's eating habits, misdiagnosed his complaints, nurtured his emotional intensity, read him frightening fairytales, and dressed him thoughtlessly no matter what the season. She pined for a quiet evening alone, away from the press of responsibility. Son adored mother; mother adored son. For the Constable, childhood comprised a montage of cheap resort towns, improvised theaters, and roaring humanity. Love pasted its bright handbills over the cracks of worry.

~

Tragedy welled. Exactly a decade before Prime Minister Olaf Palme was shot, a crime still unsolved, the Constable's father slid into the stage canon from the upward-tilted end. It was his act, the human cannonball. Wiggling down the barrel, he planted his shoes on the platform. The ringmaster goaded the crowd, "Ready. Steady."

The mob flung peanut shells. The boy grinned with pride. Yet, inside the metal tube, a button on his father's sequined suit had caught on a smoke vent. The vile stench of saltpeter flared in his nose. Metal cogs clanged. "Wait!" he demanded, his cry muted by the walls of the iron cylinder. The flame juggler mistook the muffled objection for the ready signal and lowered a sparking brand to the fuse. "My sleeve!" he pleaded—fire burst. Smoke looped. The mortal ordnance tumbled in an arc over the audience, through the parched skin of the big top, landing with a thump against the elephant cage.

Ever after, the Constable's father walked with a savage

limp. Yet the compass of his ambition refused to be constrained. He redrew his plans for the entire family. He embraced ownership of a tavern, christening it the Vole's Head Inn, though he later confessed to his son he could not remember why.

~

Being the child of a publican was not bereft of its share of enchantment. Perched alone on a stool behind the bar, the boy devoured sci-fi novels and memorized the Eddas' short passages. He studied curiosities in math and logic and tried to peek down barmaids' blouses. Above all, he cultivated the quiet superiority of the disenfranchised. The boy skipped school, frittering away his time playing pool while his father made extravagant claims to the clientele. Like his mother, the youth pined for something ever-receding. And? One ominously cloudy, cold afternoon, a regular customer realized the boy had a talent with the billiards cue. The father encouraged his son's flinty eye with strangers. Thus, the Vole's Head Inn became the staging ground for a new life, premised on the prescient conviction that innocent youth could beat a willing sucker. The Constable rose to the occasion and, to his credit, raked in kroner like a spinster at a casino. With these newfound prospects, the family found themselves eating better grades of sausage, buying factory socks rather than darning the old, and even planning a holiday abroad on two occasions, although neither holiday came to pass.

~

In the lad's fifteenth year, like a breeze coursing through the open doorway of the Vole's Head Inn, a professor of economics wandered into the dim light of the establishment.

"A thinker needs distraction from thoughts," he

confessed.

The academic ordered an akvavit, his potbelly jiggling under a thick jumper as he nestled onto a stool, his long silver hair winking in the light. He had the anxious look of intelligent men separated from what they were meant to do for far too long. He sucked in his breath when he saw the youth at billiards. He neared the table to hear the magic cadence of the clacking ivory, hearing another softer sound. The kid was reciting stanza upon stanza of an Old English poem as he sunk shots. It was Beowulf, an epic of great Scandinavian warriors. As Hrothgar's ashes floated into the air, the youth softly slipped the last ball into the pocket.

The lecturer had found his Emile.

The Constable routed several louts at billiards. The forlorn professor put his arm around the prodigy. "Why do you recite that old foreign poem, young man?"

The youth settled his buttocks on a top rail. "Because it speaks of the great battle."

"Here in Fulaflugahål?"

"Not in Fulaflugahål." With his cue, the youth pointed beyond the window to the threshing trees at the edge of the lake. "Somewhere in the country of the imagination. Two kings fought with their winter armies on the ice. Two brothers, one an insurgent. He slew his brother and usurped the crown. Fulaflugahål is too small for such things."

The lecturer offered the Constable a shandy and contrived to persuade the boy to return to his apartment. The Constable declined his increasingly melancholy pleas. The professor grew lovesick. He fawned, and he pined, and at one point, he turned up, bearing a gift. Toying with the ends of his silver hair, he handed the youth an antique manual on criminology. "Study this section," he instructed, pointing out chapters on modes of deceit by Gypsies and other nefarious tribes. In the following months, the lecturer led the Constable through the strange book's concepts within the Vole's Head Inn's improvised lecture hall. The boy learned to make billiard balls dance, spin and sink, winning rounds and occasionally divesting his opponent of his wallet, undetected.

After a season of tutelage, the boy took the advice of his unrequited admirer—who had somehow managed to bridle the colt of his yearning—and applied for early entrance to the business course at the local university. For the Constable, the benefit was free education. The boon for the professor was the ability to oversee his protégé at close range. And how was the professor repaid? The youth spoke to this or that student in the quadrangle in his shy, supercilious way. He smiled; he charmed. He mimicked cannon smoke. Whether he misunderstood his benefactor's insinuations was uncertain.

Despairing, the professor offered cigarettes and advice to the youth on sexual conquest, disguising his longing in bravado. Every moment of every tutorial rent his soul, confined with his prodigy in the quiet, smoky confines of his campus office.

At the end of his student's course, the professor came to the Vole's Head Inn, ordered an akvavit, and sat in silence. The Constable placed the strange volume on criminology on the bar top. "Tak," he said, flinty-eyed. The professor rubbed his thumb along the spine. He then touched the silver ends of his hair, a look of having been gotten the better of darkening his brow.

~

The Constable took up economics. He extended his insights on pool sharking to investment, kept to himself, grew suspicious, learned the art of periphrasis, and finished in three years with a diploma in the dismal science of quantitative analysis.

The Constable crossed over the mountains that isolated Fulaflugahål from civilization. His objective: a graduate degree in Grimke. In tutorials at the great university, he mused upon the discipline's arcana: random walks and fat tails, the influence of butterflies on hurricanes, boom-bust cycles, the infinite shape of coastlines, the drift of pollen, and tulip manias—all bound in stochastic hegemony. In addition to buffeting the rational versus irrational choice, he made burnt offerings to the madness of crowds.

He had become a quant.

~

Degree in hand, the Constable did what quants do: he took a job in an investment house, jumping from house to house for five, ten, twenty years, still pursuing an ever-receding something. Fate landed him in Icelandic soil and the nascent financial hothouse of Reykjavik. The city was humming in the early years of the new century. Construction cranes perched over the town center, archaic steel birds lining steel nests. SUVs with ballooning tires wobbled along streets meant for sheep. The quant watched as corrugated steel exteriors favored by generations of penny-pinching Icelanders gave way to basalt, a material that was expensive and impressive in equal measure.

These new stone and glass towers taunted the heavens. The Constable shunted investment money from one haven to the next, flipped ancient island companies, converting venerable brands into all-purpose investment vehicles under the umbrageous protection of Icelandic law. Then, the great banks of Europe and America went down in 2008, one after another in breathtaking succession, dead whales fulminating on a hot beach, splattering their molten gore in all directions.

~

On the evening Glitner, Iceland's most significant bank, failed, the Constable stood at the window of a colleague's office, overlooking the city center of Austurvoller Square. Glitnir was a mammoth bank, its finances melting like a polar cap. The Constable parted the blinds with his forefinger. He looked down at the dark flagstone and grey offices of the parliament and, beyond, buildings improvised from driftwood and corrugated iron and kindergarten-bright paint, the architecture of long-isolated people. He saw a crowd gathered in front of parliament. The mob was angry but silent.

His colleague, an ancient, stooped man, spoke in English. His accent was hard to place, possibly from a Baltic nation, some Siberian village, or maybe even one of the old Icelandic families' peculiar dialects. He had a penchant drawing out his words like a poker through hot coals.

"They don't understand risk. Risk means some people lose," his colleague said. The Constable had seen the euphoria and had dealt with the nay-sayers, but the old man was ripe with obdurate contempt. "Icelanders. Far too polite to carry torches and pitchforks. Too introspective. They're hippies and scolds."

The Constable smirked. "I'd give my left eyeball to see what you see."

The old man did not laugh. "Be careful about what you say. This drink will make you see things you wish you'd never seen, remember things you wish you had never remembered." He poured a drink from a bottle he had brought with him. The liquid glittered with a kind of milky iridescence, particulate as if made from crushed horn. What thrilled the Constable's taste buds was like nothing else he had tasted before: rich, mercurial, drawn from an icy spring at the roots of the world. The old man chuckled at the Constable's surprise, an undertone of menace in his voice. "You have known me a long, long while. I am older than time itself."

The Constable swallowed, letting the honeyed-sweetness linger on his palette. "My work is done on this island. I am leaving before the wolf shows up."

"The wolf is already here," the old man nodded sagely. Then, raising his glass, he said "You must remember all of this, yet speak none of it. Of this moment, you will utter only in riddles."

The Constable toasted the old man. Then, the old man reached into his jacket with his liver-spotted hand and pulled out a short instrument. The blade trembled in his grip. But the Constable had only half-seen the action, turning away from the conversation to lower the blind between himself and the crowd. Too late, he saw the curl of contempt on his colleague's lips, the grey sheen of the blade as the older man ran it into his eye.

The Constable staggered and fell to the carpet, the jelly from his eye slipping between his fingers. The old man wiped his blade on the chair upholstery and folded the instrument away. "Now, you will understand in ways you have never understood before. Now, you will remember."

The ancient figure poured his drink over his victim, descended to his Land Rover, and drove to the airport. The next flight swept him away like a black phantom into the white oblivion.

~

The Constable remained on the ice-vexed island and mended piecemeal, a prisoner of circumstance. The history lesson: Within weeks of the infamous collapse, the trillions in speculative capital that had flooded into Iceland for over a decade got sucked from its shores in a global financial riptide. The Hummers and wrap-around sunglasses were as worthless as a netful of putrefying cod. National bankruptcy loomed. International creditors pawed the shores. As Iceland sank into financial anarchy, its primary lender, Great Britain, opportunistically reinterpreted its anti-terrorism laws to freeze foreign assets. The Constable was not impervious to the mess; the government appropriated his accounts and claimed his assets. However, he was not the only one. No one had cash. The island returned to tribal barter. The Constable moved into one of his holding instruments to economize, a vast shell of luxury flats whose builder had ceased construction. The empty block was kept heated to protect against the devastating cold. Because the island sat on a continental rift, its geothermal resources were boundless, and electricity flowed without cost. Geyser water simmered in its pipes. The vacant building prickled with automatic sensors. Doors opened when approached, and lights burst alive supernaturally.

A one-eyed specter haunted the corridors, fingertips running the walls to keep his balance under his new optic discipline, his face like a bombed church. His car echoed through acres of vacant underground parking. The ruined investor was unable to arrange medical attention. As the machinery of global wealth seized and spluttered, his credit cards ceased to work. His cloven eye maturated. Late in an evening, the Constable found himself in a hidden sub-terrace of the building. He let out a hysterical laugh.

Before him sat case upon case of mead. He did not recall purchasing them, but the cache would do as well as currency in this new, old economy. He opened a bottle. Immediately, its fumes refracted in endless succession, building like thermal rollers. He tasted. Flavors lit his brain like a torch, one sensation dividing into many, bending like a corridor of mirrors. The air around him shifted strangely and became vivid. He stared into the mead as if it were a liquid gem, mesmerized by its swirling light. The liquid core of the glass deliquesced. Flavors seemed to ignite and burst into a dream. In his goblet, dimensions swirled, colliding, a globe of condensed time.

~

His ancient colleague's blade had carved an exquisite

wound. The Constable understood not merely the flavors, but also the mortal confluence of past, present, and future in the drink—pain, joy, birth, shame, striving, death. His mind glowed like a furnace. His empty goblet fell to the concrete floor.

Gradually, the winter withdrew, and softer breezes returned. The Constable located a doctor who, for a case of mead, cleaned his unsightly wound. His eye sealed shut. In exchange for steerage quarters, he then traded two palates of mead to a ship captain. The captain let him off among the industrial shipping containers and battered hoists of Grimke from which he wound his long way home.

Over time, the British released what remained of his fortune, and the Constable bought a house in the hills outside Fulaflugahål, sequestering himself behind high windows. The one-eyed man took to wearing a raked hat to hide his ravaged eye socket, a cape to ward off the cold that condemned his flesh. His footsteps echoed on honey-hued slats of wood.

"Hamlet at Elsinore," he hissed.

~

The dwarf asked, "What did you do with all the wealth? Where did the money go?"

The one-eyed man replied, "That has yet to be dreamed."

~

One evening, the pining professor appeared at the Constable's gate, drawn by the beacon of glass and light. The instructor's glorious silver hair had frayed, and thick veins of age scored his temples.

"Do you remember me? You do, my boy, you do. I have but one lesson left, an old gift." He handed his former student the volume he had trundled in a sack from campus.

The tutor then retreated with a hushed farewell into the night.

It was the old volume of crime.

The Constable overcame his ravaged vision by reading the book, chapter by chapter, repeatedly. Between sections, he studied the shadows on the sloping forest floor outside his windows and watched the wind sweep the leaves like a harp. He thought about bodies in motion, the shapes made by a spatter of blood, the drift of pollen, the trickiness of clans, the madness of crowds—the patterns and poetry of chaos. The Constable plied the lusterless tissue beneath his eye patch.

He ceased fighting his destiny. He relented.

~

Some nights, the head of his ancient colleague haunted him in dreams, only the head, detached from the body. It spoke, murmuring ancient and inexplicable truths to him. The Constable held the skull aloft in his hands, seeking its knowledge. Yet dawn would never fail to approach, the barrow of the morning split open, and the dragon-horde of the golden day would spill forth.

Part II: Aud the Deep Minded

12: Viking Funeral

The morning after the Thorkill Thorstein stabbed the truck driver, I sat at my station, bleary-eyed. The Constable whisked into the precinct house with a raven perched on his shoulder, and brightened. "It does me good to see you, boy. I feel unburdened today, light as air. And you, Kolbitter, feeling more your old self?"

The fondness in his tone was palpable. I was confused. I was expecting something to happen but not what *was* happening. Had he forgotten my dramatic refusal in his library the evening before? Was he alert to my theft?

I said, "Sir, I cannot assist with this effort." I sat in silence, feeling foolish.

The Constable stroked the tail feathers of the bird on his shoulder, a manilla packet under one arm. "Let us discuss other concerns. The shift officers interrogated you regarding the pub incident last evening."

"Yes, sir."

"Decidedly, important."

"Violent and dramatic, Constable."

"I am aware."

I presented my moleskin notebook through the window slot of my post.

"Constable, my summary notes of the brothel visit with Bergthora."

"Ah, tacit acceptance of participation in the investigation of the death of the woman in the lake. Acquiescence, if you will."

"No, sir, I mean…" I managed to find my voice. "Constable, I have your story, too."

"Story?"

"Your life-story, or diary, or whatnot. About your parents." I saw the impasse. "This doesn't belong to me, the pages I took from your library."

I placed the sheaf on the shelf between us. A vein fluttered in his left temple. He snatched up the document. "Well then, take this one," he instructed with a curt smile, slipped the manila packet from his arm, and laid it in place of the old pages.

I turned back the soft metal clasp on the sleeve and reviewed the first few paragraphs. This tale seemed to begin mid-stream in a narrative. I looked to the Constable, confused. "Is this about you as well?"

"Of course. My autobiography."

"But I just read your autobiography, and this looks nothing like it."

"This is a different autobiography for a different life. New words, boy, for another existence."

"But, still, for you?"

"You feel only one autobiography can be true? Why confine ourselves to one life?" He continued, "Enough, Kolbitter. I shall be unavailable for a time."

"For the afternoon?"

"No, for the remainder of the case. I must assist the king in locating his missing love letters some knave purloined. A dire matter, and an obligation nothing less than a duty."

Many thoughts warred in my mind. Finally, I said, "And who will take charge of the matter?"

"I cannot continue to spoon-feed everyone in this district." The Constable shook his head and muttered as he stole toward his office, "Misanthropy is never squandered." The door latch clicked behind him.

þ

As the afternoon wore on, I began to wonder whether the Constable knew what he was doing, or if he was setting us up. Was I being used as a scapegoat? Was the man a lonely crank in need of a friend?

The Constable did not reemerge from his office all afternoon. After my shift, I took a bicycle ride over the bridge's brownstone arches out of town along the marshy coast. It was a temporary respite, but a respite nonetheless. I peddled the shoreline. When the moist earth became too soft for tires, I dismounted my bike and stashed it among the rocks that lined the path, and stowed my mobile in the saddleback. Before I moved on, I felt I needed a departing glance at the precinct house. A quarter-mile back, the window of the Constable's office slipped open. With both hands, he raised Minnie carefully before him, seeming to coo and soothe her.

With a fling of his arm, he launched her into the air. The raven wheeled above the building and shot away.

I turned from the scene. I would pass over the moors on foot. After forty minutes, my hike was disrupted when, walking through an open field, a cone of a fir tree landed near me. I scanned about to resolve the mystery. Suddenly, something whipped by my left ear on rapid wingbeats, a black bird with a white tail feather. It was Minne who had dropped the cone. She jerked her head and seemed to look back at me. I supposed this was a signal, so I followed Minne, glad for the company.

Minne lead me to a set of bluffs a fair distance away, a tall horseshoe of rock overlooking a cove. The long uphill slope was arduous, easy to get winded. I slowed, approaching the top, where the stone dazzled green and salmon pink. It would not take more than a foot at the edge to trigger a long and ugly plummet earthward.

"I told her to shut up."

The voice had risen through the natural amphitheater of the bluffs. I cursed the intrusion. The voice continued, joined by another that shared the family tonality.

"She wouldn't shut up."

"What could a lad do in the face of that?"

"I have given up on reasoning with them."

"I have given up on reason altogether."

"Have you?"

The hard, nasal tones were familiar yet unnerving. I fell

to my belly and crept to the verge, the scent of wet soil permeating my nostrils. Peering down, I saw the shingle that stretched out from the limestone cliff foot to the water. Two figures loitered there. One bald, clad in black leather; the other wore a two-toned dress suit: fur collars, both of them.

The Thorstein brothers stood beside a battered skiff half-beached on the shore. The skiff was filled with dry scrub and resembled a bird's nest. Their voices rang as clear as if they stood next to me.

"The hag deserved it."

"She needed convincing."

"A few pokes with the skinny blade stopped her squawking."

"Ja, ja."

"I am working on an idea," Thorkill said.

"You're the brains of the outfit."

"Rationality is overrated," Thorkill said, returning to the previous thread of conversation.

"I have never relied on it."

"Obviously. Now, let's start with violence. A great deal of unreason flows from the refusal to acknowledge that violence is inevitable. Violence guarantees stability; a good, rock-solid society. Suburban moms, bankers, professors, doctors, vegans, hipsters, dropouts, you name it; they bury their heads in the sand. Give peace a chance? Piss off."

Minne swooped over the cliff edge, shrieking, drowning out his words. I inhaled deeply and fell still, watching. Minne repeated her cries, but the brothers did not start. Noise, it seemed, traveled only one direction in this basin, from bottom up.

Brushwood had been piled on the beach, too. The brother in the two-tone suit, Thorkill, slipped something from his pocket. After a few shakes of his hand, a tiny flame emerged from a plastic lighter, which he held to the pile. The fire expanded. The brothers' mood lightened, and they joined in horseplay, passing snide comments on each other.

The antics mounted and grew wilder. Thorvald reared his hand back and struck his brother, sending him reeling back. Thorkill snatched a stone and flung it in response, leaving a nick on Thorvald's bald skull. They laughed and boxed bare-knuckle until each drew blood. Finally, they stuck long sticks in the flames until the ends brightened before fencing with the brands. They lunged; they parried. Embers flew.

When the blaze on the shingle rose to the height of a man's thigh, Thorkill tossed away his stick and raced toward the fire. He flung himself over the flames with a howl. Thorvald mimicked the leap. The brothers took turns in daring the fire this way; their madness ripened. Then, Thorvald's boot caught on a branch; he lurched and lost his balance. Yet he caught himself like a carnival tumbler and rolled across the coals to his feet. Sparks chased him onto the sand.

The brothers remained unhurt in their carnival as if protected by a magic shield, their laughter echoing up the throat of the bluffs. Minne screeched from behind me again and swept nearer the water. Thorkill splashed into the shallows. He laid hands upon the gunwale of the skiff and pointed the bow toward the cove mouth.

Then, he barked in his tenor voice, "Berserk!"

They now seemed possessed by violence, to have left the realm of horseplay. Even from my height, I could see the brothers' faces begin to discolor. They bit the sleeves of their jackets, and frenzy fell upon them. They punched and stabbed at the air. Water flew in every direction.

Thorvald ignited another brand and touched it to the tinder in the skiff. Flames danced. It was then, in the flickering light, that I saw the skiff cradled an object about five feet long, brown as a falcon's egg. The Thorsteins shoved the smoking boat onto the waters. Soon, the skiff was rocking gently, roiling with convection currents, engulfed in smoke and mist. Bright orange sparks crackled heavenward.

Thorvald smiled serenely. "The gods were here."

Thorkill scowled. "Shut up with your romanticizing, brother."

"You have said the folkways are the best ways."

"Folkways! A lad just needs to fight."

They kicked the water and howled to the skies, yelping, and baying.

I wanted to shout. I wanted to cast rocks down on them as missiles. But I was too terrified to move.

The raven looped down again. At the second visitation of the bird, Thorvald tapped his temple. "A white feather. A harbinger."

Thorkill put his head in his hands. After a moment, he raised his face to the black streak in the sky. "A spy."

The brothers plunged from the waves back toward the beach. I now saw an inflatable Zodiac on an anchor rode, bumping the sand, and what appeared to be handlebars peaking over the rubber chambers. The brothers snatched up the tackle, and flicked the Zodiac's big engine to life. Water plumed behind the craft as they hurtled out the mouth of the cove to the open lake.

A path ran back through the moor to the lower terrace. With the menace of the brothers gone, I flew downhill to discover what strange sacrifice they had made. This journey's completion took several minutes, but the smoldering wreck had not drifted far from the shingle by the time I arrived. Icy water spilled into my shoes as I waded in. The wind carried an odor like burnt pork over the water, an almost metallic scent.

There, in the burnt skiff. I recognized the remnants of the red cap first, the shawl fluttering after it. A breeze had whipped up. The smoke and metallic scent gave way to musky, terrible sweetness. It was an odor I would never be able to forget in its entirety.

In the hull lay the husk of the old woman from the mead

hall, dead, the mother of the giantess, Aud.

After I drenched this skiff and yanked it, smoldering, to the shore, I raced on foot to a rise at the mouth of the cove where Minne sat on a rock, looking out to the water, her head feathers puffed and menacing. I looked, too, on the windless lake. The surface was as smooth as a sea of mercury, and the wake of the speedboat fanned out in a V that subsided again into stillness.

This is the cove the short-armed disco patron had told Bergthora about, I thought. But why were the brothers headed out into the lonely expanse of Lake Munch? It was time for me to call in reinforcements.

13: Crystalline Stillness

Officials from Grimke interrogated me for hours at the cove, and I spotted Freja haunting the edges of the scene. She appeared to have left the routine work to the local force, interested only in overseeing the clockworks. I recalled my impression of her that far off day on the ice. Something was missing from her. Very capable, yet perhaps not quite human.

I was released without any indication of what else was needed of me. I was deeply unnerved, given that the terror I was repeatedly witnessing made me feel cursed. It was as though a door had opened before me upon an evil chamber where bloody horrors kept piling up.

Days had now passed since that horror; I had to do something. I was weary and still shaken when I decided I must revisit the mead warehouse, alone. I knew I must speak to the giantess. When I arrived mid-afternoon, the billboard Valkyrie had been torn down, the winged helmet of the warrior maiden crushed to sticks and scattered over the car park. The bunker door flew open at my approach. The giantess had bent her head down. She pressed her fingers upon her temples, her hoarse voice full of self-recrimination.

"I am an ogre. My mother is dead; I did not protect my protector."

I followed her into the gloom of the bunker where antlers and hides hung on the walls. She shrouded herself in her beekeeper canvas and swung the bee smoker as though it were a censer. Bees rained to the floor.

The giantess crumpled to her knees, bawling. Her hands were clenched, red and tight, and she pressed them to the screen of her helmet.

"First, my friend; now, my mother. When does death end? Oh, when does death end?"

Even kneeling, her chin came up to my shoulder. I pulled the giantess close and removed her bee helmet, cradling her large sharp cheeks against my chest. "Oh, my, oh, my," I murmured as we rocked gently side to side as the smoke-drunk bees crept over the floor.

Soon, her tears wet my shirt through.

þ

After leaving the giantess, I drove to the brothel and sat in my car, staring up at a cardboard-blocked window, pondering Nils the Fat Boy, pondering the tall woman in the brothel. Pondering death, death, death.

I did not attempt to go into the building; I had no desire. And something was bothering me, too, scratching at my brain; not the case, but something I could not pin down.

I found myself wandering on foot as the hours slogged by, from the fleabag quarter of the brothel to the columned precinct house to the lakefront's piers, then to the train station. I thought not very seriously about boarding the next Interregional Express. I pictured myself riding till my money ran out, taking up busking for coins, eating crusts from the sidewalk. I imagined myself tramping a desert mountain with no possessions but a toothbrush woven into the tangles of my hair. The old bronze bell clock hanging from the platform ceiling clanged the hour, haunting the barren corridor. The evening had come. I had spent too long castigating myself; I was late.

When I entered Fadlan's apartment, I said, "Sorry I'm late for practice. I was strolling down by the rail platform. What a dingy neighborhood; I've never seen so many metalheads whizzing by on their way to dead-end jobs. That makes perfect sense when you look at the bleak stretches, the abandoned storefronts, all the desolation, the meaninglessness. After that, you want to crank up something thunderous."

"You were where?" asked Gudrid.

I sensed a donnybrook brewing. I threw my shoulders back, seeking refuge in my familiar booster routine.

"What kind of people are we?"

There was silence, but I persisted, responding to my own calls.

"We are Vikings. What kind of band are we?" I waited a beat. "A heavy-metal band. What kind of heavy metal do we make? Viking heavy metal."

Gudrid flung her drumsticks on the carpet, "Grammaticus, you didn't miss practice. You missed the gig—the gig you told us not to miss. We just got back."

Fadlan said, "We had to borrow a van."

Crystalline stillness. I dropped my arms, quitting the schtick. The events of the last few months welled in my brain—the dissonant emotions, the violence saturating every crevice of my brain.

"I did what?"

Fadlan snorted, staring. Egil did not waffle; his tone remained flat. "We've decided you're out of the band."

I felt a white heat fill my chest that made my eyes water and my heart pound like someone banging at a cell door. I knew my bandmates; they were set. The howling silence of the room stretched for moments.

I was no longer a Berserker.

14: Gear of War

The next morning, I told everyone in the stationhouse about the giantess's torment. The Constable was nowhere to be seen. Bergthora spent the afternoon oiling the pistols in the arms locker, departing promptly at shift end. "What if that five-hundred-pound monster came thundering here? No restraining order would discourage that massive troll. I doubt even chains would work."

At dusk, I was at my desk, making archival labels. Snorri had wandered into the station house and joined me, leaning back in a chair, feet propped on my window shelf. A flask of schnapps lingered at his elbow. The small man knocked back his shot, his beard gleaming white. He let his gaze linger on the back of his own hands.

"Liver spots."

I stared through my glass partition at the back of his hands, too. "At least you do not have blue tendons."

"You're glum, Grammaticus."

"I believe yesterday was the worst day of my life."

Yet I could not bring myself to tell of my shame, being kicked out of my own band. I imagined word getting out, imagined Jerker's uncomprehending grin when he heard of my passion. I imagined Bergthora stubbing the coal of her cigarillo on my instrument, grinning. I was used to being isolated, even in a crowd. Fulaflugahål was inhabited by generation after generation of souls striving not to stick out, at any cost, the Scandinavian curse. Loneliness nourishes an artist, and now I guarded my loneliness as a saint does his wounds.

Suddenly, a ferocious wail penetrated the precinct walls. I recognized the giantess's contralto: "For all that I have lost, I might as well become an outlaw." Yes, the giantess had appeared in the yard of the precinct house.

I opened the door to the parade ground. Aud's eyes were

rimmed red, her hair frizzled. Snorri descended the first step toward her.

"You don't want to spend your life in a penitentiary, lass."

Aud had abandoned her beekeeping suit. Her new outfit made her look like a medieval throwback, a creature from a popular summer Viking festival. She wore a beige tunic with a thick belt, tights of supple white leather, and turn boots big as buckets. From the skirt hem of the tunic dangled scores of animal tails clipped from the rumps of foxes, lynxes, and squirrels. A gold chain with dozens of fox teeth hung around her neck. Atop her head sat the carven bowl of a wooden helmet.

"What is this costume?" asked Snorri.

"Gear of war."

Snorri nodded to the sword in the scabbard on her belt. "And that tremendous thing?"

"My battle blade, forged from the talons of a dragon and whetted to eternal sharpness with the scales of its skin, scales as large as the disks of a field harrow."

Snorri said, "Eternal sharpness would be nice."

A dangerous smile lifted Aud's cheeks. "My mother is dead, and I shall avenge her and Misty, found in the ice. I shall avenge them both."

I recalled the dead girl in her drenched costume, the whipping wind, the travesty of the day that now seemed so long ago.

The blade hissed from the belt of the giantess. Approaching the steps, she presented a flat side of the weapon for inspection, four fingers wide at the hilt, and two at the tip. A rhyme was inscribed into the bronze:

> *Forged in fire*
> *And made to pierce,*
> *I'm deadly sharp.*
> *My bite is fierce.*

Snorri nodded. "And who shall you go against in war?"

"The killers, the Thorstein brothers."

I examined the sword poem. "This blade rhyme suggests vigilantism, no?"

The giantess released the heavy weapon, and it thudded to the earth. She smeared a tear across her cheek with a fist. "Some have greatness thrust upon them."

Snorri descended the last step and lifted the sword to give back to her. "I have had loftiness foisted upon me many times, my girl, and risen to every occasion. Perhaps I can help."

I'd hung back in the doorway, thinking. Two murders now. Time unwound before me; one route led to security and the job-funded pursuit of my music, alone. The other dissipated into a shadow play of ambiguity: treachery, criminality, perhaps death.

I was not in a band, not a Berserker. There was nothing to keep me from throwing my lot in with the giantess and Snorri, and I had to do something big to change things. I leaned into the doorframe's interior and snatched my rucksack and a set of keys from the lockbox.

Aud sniffed back tears. "We're going a-Viking!"

The giantess let the tip of her weapon snake behind her through the gravel. We boarded the only precinct vehicle that could house the giantess—a municipal van—and the giantess lowered herself through the rear doors to the floor, sword tucked to her side. The van suspension squealed beneath her bulk.

Snorri slapped his palm to his forehead, evidently recalling something. He held out his hand. I parted with keys. Snorri took the wheel, and we wound out several kilometers to the shore where the funeral skiff had rocked with flames.

þ

Yellow and black-striped police tape marked the crime area

at the cove.

"It's the color of bees," Aud murmured.

Snorri bowed under the cordon, and twigs and fragments of mussel shells crackled under his feet. He flashed an electric torch over the ground, searching. The shadow of a long sharp depression emerged in the pebbles.

I looked down at his discovery. Snorri said, "Motorcycle tracks. Looks like the brothers went around the bend at the cove entrance, then up the shore." We reached the edge of the wood within twenty minutes. Snorri placed his fingers into another gash in the soil. "Identical. I don't think there would be many motorcycles this far up the shore."

Aud drove the tip of her weapon into the sand. "Let this cut mark the threshold of vengeance. Justice begins here." She knelt, grasped the flanges of her standing weapon in one smooth move, and bowed her head, a suppliant. Her voice was sonorous, "I call upon the spirits of the mountains to trip the Thorstein brothers as they walk on precarious heights. I summon river trolls to trammel their fallen bodies. I beg the serpent that dwells at the roots of the earth to gnaw their bones and spit poison on their hearts."

Her tone was such that even the lapping waves seemed to go quiet at her words.

Snorri shouted, "Hup! We're off for glory," and bounded from the pebbled shore into the blackness of leaves.

Aud wrenched the blade from the earth and followed after him, and I followed her.

þ

Twenty minutes later, we were standing under abject darkness. Snorri stooped like a cobbler, the cone from his electric torch sweeping the way, hunting for tire marks.

I said, "Surely, the brothers would have made their way

to a road."

Aud paused to massage her shin. "Fugitives abhor traffic."

I rifled through my rucksack. "I don't have my mobile. It must be on my desk at the precinct. Do either of you have a phone?"

Snorri shrugged. "Nope. With my Lucia gone, I have no one to call."

The giantess spread a large hand. "My fingers are too big for a mobile."

I pressed my lips together. "What if we have to contact the Constable or anyone?"

Snorri flashed his torch into the surrounding night. "We'll have to get along without, like when I started as a young man at the station house, on foot and isolated."

"*Hup,*" said Aud.

Snorri seemed to want to bend and dissect every small thing coming his way. He chuckled at some abstruse revelation. "Tenacity. Sometimes, the wrong way is the right way, Grammaticus."

The trail curved away from the lake. We proceeded with just the calls of an unseen raven as company. Finally, Aud said, "I'm hungry."

In our haste, we had not contemplated food. Snorri began to clear a patch of ground. "We will not find the brothers tonight. And, I must save the torch battery." He scraped together wood for a fire, frowning at the thought of sacrificing a match slotted for his pipe. Soon, flames flickered under a roof of trees. "I'll be back," Snorri shouted, his heels disappearing in the direction from which we had arrived.

The giantess and I fed the fire. Just as the moon slipped beyond the branches, Snorri returned, a pair of lifeless hares slumped in his hands. He cleaned his catch with the edge of Aud's weapon, and soon supper smoked over the ashes. Aud feasted on one carcass, Snorri and I the other.

"How did you manage to bag two hares?" I asked.

Snorri picked something black off his tooth then flicked it away. "Eternal sharpness," he said.

Since we had no bedrolls, we made paillasses of pine needles. My eyes followed a wisp of smoke upward. High above, in the wind, an unseen bird let out a lacerating cry. I found it hard to sleep under the stars and spent hours battling the wild vacillation of worry until exhaustion brought relief.

15: Rat in the Rafters

A ferocious pain in my shoulders woke me at dawn. In retrospect this was not surprising, as I had lain all night over a rock. Snorri rose with not an ache about him. For breakfast, we snapped hare bones and licked the marrow, after which we resumed our trek. Further inland, the motorbike tracks grew faint. Every few hundred meters, Snorri laid down with his belly to the earth, searching for even the slightest trace of our quarry and miraculously caught sight of the tracks again. "This way!"

Aud chafed, "We must move faster."

Gaining on Snorri's lead, I entered a clearing ahead of the others, and a chill wind ran through me. Hundreds of black crows lay dead in the briars and scrub; their wings were torn and necks twisted, beaks wedged into the earth. I shrunk back from the carnage of lifeless fowls. Before I could warn the others of the strange horror, however, I heard Aud gasp behind me, followed up by a sharp curse from Snorri. The soft breeze that curled the mist made the feathers of the corpse-flock flutter. I do not know what Aud said next because she was gibbering, her invocations punctuated with vehement protestations: an omen had visited us.

"Nature has lost its mind," Snorri whispered.

The putrefying stench of the dead birds was overwhelming, but we managed to edge around them into the surrounding hills. Once we had passed, the trees grew sparse; another clearing emerged; and now, a stocky young man appeared, making his way along a meadow with shiny blonde hair shaved at the nape. He wore a yellow jersey with black athletic pants.

Another lad sidled in from the tree line to march beside him. A third came, and then a fourth, and by the time we saw five, I realized all wore the same kit: black athletic pants and yellow polos. Within a quarter-hour, thirty youths advanced together, identically clad, a wrangling rhythm governing their stride. We followed, hidden among the foliage.

Aud said, "And who are they?"

At another corner of the meadow, a different tribe emerged similar in number but dressed all manner of ragged jeans, cricket jumpers, black T-shirts, motorcycle boots or factory boots, and thick leather belts. About a hundred paces of open field separated the two groups. I was watchful. A few men bounced on their feet while others jogged back and forth. A feeling of agitation began to brew, and I sensed an impending conflict between the groups.

Some men let their hands drop to their sides, curiously relaxed, sizing up their opponents. The sense and possible severity of the threat grew. Then, with a roar, both sides rushed at each other over the plane, joining in battle in a flurry of slaps, kicks, and punches. Ribs were bruised, and faces pummeled; blood was drawn. Men offered themselves up to the fight, and bodies fell, yet the clash was over in less time than it takes to collect a dole check. The enemies withdrew, some limping and grumbling, others gloating. Notably, none indicated severe hurt.

"That was a shabby skirmish," Aud grumbled.

"Not out for blood," said Snorri.

I asked, "Why would they be out here in the forest?"

"Keeps combat far from authorities. Such is the underbelly of soccer: hooliganism." Snorri slipped comfortably into broad discursive motioning. "For most fans, a pitch is a sacred space. A derby is a sacred time. Every Sunday at three p.m., ninety minutes of licensed disorder, regulated misrule and jest prevail. All in the spirit of play. But then, some supporters want to go beyond rowdy cheering and chaos. Gangs of brawlers with their unwritten codes for violence. Firms are not after everyone; they're more like fight clubs and, most often, will leave bystanders alone."

"Cracking," the giantess said.

"Unfortunately," Snorri continued, "within hooligan packs, lurk sadists ever eager to inflict real harm. The casual brawler will go in for sixty seconds of rope-a-dope or smash-and-grab, followed by pub drinking and chants. These sadistic lurkers want more, but few lads want to fight someone who's after permanent bodily damage."

Aud said, "Those brothers, they're more than sadists."

The groups now merged, advancing as one body on the path, the black and yellow and the motley ruffians.

"A strange spectacle," I said.

Snorri stooped again. The grass stalks were flattened and littered with debris in the battle location. Snack wrappers. Beer cans. "They've trampled everything," he said.

Aud pointed to the soil with the vast toe of her turn boot. "Look here, Grammaticus."

I unfolded a scrap of paper crushed in the grass, a flyer that said:

> *See Olaf the Peacock speak*
> *Back from exile in Florida*
> *Patriot – Hero – Terrace Legend*

A raven alighted on a branch over the path from which the pack had entered—a sign, Aud was sure—and followed down the route. Aud spoke from behind a shielding tree. "The tail feathers of the raven. One is very long and white."

"Yes," I said. "She has been following us."

"The bird is a girl?" said Aud.

"Her name is Minne. She belongs to the Constable." But I did not get the opportunity to explain further how I had become familiar with the bird. We spotted a building of dark wood hidden among the trees. From afar, it was a handsome chalet of dark brown timbers with lots of scrollwork; the white-feathered raven arrived before us, settling on the entrance roof. A pair of youths stood sentry at the door below the raven's perch, so we crept to the back of the chalet to avoid detection

"I don't see any vehicles and no power lines," the giantess spoke in a low voice. Aud was careful not to test the chalet wall with her weight, fearful it might collapse.

Snorri pointed to a bank of solar panels. "Off the electrical grid."

Fits of laughter emanated from the building. I peered in a rear window to gain an interior view. What I saw was a kind of party in progress, with the black and yellow battlers swarming around a snack table.

Snorri joined me at the sill. "Maybe a hundred people."

I did not like what I saw. Both factions from the meadow mingled within, behaving familiarly with each other, a single group downing beer after beer and slinking about the large hall. Some folded and unfolded their arms in impatient expectation.

"A good portion rolled straight from a taproom," said Snorri.

Aud left us to creep to the front edge of the building where the youths still stood guard. Rising to her full height, the giantess stepped around the chalet corner, cooing, "Hello, lads."

I heard cries of surprise and then a pair of thumps on the earth.

Aud returned with two black and yellow kits, which we received. Snorri lifted a bony leg into his slacks. "A proper harlequin suit for a geezer."

While Snorri and I entered the hall, the giantess stayed outside, receding into the foliage. Inside, a man about my age in a one-piece coverall, orange sherbet color with vertical green stripes on the sleeves, stopped me. He wore a handlebar mustache and seemed to be acting as a guard. His eyes flitted between us, scrutinizing us. "Were you at the rumble?"

Snorri tapped the side of his nose as if the two shared a secret. "Ja, mate. You look like a Formula One driver circa nineteen sixty-five."

The guard seemed pleased with the observation. "Pass on."

At the head of the room stood a podium. Snorri steered us to the snack table at a wall, where we ate ravenously till we had our fill. There was something deeply unnerving about the people in the room, although it was hard to fix just what. My accomplice began to narrate the scene as though he was a tour guide.

"They sure are a patriotic lot. Bunting and banners. The color scheme matches the national flag."

I nodded, wary. Snorri slipped packets of crisps into his pockets.

The moustached guard left his post at the door and stepped to the podium. He seemed to be doubling as master of ceremonies. The crowd quieted as he cleared his throat. "Why are we here?" he asked the room. "All of us, though we come from different parts of town, different parts of the country, even different parts of society. We are here to unite. Hup!"

The crowd surged forward and I found myself suddenly crushed against the blond youth we had first spotted on the meadow path. Up close, I noticed his scrupulously cut wedge hairstyle, clearly a point of grooming pride.

I tried meeting his eyes, as my fingers began to flick notes. Snorri popped between us. He said, "What is your name?"

The youth raised his nose. "Everyone calls me Rudeboy. You're a bit ancient to rumble, mister."

"You're never too ancient to rumble."

The youth frowned and then broke into a grin. "Ja, never!"

Snorri pointed to the podium. "Who's he, the guy who was the door guard?"

"He is called The Viscount."

"He's a Viscount?"

"Ha! Wise up. What's your name?" The youth stuck out

a hand to shake.

Fortunately, the speaker plowed on and we turned to the podium. "We're here because politics is the continuation of war by other means. We share a common champion in a man, a renegade, a singular force…"

A heckler shouted, "Oy, your excellency, get to the point."

"Hold your nuts; this is my eloquent part. A man lately returned from exile, a man you know personally or by reputation." The crowd broke into applause as the speaker bowed and ceded the podium to a middle-aged man in a black turtleneck. Though livid red crescents scored his cheeks, his bulldog shoulders and snug turtleneck transformed his ravaged face.

Snorri slashed the tips of his index fingers down from his eyes. "Somebody carved an admission slip to the hospital upon his face. Switchblade wounds. Ambushed."

The man ran a meaty hand over his scalp. His voice was rich and resonant, like a radio voice, a music that had graduated beyond persuading girlfriends or magistrates and aimed at a larger game. "Some of you know me as Olaf the Peacock."

Snorri circled my left elbow with a strong hand. "Rudeboy, Viscount, Peacock—got it?"

I nodded.

Someone shouted, "Welcome home, Mister Peacock."

"I'm glad to be back. Each of you who was with me in Milan, Amsterdam, Barcelona, we go way back. The haul we took. Lager, lager, and more lager. Do you recall when we rolled the burnt-out taxi off the pier in Malmo?"

Laughter rippled through the crowd.

Olaf's disfigured cheeks crinkled with good humor. "Lads, the world today—this is just like when they put up the fences near the pitch to keep us penned in. They called us hooligans. Roughnecks. Brigands. You couldn't get to the loo to take a piss, and it made you feel debased. Dehumanized. And it's like that wherever you turn. You know the humiliation. You are not getting that job. Waiting in the queue for someone who doesn't have proper identification. The stink from their food carts on the high street."

Men surged toward the stage in a wave. Olaf the Peacock thrust his fist over the podium.

"We are hungry for a new beginning. We're just a bunch of loyal guys. A great movement is afoot, a sea change."

The eyes of some of his listeners lighted. They replied:

"Kebobs, tacos."

"Those oozy dumplings."

"What a stink."

"Those people eat bats."

"Worse than American food. Hamburgers and pizza. Beer like piss."

"I love pizza," a voice objected.

Olaf pressed on. "They come by caravan and in armadas. Why? Wars, epidemics, famine, floods. Their crappy existence."

"Turd countries."

"Yes, turd countries. But look at how the bleeding hearts fawn. Mandela, Gandhi. We need strength to turn all that back. My boys, yesterday I arrived on an economy plane ticket from Florida, where I have lived in a trailer home. I went to Florida because the authorities and tax hijackers here forced me out. Why pay taxes for something you don't believe in? Government everywhere is in shambles."

Olaf the Peacock placed the knuckle of a folded forefinger to his chin.

"This dole is *our* dole. We paid for it; we earned it. We must fend off bloodsuckers and welfare cheats and the southern elements swamping our shores."

A lone shout burst from the back of the room.

"Kick out the foreign scum."

Olaf punched his fists overhead. "Outlaws change history. We will change history. Who were the Vikings but outlaws? The Scandinavian spirit is founded on blade and blood."

The boots of the men made a booming and incessant thunder on the wooden floor. The sheer crush of bodies had forced Snorri to his toes. He said, in an undertone, "This is what the great heritage comes to, a wrangle over welfare?"

The Viscount stepped back to the podium before an increasingly obstreperous crowd. "An excellent speech."

Olaf the Peacock bowed deeply to the room.

"Time to celebrate," the Viscount announced.

Someone blew a rude note on a vuvuzela, a signal. Colored lights popped on, and excelsior streamed from the rafters. A projector screen pin-wheeled photo slides of the national flag, blond girls in white aprons, and forest-green skirts, with trim young men, posed majestically. Thoughtful, sensible, cosmopolitan.

Hooligans started to whistle their displeasure. Someone appropriated the electronics, and music swarmed through the speaker system, an unvaried explosive rasp. Olaf the Peacock whooped as if he was a DJ.

The men began to hop in a wild dance: legs scissoring, flailing, pogoing, slamming into whoever was nearby. The music pounded out the same artless bellow. Hive behavior. Then it dawned on me. I was at an isolated hooligan compound in a forest far from Fulaflugahål. Two women had been killed; I was in over my head. Music would not protect me here.

þ

A large shadow filled the open doorway. Aud deliberated in the entrance, eyes darting through the chaos. The moshers were too frenzied to notice her. She moved into the room, the floorboards questioning her every step.

We managed to convene beneath the overhang of the stairs. There we crouched, watching. Finally, Snorri said, "It's a dance, boys' night out."

I looked at the thrashing men. "A political assembly. But why? And why out here?"

Snorri said, "No prying eyes."

Aud unfolded herself from our stairway niche and unbuckled her sword. My arms sunk with the weight as I took it from her. She swayed into the room, snapping her fingers as if listening to bosa nova.

Some of the moshers fell back. "Fi-fi-fo-fum," someone shouted.

Suddenly, Aud lofted herself into the fray. Her four hundred sixty-two pounds flew up. Upon achieving her apex, the hive parted. Her body dropped as if released by unseen machinery. Planks and floor joists exploded beneath her thundering bulk as she hit the floorboards, a maelstrom of wood slivers driving in every direction.

I stared at the astonished faces and gasped, "Aud, your bones."

The giantess raised her head from a wrecked crater.

A thug with a bulging stomach reeled out from the other end of the parted sea of bodies. It was the bouncer from the flat Bergthora and I had visited, Nils the Fat Boy. He held some limb of broken furniture, which he swept rhythmically at knee level. The improvised cudgel went, tick-tock.

Aud clawed herself from her pit in the boards and took her sword from Snorri.

"You're a travesty of the human form." Nils laughed in an abrupt sort of way that made his laugh far exceed its inspiration. A disagreeable odor of cheap vodka and pickled fish bloomed from him. Then, Nils attempted a nun-chuck twirl with the table leg but fumbled, and the table leg spun across the floor. Hurling his walrus body to retrieve it, Nils dove and rose, wielding the leg again though as a bat eighty degrees to the shoulder.

Aud swiped her blade so that it skimmed harmlessly over the Fat Boy's scalp but clipped the table leg. The bat parted like a stick of tallow. Nils stared at the wooden stump left in his hands. Aud stepped back to *en guard* stance, as if she held a rapier, her weight shifting to one leg, the other stretched back. She was breathing heavily as she shifted her sword so that her right hand braced against the hilt and her left gripped the base. "The knife fight is a ritual, a dance." She paused. "Fat boy, would you care to dance?"

She touched the tip of her sword to Nils' nose.

The bouncer sputtered an over-eager laugh. "I failed to bring my top hat and spats."

Aud gripped the handle with two hands, swung her weapon away from Nils' face, then with surprising swiftness to the flab of his neck and held it there. Nils quivered like aspic jelly and said not a word. Then, Aud stood the blade tip down, and curled her fists around the cross-guard.

"Kiss," she commanded.

The rims of Nils' eyes were a raw pink as he pressed his lips to the metal.

"Oh, good lord, cut his throat already," someone cried. I looked around but could not find the speaker. I knew the tonality; it was familiar and coming from above. I looked up. The sight was like a truncheon on my brow. Thorkill Thorstein stood twenty feet above the mob, balanced on a hewn rafter, brilliant in his two-toned suit, hair swept back.

"Fine sentiments all around, lads, and whatever you are, giant. Male or female?"

I watched the circular swaying of Aud's blade. She said, "Female."

Thorkill crept along the wood beam, paused to swing his body around a truss, crept again, and then stopped. "The fat boy knows little, but he was right about this: you are a travesty of the human form."

The giantess gulped down a breath. "You killed my mother and set her body afire. You killed my friend and sealed her under the ice."

Thorkill's face screwed up in a squint. "I am genuinely confused. Why would anyone seal a dead girl under an ice cap?"

"You have a psychosis."

"Me? I'm offended. Everyone knows a freak like you will suffer from psychological damage. Oppressive moods, stilted judgment, and all that." Thorkill Thorstein turned again to the assemblage. "Violence may not be the only answer to societal inequalities, but it is always the final answer and, certainly, the most fun answer."

With a bitter laugh, he dug out his weezer and began to pee, much to everyone's dismay, over the crowd below.

þ

After urinating, Thorkill Thorstein leaped from rafter to rafter. Hooligans flung beer bottles at him. Someone shouted, "Nils pays for fellatio from girls at the harbor."

Thorkill turned on a beam as if he was a player on the catwalk of a theater. "You like those spraddle-legged foreign cows, fat boy?"

Starting to overcome his humiliation from seconds before, Nils flung the table leg overhead, but it harmlessly bounced off a nearby beam. Thorkill Thorstein dropped like a rat from a drainpipe, landing on the sill of an open window, slipped out the opening, and clattered down some exterior fixture.

The throng heaved toward the door at the back of the hall. I felt squeezed by bodies, moving higher on the comb of a wave. Outside, a motorcycle revved, jumped to high gear, then dopplered away. The crowd thinned as men scurried from the building, like bees from a dying hive, with only a couple dozen hooligans gathering outside. Nils slunk up beside the lingering mob, having found a bottle of vodka, and was taking nips.

"Time for a good scrimmage, eh, mates?" He mimed a sharp sideways stomp with his boot, the kick of someone who knew how to break a thighbone in an alley and be off before the howling began.

Olaf the Peacock, arms crossed over his chest, fingered his biceps. "Nils, son, the empty drum makes the loudest noise."

The men began sorting themselves back into factions. Black and yellow kit migrated to one side of the shading boughs; T-shirts lounged against the chalet wall. Intense and protracted silence fell, then Olaf pointed down a bare and smooth path.

"Let's make a pincer. We shall reconnoiter at that little harbor village down at the lakeside."

Aud rested the blade of her sword flat against her left shoulder, one hand under the pommel, rifle-like. "Count us in the scrimmage."

The chieftain's laughter echoed down the colonnade of trees. "You and the twitching idiot and the dwarf with a face like a shovel?"

I watched the cadre of black-and-yellow clad youths disappear up the path, Rudeboy at its lead. Olaf, the Viscount and their jean-clad entourage disappeared noiselessly, mercenaries into a jungle. Nils tucked his vodka flagons at his elbows and whisked himself into the dim light of the forest.

16: Into Open Waters

Snorri raked his fingers through his beard. "We must arm ourselves and follow."

I sat on the spongy soil. "Arm ourselves with what?"

"Aud, check the armory, I mean, the garden shed," Snorri instructed.

The giantess disappeared behind the chalet. When she returned, Snorri inspected the booty of her errand, a field ax and wooden pole. Scooping up the ax, Snorri regarded the blade with the discernment of a gourmet fingering a cheese.

"This is a woodchopper, the edge notched."

"What do I get?" I asked.

Snorri nodded to the other implement.

I frowned. "A rake-handle?"

Aud set her chin in her hands. "It is a quarterstaff. A quarterstaff is used to strike others, block strikes, parry, and otherwise defend yourself. Simple actions, difficult to master."

The overhead branches clashed with a sudden breeze. Aud and Snorri quickly rounded a bend ahead on the path. I gathered my rake handle and strode after them.

þ

A mat of pine needles ushered us into the blue-green light. Aud's pace had been waning. She let out a muffled sigh. As if to give her brief respite, Snorri knelt and tested a suspicious mushroom by blowing on it; it released a cloud of spoors. He crushed the mushroom with his right heel. "Don't eat those," he instructed.

We hiked up a final steep slope and stared down the other side of the crest at an old lakeport village. A new odor filled the air: the scent of burning. As we started our descent, we saw smoking timbers, shattered glass glinting along the narrow lanes. Three cars parked along the street had doors beaten in. A fourth car had a small cube refrigerator wedged through its shattered windscreen. I watched two elderly women in the street below rushing along the walk, dressed in black like dowagers. They fled into an alley and disappeared.

Aud thumped downhill ahead of me. A thin, blue-veined woman slumped in the doorframe of a packaged food store, her hands resting on the ground, palms up, despondent. One foot was bare, having lost a leather clog. Smoke from the wreckage formed a green haze around us and she winced when she saw us approach.

Snorri attempted to reassure her: "We are working at the pleasure of Fulaflugahål precinct leadership."

The woman rubbed her red ears. "Lots of syllables in those words," she said, regaining herself, and started telling us her story. A group of thugs dressed in black and yellow had poured into the village from the north shore, and another had come from the forested western edge. She rattled off miscellaneous details of the thug uniforms: black boots, black jeans, ragged T-shirts, handlebar mustache. They worked fast. Brutes piled into her shop and stripped the shelves, howling, stuffing their jackets with beer, biscuits, and soda. Then, a lad with a fancy wedge haircut disappeared up the back steps. Seconds later, a little cube refrigerator flew out the second-story flat window and smashed the windscreen of her car.

"Not a penny is left in the till," the shop woman sobbed.

Aud called to her, "Did anyone get the police?"

A sly, defeated smile crept over her face. "It would take half a day before the cops arrived. About twenty roughnecks descended from the northern forest, others from the western shoreline."

"Where did the hooligans go?" asked Aud.

The woman slowly lifted her arm as if she was an oracle pointing to another dimension, "One must fear the power and danger of crowds."

"Some crowds are brave," Aud said.

"The mobs I know are drunk or angry, or a combination of the two."

"Democracies are mobs," Aud said.

But the woman had crumpled into herself, her lusterless eyes drifting to a tugboat tied at the dock. "Your friends are resting after marauding."

Snorri and I were still wearing black and yellow outfits. We bid the woman farewell and made our way to the waterfront.

Yards beyond the pilings, men in their motley garments sprawled on the tugboat's open deck, sleeping, as the hulking vessel lifted and settled with the swells. Beer cans rolled serenely across the timbers; an odor of mayonnaise and urine mingled on the breeze.

Suddenly, the whine of small, powerful motors burst into the silence. My eyes flitted back to the village lane. I recognized the brothers at once. They straddled Husqvarna motorcycles and they barreled down the jetty. I raised my rake handle and drew back on my left foot. One engine blasted to my right, the second blasted to my left as the brothers split along either side of me. I closed my eyes and lunged, swinging.

The next sensation I had was of a violent physical shock to my shoulder. My eyes popped open. I found myself spinning one hundred eighty degrees, still standing. One bike lay on its side. Thorvald Thorstein clutched his leg at the knee, his straight mouth bracketed with lines of pain. My quarterstaff had struck him just above the boot top. I did not see where Thorkill had gone.

To my astonishment, the dismounted rider stood the cycle up, swung back onto the seat saddle, and aimed at the open lake waters. He sped full-on toward the end of the pier. At the last moment, his tires screeched, mudguards shivering. In a series of well-timed hops, he bounced his cycle over the low railing. Rider and bike vanished below the horizon of the dock.

"Are they drowned?" said Aud.

"No splash," said Snorri.

It was then I realized Thorkill must already have vanished from sight in the same mysterious way. An outsized engine roar kicked up from below the dock, a thundering far louder than the motorcycles had made. Then a motorboat burst suddenly into view. Instantly, I recognized the inflatable rescue boat from the day Aud's mother had been set ablaze. The handlebars of the Husqvarna bikes rode heavily on the rubber pontoons.

"How shall we chase them now?" Aud moaned as the Zodiac disappeared past a green headland into the rolling void of the lake.

Not one of the wretched souls on the tug boat had roused. The beer cans continued to rock back and forth with the sea. Aud, Snorri, and I approached the jetty's end and peered over at the narrow, hidden dock. Close by was a weathered gig cleated to the wall, an antique lapstrake affair that had only a mainsail on the boom, no foresail, no oars, and no engine.

Aud's brow furrowed.

"I see no other choice," said Snorri.

I leaped with the little man down to the gig, and together we gingered the giantess near the keel, placing her sword beside her. We pushed off the pilings, drifted a few meters, and raised the mainsail; the wind filled the canvas. I took the tiller, and Snorri's eyes grew narrow as he scanned the waters. Aud nestled deep in the narrow cradle of the hull.

"It smells like fish down here," she grumbled.

The village's grey wharf fell away, and, as we proceeded onto the open waters, the sky melted from eggshell blue to cyan and from cyan to vermillion.

"We are moving at a snail's pace compared to that rescue boat," Aud said.

"The wind is strong, a good sign, but I do not trust it,"

Snorri advised.

Lake Munch was infamous for its ferocious, short squalls. I, too, did not like the forbidding sky. Our mood settled into a gloomy slog. Aud said, finally, "We are not entirely without good omens. We have our comrade, who has joined our expedition again." The giantess pointed from her recumbent position to the spreader up the spar, where a raven with a white tail feather sat.

Interlude Two: Rain, Wind, Fire

Aud set one of her colossal feet against the mast base. She appeared to spend some time feeling the wood with the sole of her boot, her eyes tracing the bending spar skyward. She addressed her next words to the bird.

"This is how I predict the weather, Minne. Usually, the wind will hit high up first and then shake down the length of the mast. If I feel the spar tremble, the weather is changing, maybe a storm. But the wood of the spar must be tight as an archer's bow for the trick to work."

Minne took one step toward the mast and trilled *kra.*

Snorri watched the raven swaying with the spar. "Out onto open waters, friends."

"Monsters. This shall take care of them," Aud said, tapping the ball at the end of her sword

"Great passions from a lady of great heart," said Snorri.

"Too much heart, too much everything; my limbs ache with ceaseless growth."

"Giantesses are mortal, too."

"Sir, too mortal."

Snorri reached across the cockpit and tapped my tiller. "A little more to the west," he said.

Our journey would be west and southward, of necessity, since Lake Munch formed a long craggy oval about fifty miles in length, with Fulaflugahål at the very northeastern end. As we bore on, silver slips of spray at our bow, I remembered the mysterious packet the Constable had dropped at my desk window in the precinct house was still in my pack.

I drew out the envelope and tore it open.

This time the Constable's handwriting was almost illegibly small, with sentences creeping around and up or down the narrow margins. I had the impression of a private document written in haste, like the pages I had spirited from his library, mixing history and magic, farce and tragedy. The pages of the manuscript were numbered, and the first three of them had been omitted:

The Constable's Second Autobiography

. . . regained a full cycle of the moon. This outcome was perhaps not what my parents desired, for I was an unpleasant youth at that time, and they had the ill fortune to endure one more annoying episode of my churlishness. We rehearsed a familiar dispute. Father foresaw the twilight of our existence. The old guard must be replaced; such was the nature of epochs. But I demanded more of my parents. Could they do nothing other than lament? Nothing but scavenge the world for a few dismal moments, like carrion birds? I considered my parents selfish to the core, imprisoned in self-regard.

The scent of cardamom wafted from Father. Mother wore a liripipe of azure silk that drew out her narrow chin, hazel eyes, and the grey streaks in her hair. I watched Father's gaze dart among the hills. Columns of smoke crept through a windless sky.

"The mines," my father lamented. "They have broken out from the mines."

I watched a mob army thronging over the plains from their hovels on the steppes, the swelling band feared and loathed by Mother and Father. Unlike my parents, however, I held these dim figures from the pits, with their leather caps and makeshift weapons, as symbolic of an impending uprising we may have deserved but were not doomed to accept or repeat. Compassion. Oversight. Guidance. The future was forked, and infinite, and might contain any of these. In the guise of self-imposed rebellion, I feigned nameless psychopathy, lounging about the manor, refusing to bathe, flinging myself to the ground at the slightest provocation. I quoted nonsense and pretended not to understand the most straightforward questions. I fasted inordinately.

Father sent for the lawgiver from Grimke to speak to

me. The man wore a merry jerkin embroidered with tulips and river barges and a tall black cap with a single white feather. Evidently, he had been warned of my mood.

"Your grace," he swept his plumed hat to his breast.

I sneered. "Lawgiver, are you here to break into the coffers of our women and steal the goldenrod?"

"No, lad, I come to give, not take."

"You should have brought jesters. Fiddlers. Carnival masks with beaks and felt mustaches. Or, are you the jester? Where is your paper crown?"

The lawgiver coughed an artificial cough into the knuckles of his hand, "My liege, festivities would jeopardize the calm that is essential for your health."

"My health?"

"You have grown thin. Dark pockets under your eyes. You must eat." From his jerkin, he withdrew a green leek and fell to one knee to present it. "I shall roast this vegetable for you. It has magnificent nourishing properties."

I sniffed the leek. "It smells of death."

"How so?"

"Blood. Stench. Rotten as the stew of earth from which it sprang. Where was it grown?"

The lawgiver indicated a nearby peasant farm known for the large ash at the edge of its fields. I replied it was no wonder this harvest tasted of death.

"No wonder?"

"That ash was a gallows tree. A gang of highwaymen came riding. They were caught and hung from its boughs. Vultures perched on the napes of their necks and tore their flesh. It is their blood I taste."

The lawgiver retrieved his leek from my hands and bowed his big oblong head many times over as he backed away. His cheeks had gone pale. "Lad, I beg pardon, you are right. You are indeed right. I have failed and am a miserable wretch. I ask forbearance…" Etcetera. At last, he disappeared out the heavy oaken door, the plume in his *cap dancing with shame.*

~

Mother, Father, and I bickered through half our days. "You think this mask of silliness will help you gain your so-called freedom. Well, it shall not." Mother tossed another empty mead bottle into the garden pond, where it bobbed on the rippling water before it sank.

She tested her theory of my mental state by bringing a highborn maiden to sport with me. When the girl arrived, I was alone in the garden practicing my fencing: right foot forward, hand down. Left foot forward, blade extended, sweep and feint, and so on, through the exercises. I heard a rustling behind me and swung about, my weapon poised.

Her teeth were the color of almonds, and her hair had all the ribbons of a maypole. I smiled but offered no greeting before turning back and saluting my invisible fencing opponent, bringing my saber up. I then turned my torso to the right, and the blade pointed diagonally to the ground.

"A gallant weapon," said the maiden. "You move smartly."

"Your name?"

"Freja."

Her eyes were violet; her lips made the pallor of her skin almost startling. I replied without altering my guard, "Mother thinks that having a pretty girl near me will prove my phlegmatic state is simply an act, that I will reveal my sanity by the earnest pursuit of you."

"Eccchhh. We all <u>act</u>." She hesitated. "You are not of this world."

"And you are as a mermaid longing for the sea."

"Am I pretty?"

"Delightful. Am I mad?"

"You are rude."

"You are haughty."

I raised the tip of my saber to a ribbon above the maiden's left ear and flicked it gently, so the silk separated and fell among the stems of grass. I will admit my blade struck closer than I had intended, and the lobe issued a tiny drop of blood. The shocked maiden fled, shouting protest.

My parents descended on me with magnificent outrage. "Wicked fiend," my mother shouted.

Father's velvet robe swirled as he tromped along the granite balustrade. "Do you not want to enjoy our peaceful existence? You are not to be trusted."

I replied with the unwavering gusto of youth, "If it is fated that we must clash with that horde, then let us do so. Give me war over occupation."

My father snorted, "Occupation would be a mercy in this age of swords, this age of axes when betrayal is certain." Father stared as if transfixed. "Devilish rationalism has kicked the stilts out from under everything. No certainty, none. In the absence of certainty, they will kill each other over a minor slight. They will seethe with resentment and oppress the tiniest difference. A warm pot and strong drink, is the answer for them."

I surveyed the plain. The evening seemed to have lurched forward unexpectedly; a bright moon showed upon the gloom. The clattering masses had encamped for the night. Their cooking flames danced among broken tumbrils and staves as they boiled stews of chaff and scavenged meat. A rancid fetor drifted down from the tents.

~

I resolved to escape. The moon had lifted, a milky lozenge glimmering through the boughs. I slipped my spurs over my bootheels and crept to the stable to find a mount, a grey stallion with muscular hocks. The painted birchwood saddle chafed my thighs; I dropped my steed's pace to a canter. By dawn, I arrived at Grimke, a metropolis compared to the villages scattered about our estate. By afternoon I was stumbling from one public house to another, adamant about spending my final hours in a hedonic blur. I ended in an establishment with the unfortunate name of The Vole's Head Inn, a lamplit cave with hams and ropes of garlic strung from the rafters. A carboy of cognac found its way to my elbow and a plump redhead to my knee.

"You are darling, Love," the redhead whispered, her voice rough as coals scraping on a grate. "Such a comely face, with your flowing dark hair and skinny arms, hands always twitching. I bet you can work magic with those fingers. Shall we go upstairs, Sweet?"

A man of late middle-age with a pocked nose stood aloof by the belching hearth throughout my cavorting. A hairy cap on his head, he had laced his hands behind his back in a posture of restraint. What he thought as he watched remained uncertain since he showed neither patience nor impatience.

I dropped my voice to the lass. "Who is our friend?"

The redhead was half-turned to him. "Never seen that old runestone before."

I portioned a drink from the carboy, extending the goblet to the stranger. "Mister, you look hard, as if hewn from a block of granite. Split by great forces, were you? Come, sit on our plank and tell us a tale."

I jiggled the redhead on my knee to make the invitation more inviting.

The visitor received my cup with a curt, "Tak."

Yet soon enough, he was on the bench, with us elbow deep in cards and cognac. Hangers on collected about our table, filching drink, and harvesting fallen coins. "Let's play that old game so popular deep in the forests of the West." Before I knew it, the stranger was dealing a game with a deck not familiar to me, cards backed with an assortment of boars, wreaths of flowers, knights on horseback, and skeletal harlequins. The rogues took positions on the benches on every side. I made my way about the table, asking names.

"Who are you?" I asked.

*One held his clay pipe with tongs. "Dirk Dogstoerd,"
he replied.*

*"Jan van Hogspuew," offered the second, having
staggered in after pissing in the dark.*

*The last, an ancient geezer, sat in silence, his skull fire-
lit, and opened mussels in a bowl. "And him?" I asked
upon hearing nothing from the man himself.*

*Dirk Dogstoerd gobbed at the grate. "Old Prijk," he
said.*

*The dealer shuffled out cards. I understood none of the
rules if there were any. Round after round, I declared by
my losses and spread my cards face up.*

*"Rain, wind, fire. A secret bestial peace," Old Prijk
cried at last as if summoning a forgotten prophecy.*

The others stared at him as if he was mad.

*I had forfeited my gold within an hour. Finally, the card
dealer slid back on the bench and tugged his hairy cap.*

"Do you want to break the curse?" he asked.

*His eyes looked as if they had been dredged from the
bottom of the sea.*

*Redhead tugged the small hairs on my neck. "Be still;
he does not mean losing at cards," I muttered, tracing my
fingers under her skirt. Her eyes fluttered, welcoming, and
I pulled back my caress and turned to the visitor. My voice
rose at the man, perhaps overdoing my incomprehension.
"The curse?"*

*As if at a signal, the rogues cleared from the darkened
room, my coins jingling in their pockets. The dealer
removed his hairy cap and produced a silver flask from
deep in its folds. "There is one certain remedy against
rabble."*

*By now, Redhead had her lips very tightly set. The toes
of her feet pointed under the table toward the staircase, as
if readying to leap away. My heart was pounding, the thick
blue tendons of my hands went taught. "And what is it, you*

say, that will beat back a mob?"

He seemed surprised I had asked and paused before responding, *"A good memory, lad."*

Redhead snorted laughter. *"That's your secret, old cuss. That's really your secret."*

A burning hearth log popped and reported like a pistol shot. Misconstruing the noise, Redhead squalled indignation. Her clogs slapped the bottoms of her heels as she disappeared up the steps alone.

The card dealer cackled and sucked at his teeth. *"A mob has no memory. It only acts. But an individual with a certain immortal gift could surely hold the brutes at bay."*

I stood and buckled my saber to my waist. *"Show me now."*

"Come into the hearth light. I have the most delicious liquor, a dream of a dram summoned from a thousand lost ages, and summoning those ages too."

"Drink, again," I murmured to myself. *"Why all the magical drink?"*

The man intruded upon my thoughts, *"Impossible to say; this drink, however, is liquid poetry. Sweet yet bitter, musky yet clear as starlight. Taste, oh, taste, and see."* The ancient brute unhooked a drinking horn from its peg in the hearth board, steadily filling the vessel. *"There is a price, lad."*

I drew back. *"All my gold was not enough?"*

"Alas, it was not."

The silver liquor lapped at the rim of the horn. I thought of my parents, and then of my scorn for them. Perhaps there was something that could potentially become momentous. Perhaps I could persuade my father to shed his ire and my mother her taste for afternoon mead. Perhaps I would shed my feigned madness. Perhaps the bargain would lead to a united front against the chaotic legion. Perhaps. I said, *"This magic drink will dispel that inhuman concourse forever, and we may live in our great hall, unmolested?"*

The card-sharp cackled and sucked at a tooth. *"Ever*

after. Straight from my well, lad, the finest liquor in heaven or on earth."

"Liquor from a well," I scoffed. I had to prevent my fingers from leaping at the drink. *"What is your price, mister?"*

"Vision."

"Do not speak in riddles."

"No kenning, lad. Vision for vision, sight for sight."

Impatient with his puzzles, I seized the horn from that miserable carcass. The drink was icy and stung my throat. It was as if a shard of a glacier had pierced me; yet, simultaneously, as if I had licked honey straight from the comb. The taste was richer even than the herbs of the grove my mother crushed into her mead. Thus, I expected the tributaries of the ages to mix and eddy. Did I expect to regain something—time? A new life?

But I remained as I was—in place, at that hour—with no wave of the hours drawing me back. I said, *"I shall not be enamored and held hostage by false promises."*

"You shall not be."

Thus, swifter than I could have supposed, the old corpse made a poniard appear in his claw and thrust it at my face. I threw my forearm up in what was a useless gesture. The steel slit the flesh of my left eye. I fell to the floorboards. The liquor winked silver on the hearthstones. Blood ran between my fingers.

"You wanted release?" the mad stranger hissed. *"This is your release. The vast cycle of ages will advance without disruption. The price? Sight for sight; vision for vision. You will remember everything, and see everything, and you shall wander haunted among mortals, seeking meaning."*

I managed to spit out an insensible reply, *"The future is forked and infinite."*

"Yes. And you shall know every possible path on the way to your mad destiny." Flat on all fours, I saw, with my remaining eye, the pointed toe of his narrow leather shoe rising to strike my ribs. Nauseated with the extreme pain, I

collapsed again to the hearthstone. He said, "Your wisdom shall be vast. Call this vision and this curse what it is: a gift."

~

My foe disappeared out the inn door, a wraith into the moonlight. Redhead bounded down the staircase at my howls and wrapped my ravaged face in linen undergarments retrieved from the loft. What a fool I had been, she chided, for not only was I missing an eye, my gold was gone, and she would not see another kroner of it.

Once I was out of mortal danger enough to think and bandaged sufficiently by my nurse to ride, I ordered my stallion to be saddled. My spurs clattered on the stair as I descended. When the lackeys had finished their task, I leaped onto the back of my mount and made off at a gallop. The horse's shoes sparked on the cobblestones. Women screamed, and windows slammed shut as I escaped. Farmers stabbed their forks into the turf and made foul cries. I hurtled through the thick forest, covering more than thirty leagues in six hours, spurring and whipping the beast until it reared in misery. Occasionally, I stopped to listen, only to hear the laughter of my thieving companions haunting the glades. My determination grew into a fury. Dawn advanced, and soon, a fiery spot of orange hovered low in a hidden sky. At last, the forest's darkness broke and a meadow opened before me.

I wiped the dripping sweat from my brow. The horse was entirely winded from the long crossing. I may have killed the poor beast, I thought, dismounting, and followed the path from the trees' edge. My spurs clattered on the stones. The wall of my family compound emerged; the ravaged palace grounds were scored with buckshot. Broken hafts of farm tools and wooden helmets littered the way. I threw open the splintered wooden front door. The interior was a ruin. Rust showed on the iron fireplace, the spit caked with half an inch of char, and the once-gleaming ancestral table bore the scars of crude knives. I strode down long passages until I reached the small paved courtyard, ever the last sanctuary of my parents. Rank shoots wilted in a corner garden bed; the wind caught the scent of rot and cast it in eddies about the space. Light played on the shattered lead windows.

I immediately recognized their forms, impossibly hardened into statues of glass. Clear, shimmering glass, glowing with a misted light from within. Deliquescing. Father in his opera hat, worn too low, the corners of his thin mouth sloped down toward the folds of his cheeks. Mother, liripipe framing her face, clutching a sprig, staring off into an unpeopled country.

A black raven perched on the head of each statue. One had a white feather in its tail; her companion was black as onyx. Summoning the ravens to my shoulders, I bid them tear strips from my neck. Yet the birds seemed to refuse my imprecations, cawing to me instead.

"Min-min-minne," the raven with the white tailfeather chided.

"Tak-tak-tanke," her mate echoed.

I read in solitude with perhaps sporadic vocalizations of bewilderment or despondence. Watching me lower the folio to my lap, Snorri said, "Young man, tell us what your noises mean."

The Constable is crazed as a box of frogs, I thought privately. I also wondered whether his variant stories were preparing me for something. But what? Why would he create such wildly different versions of his life story? What was meant by this eccentric puzzle?

"This manuscript purports to be an authentic autobiography by the Constable." I recited the first tale and then the second, refraining as much as I could from editorial commentary.

Aud's large eyes widened and rolled. "I see the

problem. It cannot be possible to have competing autobiographies. Or, so it would seem."

I shook my head. "I do not believe the man would know *authentic* if it plowed him under the earth." I added, "Perhaps the tale tells us what we need to know. Sometimes, the Constable seems like a feckless wizard, stuffed only with troll lore and magic."

Aud took the document from me, in her hands the pages as small as playing cards. She bent her head to them. When she was done reading, she handed them back without making any comment.

I crumpled the pages in the Glinter stationery and tossed them over the rail. The giantess watched the paper swirl away among the waves.

"Sometimes," she said, "sometimes the straightest line is not the swiftest route."

Part III: A Wild Hunt

17: The Isle of O

The long-keeled gig rose and dipped smoothly against the waves.

Snorri clapped a palm against the gunwale. "Surely, Minne will navigate for us."

We sailed on half an hour, scouring the horizon in every direction without spotting the fugitive brothers on their escape boat. A veil of darkness was falling from the western shore, an imminent storm. Minne hammered the mast with her beak, then leaped off her perch and soared ahead two or three boat lengths. Snorri instructed me to steer after the raven. I nudged the gig this way or that over the seas after her. Our vessel was soon bursting over the swells.

I said, "We appear to be headed out toward the middle of the lake, the same direction the Thorsteins went in their Zodiac."

"She must know something." Snorri pointed to the grey lump now visible on the horizon.

"What is that?" I asked.

"A small island," said the little man in a grave tone.

From our still-great distance, I could make out the eerie rock formations, the rugged profile of the bluffs, and the dense, warty tufts of a forest.

"An island?"

"A two-hundred-meter-tall, fifty-million-year-old lump of granite rising from the water, to be more precise. It is called the Isle of O."

"Why would the Thorsteins go there?"

"Remoteness lends protection. No one goes there. In the eighteenth-century, ore was discovered, and a mine started there. The mine was abandoned long ago though caverns remain, a warren of dangerous tunnels."

"Why was it abandoned?"

Aud lifted her head from the planks. "Because of the witches."

I looked to Snorri for confirmation; he grunted agreement. Ahead, the raven tilted her wings and squawked back to us, *grawwwr-grip*.

"I feel the spar timber quake, Minne," said Aud. "A squall is coming."

The slate-colored clouds suddenly burst upward in immense towers. Within moments, the wind clocked toward the gig's bow and settled hard against us. Spindrift frothed over the lake's surface. Rain flew down, and the wind drove the hard drops sideways, pelting my face and stinging my skin.

Aud curled as close to the hull timbers as her bulk would allow. I followed Minne with the tiller as she ghosted in and out of the gale. The frigid lake water numbed our limbs; we warmed only when the rain drenched us. Ninety agonizing minutes passed. The gusts built and built, with wild and conflicting seas finally culminating in a ferocious blast that knocked the mainsail hard. We were pitched leeward, the wild eruption of wind accompanied instantly by the shriek of splintering wood.

With that crack, the hull suddenly righted; the mast had gone down. A stump of shattered spruce poked up through a saw-toothed gash in the sail canvass, now useless. Minne screeched somewhere in the swirling gloom.

Snorri crawled among the strewn parts, inspecting, his bony shoulders hunched. "The spar is broken in two places, an impossible repair," he shouted.

We banged among the waves, our sail dragging in the milk-white water. Snorri instructed the giantess to pass him her sword. Slowly, the little man worked the lines over the blade, sawing. Freed of rigging, the mast slipped beneath the lake surface just as the roaring abated; the storm was passing. A trail of foam grew behind us, the haze fell away, and vaulting pale cliffs emerged to starboard. I heard the crash of the surf against the footing of the escarpment.

Minne flapped down to us and settled now on the rail. Aud said, "We can use my tunic as a sail; there is much cloth in it." After a pause, she continued in a stricken tone, "But I cannot be naked before men."

Of course, she was still a teenage girl. Snorri and I turned our backs; I heard the sounds of ripping cloth. Cheeks red with blushing, Aud handed Snorri the great majority of her garment. She had torn the decorative hem from the bottom of her skirt, fashioning it into a kind of halter top, the animal tails a fringe at her midriff.

Snorri stood her sword with handle skyward, wedging the blade tip into the shattered stump of the old mast. He passed my quarterstaff through the garment's sleeves so that it resembled a scarecrow and lashed both arms of the contraption with lines.

"A new mast and a new sail, square, like a proper Viking ship," Snorri grinned.

Minne circled an opening in the rock wall that loomed above our battered ship. I steered the bow toward the inlet. Rushing walls of water stirred fear in me as the gig raced to the entrance. I heard the waves breaking on a gravel beach, yet a series of small granite outcrops broke the swells. We ran smoothly between the rocks of the inlet opening. Once inside, the lake waves bent and dispersed upon a lagoon.

"The witches have spared us," Aud said.

We disembarked from the gig and fell on the shore, exhausted. Aud removed her sword from the mast stub and managed to drag the gig up the sand. She turned over the hull for use as shelter and gathered juniper from shoreside for our sleeping pallet. I knew that, like me, she and Snorri were too spent to hunt down food. Aud's complexion had grown chalky. We were cold, miserable, and weakened as black night fell.

"Sleep now, grub later," said Snorri.

"I will be there in a moment," I said to the others as they crawled under the gig. Though exhausted, I needed to gather my thoughts. I retrieved my rucksack from the hold, sat on a rock, and took out the moleskin notebook; the pages were thankfully dry. I tried to think a bit about the case. But as usual, my mind wandered. I thought of music and fingered imaginary keys. A tune came, released perhaps by exhaustion. I wrote down lyrics in my moleskin notebook before they could escape back into the brainwave from which they had leaped. I felt these lyrics were, finally, the Viking words called for by my bandmates. I sang them quietly to myself, sure that Snorri and Aud were sleeping too soundly to be disturbed.

Then, tiring, I stuffed my pad and rucksack back into the gig hold and set out our weapons: ax, quarterstaff, and sword, propped against a nearby boulder. Lastly, I slipped beneath the overturned hull to join my companions. Snorri curled under one great arm of the giantess. I took up shelter beneath her other arm. Minne's claws clicked on the hull shell overhead. I gave myself over to lulling waves of oblivion.

þ

I opened my eye to find myself staring at a stone wall. Sunlight heated the skin of my feet, which stuck out from under the gig. The morning had come. I tried in vain to move. Aud had stretched her legs in the night, pinning me between the wooden planks of the gig and the base of the granite bluff. I nudged the giantess awake.

"You're crushing me, Aud."

With a sleepy smile, the giantess rolled to her other side, releasing me. Meanwhile, Snorri had awakened earlier and located the rubber escape boat the Thorsteins used, tucked behind a boulder.

"I found these onboard." Snorri tipped back on his heels and laughed. In one hand, he held out packets of crisps; in the other, a substantial, thick white lump, sealed in plastic. "Seven kilos of salted cod."

Minne stretched and gurgled. She snapped something off from the muck and made the morsel disappear into her beak.

We ate the cod and crisps, then after our gorging, Snorri pointed out the recent churn of soil up the shore. "Motorcycles—we must go that way about the island."

Aud fastened her tunic about her shoulders like a cape. The upward grade of the path was moderate. Occasionally, a compressed layer of rock showed through the ground cover, fragments almost like tarmac. Snorri plucked one up, turned it over. He smelled it. He tasted it with his tongue. "Bitumen. Must be this route was paved with macadam at one time."

As we trudged along the old route, Snorri narrated the history he knew of the remote place. "Who knows what we will find when we get to the top. The steep shore rises from an underwater mountain. Clans started mining here, some think in late medieval times, Viking times, the ore being dug from the summit until the shafts spread deep into the earth. When the veins finally ran out, the modern miners abandoned their equipment, and the island community never recovered."

"The mines should have flooded with lake water after all these years," I said.

Snorri said, "Perhaps. We will find out."

"You have been here before?" I asked.

"No. This island is not a hospitable place."

"Except to witches," said Aud.

I calculated that we had landed on the island's northernmost shore. We started our trek near the top of the "O" and were advancing west around its rim. By late morning we had discovered nothing but endless miles of crumbled macadam. Snorri announced we must forge into the interior, yet a hike straight up the bluff was impossible. Likely a mine entrance sat atop the dome, an opening that might make a good hideout surrounded by thick conifer forest. Gravel spills and rubble would clutter any obvious route upward. We would have to wind back and forth up the switchbacks.

Minne hopped on Aud's shoulder, signaling her contentment to let Snorri lead the way. Aud and I hurried after the little man. On either side of the macadam path, scrub shot up about eighteen inches in height, stems topped with a shag of pale purple flowers.

Aud plucked a bloom and crushed it to her nose. "A beautiful scent."

Snorri's eyes suddenly lit up. "Same as the perfume Lucia wore."

"Lucia," I echoed, pleased with the sound. "Lucia," I sang softly, a mock-Pavarotti.

Aud shushed me. Snorri went on, "Dabbed on the inside of her wrists, her neck, under the ears. Poor dear Lucia, six years have gone," Snorri sighed. The little man waved the sprig at me, and the scent permeated my nostrils.

"Smells like a mortuary," I laughed, intending a joke, but Snorri's smile faded as soon as these words escaped my mouth. Once they were out, I could not retract them. Snorri looked away, squeezed both fists about his ax, and scrambled up the broken piles. Soon he disappeared from our view, hidden in the folds of the escarpment.

Aud shoved a branch away, revealing her searing glance. My eyes fixated on her wide lips, which appeared to reflect the grey light of the rock. She scolded, "Now you've done it, he may abandon us here to founder."

I hung my head as Aud stood and paced. My hand began to work unheard chords.

My quarterstaff lay flat on the loose soil, where I had abandoned it. Aud tapped her great toe on the weapon, and there was adequate spring in the wood handle that the thump made it jump up into her hand. Wielding the handle as a pointer, she tapped my jittering fist. "What are you doing?"

"Nothing."

She frowned.

"Practicing," I corrected.

"Practicing what?"

Though still glaring at me, she flicked her cape away from her shoulders and began to give me a lesson in rake handle offense. "Stretch your back, Grammaticus, stretch your neck, stretch your legs. Adapt flexibly to successive action. Plasticity will help keep your weapon's rhythm from becoming deranged."

"Deranged?"

"Deranged." She poked the quarterstaff between my shins. "Here, a derangement."

She made her illustration with a gradual lateral rotation of the weapon. A twist of her wrist brought the staff from my shin to my opposite knee, the pain sharp, and I was on my back, the giantess drawing figure eights over my nose with the end of the rake handle. "Learn your body, learn your weapon," she pitched the rake handle to me, and pulled her sword from her scabbard. "My weapon is of ancient design, Grammaticus. From the tip to the hilt run grooves, on each side, to give strength and, some believe, aid in draining blood away. The pointed tip can drive through chainmail. Though hilts of such weapons are often embellished with carvings, I prefer mine simple. My grip is too course for finery, and I sweat."

Aud returned the sword to her hip, loosed the scabbard from her belt, and leaned it on a tree. She continued. "Some ancient warriors fought standing in place. They relied on strength and the mass of their weapons to deliver wounding blows. My blade is for slashing. While your weapon is not a sword, of course, it is the staff. A staff demands other skills. You must be agile."

Aud pressed the tip of a massive forefinger into the spot in the middle of my brow; the pressure sharpened. "This is where a sword can go. Remember the grooves in the blade for running blood."

Aud gestured for me to stand, bearing my rake handle in front of me, and with her left boot toe, she tapped my feet apart until I had a proper stance or at least a facsimile of one. I clasped the stick *en guard* fashion. The giantess lifted my elbows and pressed my right bicep back, adjusting my shoulders to face an imagined adversary.

"Do not look pleased, do not look displeased; be tranquil. Have a comely, radiant face."

She showed me how to raise on my toes and push off from the heel always in the same manner. If I favored one foot, she prodded to remind me of the use of the other.

"Examine this well," she instructed.

After forty-five minutes of these exercises, her eyes resting on my contortion, she wordlessly pressed a heavy finger into my forehead until I eventually lost balance and fell. I leaped up, peeling pebbles from the skin of my palms.

"Burnish the powers of your mind, Grammaticus; make detail acute. It is difficult for me to communicate a simplicity. Accept that you are a traveler in this world. Battle is governance of moving energy."

For reasons I did not fully fathom myself, I asked, "Where was she from, the girl in the ice?"

Aud paused. "She never said. Do we have the right to raid the history of her life for our solace? In death, the secrets of her heart are away from us forever. You remind me all too clearly why we are here. Death: hers and my mother's. Slaughter and madness."

"But, Aud…" I knew now why I had asked about the girl. The giantess pushed strands of hair sneaking from beneath her wooden helmet, back towards her temples.

"Yes?"

"I cannot fight for vengeance."

This comment unleashed something in Aud. Her voice was like the rasp of blades. "Not vengeance, Grammaticus, justice. You may grow into a great musician, a spiritual giant, by acts other than your art because those acts may feed your art. Lay down your fears. Lay down your woe. Ripen toward your destiny."

A sound came from behind me, and then Snorri, whose

face was glossy with sweat, slipped back into our circle. He still had his ax with him, and, shuffling before him, was a black raven with a white tail feather.

Aud cooed. "Minne, I did not even see that you had gone."

The bird released a soft gurgling sound.

Snorri batted the dust off his pant legs. "There is a plateau, a relic of old excavation, which I did not try to go beyond as I did not want to be gone too long. Come." As soon as the words were past Snorri's lips, he turned back towards the path from which he had come. We chased after him. Stone pinnacles swept by, and creatures croaked among the shadows, sounds Minne replied to with a hiss or gentle flap of wings. The wind whistled in the overhead crags. Finally, we stood on a basalt ledge.

The plateau we had aimed for opened out at our feet. The flat space was, by all appearances, a way-stop for the old miners, stones from toppled cairns strewn everywhere. Industrial debris and tools lay about in piles. The afternoon sun had seared the mist off, and the lake's vista lay to the west, a gaunt cliff on the inland side. We sat far from the edge for safety. Snorri shared out handfuls of cod, meat that went down hard without drinking water.

"We have climbed three-quarters of the way up the mountain," Snorri said. He stepped toward the overlook where he stood silent. There was no comfort in his manner. At my side, Aud released a slow exhalation.

I looked back at the direction from which we had emerged and saw the shallow trench that Aud's dragging sword tip had cut along the path. Minne let out an extended cry, full of sepulchral warning.

The sun bent over the summit, and a strange yellow halo lit the broken peak. We pressed on.

18: Casting Runes

The steep walls of the stone channel through which we walked, buried the sun, and Minne darted through the shades ahead of us. Snorri following her, lead us through an even more confining passage of stone, weaving left and right, right and left, then left, and then left again. At last, we passed beneath a rock arch that formed a threshold to a stand of knotty pine, the carpet of needles soft to walk on after the hours of broken boulders. The air had changed as well, and a layer of mist rolled over the ground. I marvelled at the dripping arbors, the great contrast. A glimmering emerged ahead. "The yellow aurora," I said to myself.

When a toad leaped into our path, croaking, a second toad followed it, then a third. Within moments, scores of toads were trilling at our feet. "They may be guardians," said Aud, but Minne darted from the foliage, pecking wildly, and the warty brigade scattered.

Further up the path, I was startled to distinctly hear three female voices, the calm, coordinated interplay of women preoccupied with tasks. Cracking inelastic throats, older tones, and frank, coaxing, acknowledgment of duties well done. Minne vanished into the soft glow.

The glade we entered was a watercolor tableau, a circular court of pines with a massive ash tree at the center. Under its canopy, a trio of women labored. All three were of great age and wore cream-colored wool sweaters. One had oversized plastic-rimmed glasses, a second a peasant skirt, the last buckled clogs. They had identical locks that shone in white glory, skin mellow with golden undertones.

"Three beauties in the forest," Snorri said with a pleased sigh.

Minne had taken a perch on a bough over the laboring ladies. Two of the crones pulled water from a well near the ash, ferrying bucketsful to splash at its base. The third in the peasant skirt directed them, though her eyes were cloudy with cataracts, and her companions stumbled and meandered under her guidance.

Snorri stepped into the ring of trees, yet the women toiled on. Then, the woman with plastic-rimmed glasses turned, by degrees, as if drawn from an abstracted state. She described Snorri to her companions.

"A visitor, sisters. Bearded, swarthy, and talkative. And brandishing a woodchopper!" She addressed Snorri directly now. "This well feeds our great ash and is not for usage other than nourishing this tree. The water in our well is not for use in the smithy, dwarf."

The deep voice of Aud came lilting over my shoulder. "Dwarves are ironmongers, and it appears she thinks Snorri is a dwarf."

Snorri gave a sharp laugh. "My name is Snorri, and I am a retired police officer. This gentleman is Grammaticus, a clerk at the precinct, and this young lady is Aud, a friend we are helping."

"A dwarf, a giant, and an elf—a curious tribe. Dwarves are small and uncomely yet are handy with things. Giants are thwarted romantics. And elves can be marvelously clever, but I regret to say, this elf is a sad specimen. Look at those skinny arms."

My hands were beginning to twitch. Snorri said, "My colleagues and I believed nobody lived on this island, but here you are. How did you get here and up the steep slope?"

The old witch pointed around her circle, first to the woman in the peasant skirt, then to the woman in buckled clogs. "We are seers. These are my sisters. My name is *Happening*. Her name is *What Shall Happen*, and she is known as *What Has Happened*. We rode upon the currents of fate."

"A living allegory," the giantess said.

Assessing their frumpy clothing, I said, "Nothing about them looks especially supernatural."

Snorri cast his gaze from one woman to the next. "Ah, I

see, ladies. I understand the sixties. I was there. We experimented, but may I say, it seems the decade was a little too good to you?"

The leader arched her back and cocked her head. She seemed to listen to something far off, even as she spoke in a firm voice, saying:

> *We worship this ancient ash, tree of life,*
> *And water it to keep its roots alive.*
> *This tree brings mist flowing from the hills.*
> *We nourish it with visions from the well.*

Aud understood this babble better than Snorri or I. "Tell us, wise woman, what the future holds."

"I shall do just that." The crone narrowed her eyes, the eyes of a cat. "I take back what I said before. For you the well will make an exception. You and your friends must refresh yourselves with a draft of our water."

She summoned What Has Happened to bring over her drinking pail and removed a packet from a fold in her skirt. She tapped powder into the water.

"To make it potable," she explained.

Snorri nodded, "One of those ashram hacks."

We drank deeply from the bucket, the water satisfying after the long hike up the mountainside. Within moments, however, a strange silence blanketed the forest. I looked around, finding it hard to focus my thoughts. Aud smiled, tottered, and crumpled quietly forward. With a squawk, Snorri tumbled too. My head buzzed, and I reached out to steady myself, struggling to get my words out.

"That powder was not to make water potable."

Happening laughed. "No, no, it wasn't."

My cheek hit the spongy soil, and then I recalled nothing.

þ

Salmon-colored light crept between mossy branches. Toads droned nearby, unseen.

"Dawn," Snorri groaned. "I feel someone has pumped sludge through my veins."

I knew what he meant. My head was pounding.

I examined my situation. I was sitting with my back against a tree, wrists tied in a leather pouch before me, my feet bound the same way. A rough manila rope was cinched around my chest, disappearing beyond the scope of my vision on either side. The sisters had laid our weapons at a distance, and when I struggled, my wrists burned as if on fire.

"You're tied up, too, Snorri?" I whispered.

"Wrists, ankles, chest, all fast, mate," Snorri replied. "I think you're on the other side of the tree from me."

Aud was trussed between two nearby pines, on her back, her hands strung over her shoulders, fastened to a pine, her feet drawn in the opposite direction fastened to another. The tails of her tunic spread sadly over the soil.

"We must have slept through the night," Aud said. "It's like my entire braincase has been rattled violently."

"Our second night on the Isle of O," I said.

A sharp clap of hands and the sisters emerged from the trees. I craned my neck. Our captors had changed clothing and now wore ragged deerskin dresses; spiky horns jutted from the tops of their heads. They had blackened their eyelids, and a stroke of black char ran from their lower lips to their chins. The leader clutched a curling staff.

"Rattled your soul," Happening corrected. "The ancient poem tells us:

> *Three wise women, three in all,*
> *Whose hideaway stands under spreading boughs,*
> *Make the eternal laws and choose survivors,*
> *Forging the fate of the children of men."*

After a pause, she added, "*We* chose the survivors, girl."

Snorri said, "What drink did you give us?"

The witch laughed. "A potion, the draft of oblivion."

Before Snorri could reply, Happening took her staff and used it to draw a series of concentric rings in the forest floor, the widest of which was about three meters across. "Now, we are prepared to penetrate the future. This diagram shall help us sort it out."

The sister who formerly had worn the peasant skirt— What Shall Happen—stepped into the nested rings. She immediately began to writhe, cycling her body through various postures: elbows lifted, forearms crossed, arms stretched out and upward, an endless sequence of balancing.

"The dance of runes," said Aud.

"Giantess, we shall divine your rune first," Happening said, and gave her writhing sister a poke with her staff. The woman tumbled to the ground with a wet slap, landing back straight, right arm pointing up, and left arm pointing down, forming an acute angle. The head crone stared at the shape and scratched a form in the loam beside her fallen sister: þ

"This is your rune, giantess. It is called *thorn* and means, 'the giant.'" Happening's chin trembled. "You have been through much and seen much. You are both mighty and kind, a rare combination."

Snorri's eyes grew lustrous as he listened.

"You are next, dwarf." Happening hoisted her fallen sister and replaced her in the diagram with the woman who had worn buckled clogs, What Has Happened. Happening poked her second sister over and studied the new shape. Beside her, she scratched the rune ᛒ and said, "This is the rune known as 'the boil,' whose meaning I will render as a poem:

> *You are like unto*
> *a raw blister, little man.*
> *You maketh the corpse*
> *grow sallow.*

"Dwarf," Happening concluded, "You wander in a cavern of loss and loneliness."

The glow faded from Snorri.

"Next you, elf. A troubling specimen," Happening said.

"Lack of character," What Has Happened called from the mud.

Happening paced, frowning, then raised her right hand, touched the thumb to the crown of her head, and then let the hand fall to her side. She motioned for What Shall Happen to return to the magic circle then poked her again with the staff. What Shall Happen landed on her buttocks beside their sister, then brought her knees up, her feet flat on the earth, forearms poised forward.

Happening uttered minor grumbles of delight, then inscribed this mark upon the earth: ⊏

"What does that mean?" I asked.

"I hear mad sounds and rhythms, tumult, strife—a ferocious racket."

What Shall Happen said, "I hear it too. Great weal and woe, but melodious."

What Has Happened closed her eyes tight and, as if in a fit, said, "The elf is a musician though not *just a musician*. Look how his hands quake."

Together, the three sisters chorused, "Fie. He is a heavy metal musician."

I ceased moving. I felt my cheeks flush hot. Vision complete, Happening curled her fingers like sticks of tallow around the staff, "These runes will give no more."

The sisters bowed as if having completed a show.

"Now, we will return to our sacred duty, tree-watering." They resumed toiling quietly. Sweat gathered on their brows, and their eye-blacking grew runny. After half an hour, Snorri's brow had furrowed at their arduous method.

"I can take it no longer," he burst out. "Ladies, dear ladies, your process is as efficient as irrigating an acre with a teaspoon. Work *with* gravity, not against it. If you allow me, I will show you how to make a rain catcher."

"What dwarf-devilry do you say?"

"A trap, a canvas that will channel rainwater to your tree."

The witches huddled a long time and seemed to speak in some ancient rough tongue as incomprehensible to my companions as to me. Finally, they stepped back.

"Agreed," said Happening, "but beware. No tricks for which dwarves are so famous. You shall not fashion a magic dagger of iron; nor will you produce a gemstone with a glowing center; nor shall you walk upside down upon a ceiling, nor make eyes appear to move in paintings. If you break your oath, we will summon a mob of toads to rub their poison skin upon you — a dire fate."

"I promise to do none of those things."

What Has Happened and What Shall Happen departed. I listened to the shushing forest and, after a while, the toads resumed a rhythmic pulse. Happening drew a symbol on the earth with her staff.

"What is that sign for?" said Aud.

"To hasten the passage of time." Bending toward the toad chorus, she cried, "Hurry!"

The sisters suddenly returned arms laden with deerskins, a knife, twine, and other equipment. They handed Happening the blade, who loosened Snorri from the rope and cut his wrist bonds. She then presented Snorri with the knife and an awl.

Snorri set to with his tools. He laid down two large hides, one atop the other, and with the awl and twine, joined the pieces creating an enormous pouch. Then he cut long, narrow strips of hide and repeated the operation, fashioning a hose that he attached to the bag with a sturdy stick for twisting. Lastly, he hung the contrivance between branches with the manila line and passed the makeshift tubing to the great ash's roots.

Snorri stood back, his hands on his hips.

"Looks like a huge pig bladder," said Happening. Her

sisters murmured their accord.

"A water-butt, ladies. Let the rain fill it; twist this stick like a knob to release the water, and twist it back to shut off the stream."

Snorri slid his hands in his pants pockets. "Look here, ladies, I kept my end of the bargain. Let my friends go."

My release was as easy as had been Snorri's, and within moments I was away from the tree, rubbing my numb limbs. Aud, however, was a different matter. She had struggled, and her massive limbs wrenched her bindings so that her shoulders bit with pain and her hands grew purple.

Snorri knelt beside her. He eased the tree lines, then clipped the rope that bound her wrists and ankles, plying the blade like a doctor with a scalpel. However, it took her fifteen minutes to lift herself back to standing, and she was reticent afterward. Finally, I said, "Snorri, where did you pick up the sewing skills?"

"Running with soccer mates. You never know what will need mending—a jacket, shoes, a game ball." The rope-cutting business had turned Snorri somber. To Happening he said, "We are pursuing thugs who committed murder, and they must have passed very near here."

The crone pointed with her crook to the summit that still towered hundreds of feet above us. "Two evil trolls have taken up residence in the mountain cave uphill."

"Just the fellows we're wanting," said Snorri.

The woman's mouth flattened into a crease. "You shall never approach those beasts without our help."

"Why not?"

"Even if you get to the top, you shall see their fortress is enclosed in an iron gate, a great barrier." The crone patted down her garments once more, drew out a small iron band, and handed it to Snorri. "A fearsome engine," the old woman continued, her eyes on the ring. "It was hammered on the ancestral forge of your people, in the time of mist and dragons, and possesses potent magic to open the gate."

"A princely bauble," Aud ventured.

Snorri slipped it on the same finger that held his still-worn wedding band. "It fits nicely. Anyway, it will protect Lucia's band from slipping off again."

The women now stepped together where the nested circles had been. Their voices rose in unison. Their wailing intertwined in what emerged as a whirlwind of harmonic despondence. The voice of the rune-reader Happening rose above her sisters' as she sang,

> Brother will battle brother till ruin comes,
>   and family betray family.
> Desperation overtakes the world.
> Time of swords, age of axes, when shields
>   splinter;
> Age of wind and wolves, and prowling
>   destruction;
> Now, weapons of warriors shall show no mercy.

After the song, I toe-bounced my stave, so it sprung up into my hands, the trick Aud had shown me.

"*Hup*," I cried.

The giantess raised her right eyebrow. Snorri snatched up his ax.

Happening bowed to the raven. "Farewell, Minne."

My comrades and I clambered down the tree barrow toward the path. After we had cleared the court of pines, I said, "Do witches always come in groups of three?"

Aud shouldered her sword like a rifle. "Most assuredly, Grammaticus. It's a thing."

Minne waddled on her claws before us, crying *kooor-kek*.

19: The Death of Nils the Fat Boy

The great ash tree and watering well vanished among the pines, and a branch clicked to the ground as if locking a gate behind us. Distant enough now not to be heard by the peculiar women, I said, "I feel as if something significant has happened though I can't put my finger on what."

Minne burst from the ground into flight. Much of the oyster-grey lake was visible from our new height nearing the summit, and down the steep western slope lay an old industrial dock previously blocked from our view. Derelict hoppers, mine refuse in melted piles, a ruined dock hoist bowing its head to the pier—it was easy to imagine a phantom fleet hauling ore away.

Then, a startling sight: hooligans. Men who had been at the rally, who burned the town, dozens of them, roughnecks who appeared from our roost to be the size of rodents. At the crumbling dock below rested the tugboat they had confiscated in the harbor village. The hooligans hurried over the planks, shouting, tossing lines. All I could hear was the rhythm of their hard voices as opposed to specific words. Some were calling, a few singing a match song.

I now saw the stubbled scalp and heavy-muscled form of Olaf the Peacock standing on a boulder, a dais from which to issue commands. His muddied voice carried the stern notes of one used to quelling insubordination.

I clutched my quarterstaff tight.

"Look," I cried, barely able to contain my distress. The hooligan mob moved quickly, advancing up a mirror path to ours, as though two threads wound from opposite ends of a spindle.

"We are defeated," Aud breathed over my shoulder.

Snorri shushed us, "We must not risk attracting their attention, even from here. We are closing in on the island summit."

Twenty-two hours had passed since our little troop made landfall upon the shore so far below. I felt I must better decipher the impending danger. I crept to an outcrop and peered several hundred feet down. The chieftain now stood with his group at a wayside niche. To my surprise, colossal cheer seemed to have gripped the men. Olaf the Peacock was giving instructions, and I could not hear distinct words; only the baritone swells of his voice, followed by a burst of laughter from his gang. I returned to my companions and told them what I had seen.

"No doubt, they are conspiring over what they will do to us when we are captured." Aud was panting under redoubled exertion. The forest growth was ancient. I stopped before her every few paces to clear tangles and ease her way. Her wooden helmet had gone askew on her head. Did I detect a slight limp in her gait?

Ax in hand, Snorri hopped and skipped over emerging slag mounds. Finally, we rounded upon what turned out, to my surprise (so used had I grown to adversity) to be a gate of heavy iron. It rose thirty feet into the air around what must be the mine entrance, a hollow descending like the postern of a fortress to a door woven of iron bands like a tapestry of metal. No approach was possible but through the locked gate. The familiar knobby-tired motorcycles lay on the soil just inside.

There was a massive latch on the gate, and above the latch were five rotating disks inscribed with the letters of the alphabet, the tumblers of a combination lock.

"Usch," said Snorri. "Such complex mechanism; the old iron masters were too good."

Aud stepped to the gate, throwing her might into rattling it. The old iron shivered but would not open. I slumped, dejected.

Aud said, "The witch said Snorri's ring had magic to open the gate."

Snorri passed the band to the giantess, who waved it like a wand over the latch. Nothing happened. She tapped it against the metal. Again, nothing. Aud turned the ring over and over, searching as, now and then, Olaf's booming voice echoed up the slope. After countless minutes, Aud paused in her movement, staring at the interior of the ring.

"An inscription," she murmured and read aloud:

> *Discover the code*
> *And pass through me.*
> *The answer lies*
> *In G-r-i-m-k-e.*

"We have to go back to Grimke," I groaned.

Snorri sputtered, "Everything leads to Grimke."

Silence extended itself into every crevice of the surrounding rock. "But why spell out the word?" she said. Aud pressed her fists to her temples. Another desolate pause, she rotated the discs. I saw that she had tumbled the sequence G-R-I-M-K-E. The giantess pressed the iron bars and the door swung silently open.

"Five discs, five letters," she sighed.

"Fantastic magic," said Snorri.

"Aces," Aud replied.

Inside the gate, an antique windmill towered on lattice legs, and atop the windmill sat our raven with a white tail feather. A wire from the mill snaked beneath the lid of a battered locker. Another strand of copper exited the box below, disappearing under the mine doors.

Snorri lifted the box lid, which came up easily.

"A trickle generator," he said. A bank of vehicle batteries occupied a portion of the box floor. "Ultra-low voltage from the windmill charges these power cells. Someone revived the rickety old windmill for this purpose. Ingenious. We must find out what this electricity feeds."

Even as Snorri moved to open the iron gate, a disembodied voice emerged from the other side of the crown of slag we had just crested. I ducked behind boulders lined like broken teeth before the door. Where Snorri and

Aud hid, I could not tell.

Nils the Fat Boy appeared. He maneuvered about, oblivious to our presence, and wrestled himself down the slope of broken rocks, back to us, the fish-white crevice of his buttocks showing at the top of his pants. His tone carried the ache of a wounded animal, singing as if to boost his courage:

> *I am Nils, and I've come here*
> *To shag your girls and drink your beer.*

At the bottom of the hill, Nils passed through the open gate and approached the woven metal door. He hammered it with a rock only a few paces from where I crouched, unseen.

"I was loyal, sods, let me in. Dedicated, unswerving I was." His cries quickly turned hysterical. Nils threw himself at the door, convulsing with silent tears. The silence grew protracted. Finally, some shuffling noises emerged from within, followed by a cough. Thorvald Thorstein appeared at the door, his visage disordered, his rigid flat beard filthy with dust, his fur collar torn, Doc Matins caked with earth.

"Who are you?" he said.

"I'm the bouncer from the chicken ranch at the Fulaflugahål quay."

"The what?"

"The brothel where she worked sometimes."

Thorvald Thorstein said, "She who?"

"The wog girl in the lake ice. She worked there, like all the girls you got working permits."

"Go away."

Nils' gaze darted feverishly about the slag rim. "Hurry, my father is coming."

Thorvald called back beyond the door. "Some obese prat is here, brother."

Nils proclaimed his great admiration for the handiwork

of the siblings. At intervals, Thorvald checked over his shoulder on his brother's progress. In time, Thorkill stepped into the muted light of the gulley-like postern, squinting. The breeze coming off the lake tousled the fur on his collar.

Nils gestured wildly while making his point. "Let me say this, gents. In January, I was in the pines while you were on the lake ice doing your business. I remember everything."

"Everything?"

"I had a clear view, and voices carry over the ice. The girl screamed. She broke away, but she slipped. The wings made it impossible to run. You put your boot on her neck, and she shut up. She was like a little girl, terrorized. Then the blade. Three jabs."

The brothers exchanged glances with each other.

Never one to know his best interest, Nils continued. "People ice fish out there. A few scrapes with the blade got the hole bigger. Getting her in was a bit dodgy, but you did it. After you left, I had a look-see. She was impressive in the wings, lovely. But she kept floating up, right, the corpse, and then she folded over. Imagine it. Ugly down in that hole."

"Was he at the rally at the chalet?" Thorvald asked his brother.

"I recall him," said Thorkill.

Nils gulped, "I tidied her up. I went and fetched my kitchen torch from my flat and fashioned a frozen window above her, very neat and clear as a lens."

"A culinary torch. But you seem more an acetylene guy."

"Big praise, mate, but you work with what you have." Nils was feverish with the recollection. "I welded a lid onto the ice, so to speak, and made her into a sweet ballerina dancing in a crystal."

Thorkill seemed to contemplate the information. "Remarkable."

"I have it here." Nils rummaged through a secret cavity in his pants and, grinning upon locating the object, produced a short silver cylinder with a hooked nozzle.

"You covered the corpse by melting ice over her with that instrument?" Thorvald asked.

"It is hard work to lay down the ice and then smooth it over," said the fat boy, looking simultaneously frantic and pleased with himself.

Thorkill pressed the index finger of his right hand to the right side of his nose. "Something in those foreign girls demands to be treated that way, demands victimization. They expect ill-treatment." He yawned. "They know they are beaten before they start, which brings resignation. Their faces haunt you; the sweep of the lashes, the pulse at the base of the neck. They can invade your dreams and lead you to corrupt places. It can have a powerful effect on you. You can become a victim yourself. The arm of the executioner must fall."

"So true," said Nils.

Thorkill said, focusing now on Thorvald, "Perhaps you agree with me, brother. Follow my logic. Nils is a witness. The trouble is, this witness, this personage, did a neat puzzle for police to figure out. He sealed the girl in ice, as he says, leaving quite a mystery to ponder. But puzzles don't stop the law; they only make them more determined. Puzzles can be linked to puzzle makers. You see, the kind of problem that arises?"

"I do," said Thorvald.

"The fat boy is an even bigger idiot than he looks."

Thorvald gripped the nape of Nils' neck with his thumb and forefingers and pulled him inside the open door.

A male voice floated over the hollow, deep, authoritative, "Nils, you idiot."

Olaf stood above us in the same spot where Nils had descended the slag ridge moments ago. His gang filled around him, the men I had spotted on the harbor tug gathering on the berm. Half a dozen in the black and yellow kits mulled to Olaf the Peacock's left, the ragged crew in eclectic garb to his right.

Nils wailed, "Dad," and clutched at the stones around him, trying to scramble back out the doorway. Thorvald snatched the rock Nils had used to hammer the door, clubbed the fat youth, grabbed him by the ankles, and dragged him back inside thrashing. The metal door swung shut with a clang. I was so close that the noise thundered in my chest. From behind the door came loud baying; the brothers imitated the howling of wolves, Nils' shrieks intermingling with their uproar even as the sounds faded into the depths of the mine.

"Sometimes the apple falls far from the tree," said Olaf.

The Viscount said, "Is that fat one your son then?"

Olaf turned his eyes away. "A sad truth."

The black and yellow gang had refrained from descending to the mine doors; their eclectically-dressed counterparts likewise refused to budge. Olaf admonished his followers. "Be united. We've got work to do. Infighting is the bloody issue with this movement."

The men drew close to their leader. Rudeboy rhythmically tapped his thigh with a switch. "What do you advise, generalissimo?"

Olaf the Peacock patrolled the circuit of the berm, ranging to and fro over the heaps. Broken, rusted chains hung from the crags. For him, the arena became a theater of sorts as he shouted, "Foreign scum willingly die in great numbers to get to our country. Why betray each other? Those two in the fur collars, in their wolf hole—we have to put them down. But…" Olaf licked his upper lip. "We also have to adhere to the purpose. Doctrine. Principles. Policy. These are things you stick by."

Olaf smiled, confirming he was a mate and would tolerate a lack of understanding for now. He continued speaking.

"Our doctrine is this: Boots to suits. Up your game, boys; infiltrate and integrate. Don't get me wrong. The thrill of physical confrontation is exquisite. There's nothing like the feel of a blackjack in your pocket, nothing like the sound of five thousand feet stampeding through a stadium. But murder is bad press, and we have to get the Thorsteins."

"The Thorsteins are foreigners?"

"Far from it. Fulaflugahål born and bred, but they raked us over the coals. Let's examine the matter of Anders Breivik. Seventy-seven people slaughtered at a summer camp, mostly kids. He set the movement back years."

Rudeboy scratched his back with the switch. "I thought Breivik made things quite exciting. Handsome he was, whereas the slant-eyed people, the smelly people, we need to cleanse the planet of them."

Olaf the Peacock searched the youth's face and then the faces of the others. A stiffening wind made the fetters of the hillside machinery clink. "That's old school," the Peacock preened. "We have a new doctrine. We believe that someone needs to represent the white identity in a diverse society before whites are stamped out of existence. Stop the vermin from using up our money. All we have to do is get them out of the country. We don't want blood on our hands. Get this in your heads."

Olaf the Peacock directed The Viscount to approach. As he neared, Olaf snagged a long stray whisker in the Viscount's moustache and yanked. The Viscount yelped and gave a black look. Olaf proudly displayed the plucked hair.

"One hair, easily removed. Now, observe."

He closed his fists around the large clumps of hair that were the man's sideburns. The eyes of the Viscount grew red-rimmed and watery with each tug. Olaf the Peacock released the beard and spread open his clean palms.

"It is easy to uproot a single hair, but not many together. Same with men. As a firm, we are stronger. An isolated man is bound to fail." He approached the pit gate and studied the woven iron and the crumbling buttresses. "Men need to fight. Otherwise, they are not men; they are girls."

Rudeboy said, "Follow the boss. Follow the way of the gang."

The Viscount massaged the red knob of his chin, "No outliers."

Under the watchful eyes of Olaf, the men hoisted up a length of rusted drill pipe and, this ram tucked under their arms, plunged at the metal door behind which Nils' cries could no longer be heard. With each blow of the pipe, the door emitted a leaden *thunk*. The hooligans repeated the assault until they grew tired.

The booming shivered my bones. In the hush between the last thrusts, Snorri responded in a low tone, "The iron gate was locked, but this one, too? They should pull the barrier outward, first, to see if it opens."

As soon as the little man uttered this observation, Rudeboy stepped silently forward and tugged. The doors swung smoothly toward him. Olaf's voice was suave, arrogating the discovery to his credit. "Go on, lads. Maim them, if need be, but do not kill them."

The youth with red cheeks asked in premature elation, almost spitting, "So this is a capture and release operation?"

"No. Apprehending those brothers will be excellent press. All will know we are genuine."

As the fighters entered the doors, they loosened their fists at their sides and eased their postures, assuming a familiar street fighting stance. They filed gravely in, and blackness swallowed them whole.

þ

Once the hooligans had disappeared inside, we emerged from our hiding places and followed. Minne darted about making high-pitched mewing calls, caught a draft, and swooped up, wheeling above the ravine and refusing to enter the mine.

Aud watched the sky. "The Thorsteins have abducted

the fat boy, and Olaf's gang is in hot pursuit. The Thorsteins must know this mine and could disappear into the mountain, and none would find them."

Snorri stirred slag dust with his right foot. "We could wait them out."

"There may be another exit from the mine, or they could have deep provisions."

Snorri retorted, "Olaf the Peacock's gang is a dumb force feeding on itself. They will root out the brothers."

I added, half-joking, "How much magic is left in that ring?"

Aud rubbed her nose, uncertain. "Enough, I hope."

The chamber within blushed an eerie yellow, and Snorri traced the line from the windmill batteries. "Diodes on a string."

Unexpectedly, the passage had ample clearance for the giantess. The clacking from the windmill blades fell off, and the black grew peaceful, the air chill but not unbearable. Vast struts of wood, often half a meter wide, braced the rock; they had buckled over decades into fantastical shapes and wild bulwarks. They evoked the whirr of augers, dynamite charges, and men used to harsh tasks. Every hundred paces, a cone of pale light shone from the diodes at foot level. I learned to creep along half-bent to avoid banging my head on the beams and carrying my quarterstaff dangling like a spear at the end of my arm. Aud cursed when her back scraped the unforgiving roof, or she grazed her elbows in narrow passages.

Snorri said, "There likely won't be any dangerous gases floating about; they'd have drifted away ages ago."

I did not smell any taint other than dry, dead wood, emitting a scent similar to cardamom. A barrow handle lay on the ground, marbled with flaking fungus and clumps of toadstools. Yellow moths flitted through the low-lit stretches, and I felt their feathery wings on my skin. We trod slowly, stopping to listen at each bend. I repeatedly stumbled on railroad ties, the remnants of a track once used to move the tubs of ore.

After thirty minutes, we came to a spot where the crumbling ties disappeared into the earth. It was there that the string of diodes lost their flicker. I stood with the rake handle under my arm, bewildered as to our direction.

Snorri dropped to his knees, "I can't find the wire."

Ahead, the cavern split, the passage on the right advancing level with the ground we were on, the left descended steeply. The little man froze, motionless, and cocked an ear. Muffled voices reverberated along the right path, remote and scarcely audible.

Snorri crawled next toward the steep, downward sloping shaft. I stooped beside him, the cool, silent air flowing over my cheek.

"A breeze — it could mean a second access point further on, somewhere in this direction, or a ventilation chimney. The Thorsteins would go where the new air is."

Suddenly, Olaf's voice rang clear from the level gallery. "Stand together, lads. Working in a tight space like this brings guys together."

The gang sang out, "Right!"

Clammy sweat broke out on my forehead. They had figured out they had taken a wrong turn and were retracing their steps. We quickened our pace downhill like insects feeling along a crack. However, the voices rapidly faded as the gang retreated along the main shaft, back toward the entrance. I breathed relief. After a long scramble, tight-lipped and wary, we passed a metal door.

"A vent?"

The door had a round glass window as thick as a submarine portal.

"Behind this door will be a collapse-room," Snorri explained, "a reinforced shelter for miners should the roof come down. It may be a place to hide if that lot come storming our way."

The corroded metal glided smoothly on its track when Snorri pulled the bolt. I stepped back. The movement had caused a black ooze to seep from the bottom of the opening and spread along the floor. Snorri touched the fluid, sniffed.

"Blood."

Aud clutched both hands to her mouth. My head swam, and I placed a hand on the iron jam to steady myself and felt my lips tremble. Nils lay prone, chest-down, in the crumbled grit, his lined face turned to the side, with his arms splayed forward. A spongy mass of organ tissue bubbled from the fat boy's back, and his open eyes glistened, lifeless.

He was, of course, only recently dead. His face muscles slowly relaxed until the lids crept closed, not entirely shutting, a sliver of white remaining. It was a grotesque assemblage, and I could smell the awful odor of his innards.

"Poor Nils," said Snorri. "He looks more swine than ever."

Suddenly, we heard the sound of men tramping our downhill alley like a herd.

20: Barbarians

Snorri's rough hand grasped my jaw as he wrenched me into the collapse room, a muzzle to prevent me from making a sound. Aud had already slipped through the iron frame, and Snorri sandwiched me against her, all of us obscured by the half-closed door. Nils' body had slid from his bier; his face pressed into a puddle of coal-black effluent. The weight of the stone walls pressed down around us, a brooding weight.

The mob stopped, motionless, on the other side of the barrier. I heard the crackle of a flare being lit and shrank from the sparking glow.

"Good god," said the voice of the Viscount.

Olaf the Peacock began panting and grunting, then the cavern exploded with his wrath, like the roaring of a subterranean foundry. The gang sprang to life and hurtled on beyond the splayed corpse.

Snorri released my mouth, and we followed.

The path resumed its sharp decline; we hung back from the troop to remain undiscovered. Within half an hour, the flare-light had vanished, and the war cries passed beyond earshot. The walls began to show signs of moisture, with water seeping through in some places.

"We have reached lake level," Snorri said.

Aud touched a finger to a weeping wall. "The mine hasn't flooded yet, though it seems one day it may."

Snorri warmed to an explanation. "One day, these are not the efficient pits of modern industry. Generation upon generation of laborers would have worked digging channels that looped along the seams and depended entirely on the day's tools. Often, a path would end wherever a lamp dimmed from bad air or a vein ended. Nonetheless, these shafts were dug by Nordic miners whose efforts will have been thoroughgoing. If the engineers did their job, these barriers could last hundreds of years."

Great lengths of timber enclosed us, shimmed with wooden wedges and sealed with pitch. It was as though we were walking through a mammoth, capsized hull of a Viking longboat. The dripping made the cool air humid and thick as that of a crypt.

"These are the water table barriers, which will hold off water from the water table that is connected to the lake," said Snorri. "A water table is not a still thing; it is dynamic, with surges and shifts, no doubt this one especially. The pressures could be immense."

"Churning water on all sides," murmured Aud.

As we trod on, leaving the barrier of wooden staves, we observed more safety rooms at uneven intervals, some with doors broken from their hinges, others sealed forever behind rockslides. Because the stone was full of unpleasant mysteries, we kept our distance. The walls wept still lingering poisons: mercury, cadmium, and arsenic. Disparate trickles merged along the center of the path, snaking downward.

Aud's face was a pale saucer in the dim light. The passages were only as high as the old miners could reach while tearing out the clods of iron. She paused, rubbing her scalp. Blood streaked her dusty face, her lips grew red and contorted, and her frame shuddered. Wearied by the torment from her abrasions, the giantess lamented, "My mother ended in fire, my friend in ice."

Snorri and I each took a hand of hers and cradled it. The little man continued to soothe her. "Ice and fire, great poles of existence, lass."

The giantess's snuffling reverberated through the tight space. "I find freedom in knowing another person, especially someone unfamiliar. A new face arouses goodness."

Snorri said in a low voice, "Not in the Thorsteins. They hate a new face."

We renewed our descent; the darkness was terrifying. I

wondered where the hooligans had gone and, more worrisome, whether the Thorstein brothers were perched among the crags, ready to spring at any time. We came to a spot in the footway that marked a threshold. At the far end of a corridor, I saw tiny lights twinkling little beams in the dark, scores of them sprayed across my vision like a sprinkling of diamonds caught midair.

Aud raised the tip of her weapon toward the still, glittering array. "A supernatural glow."

As we approached the lights, the frame of another iron door emerged. The tiny constellations of luminescence were pinpricks made by the corrosions of time, flickering from beyond the other side. Aud pressed her shoulder to the metal, and the hinges did not squeak when the barricade opened.

þ

We peered out from a rampart into a splendid expanse that seemed to be the terminus of the old miners' digging. The vault was large and bell-shaped in the manner of an enormous granary, with the largest collapse room door I had seen yet on a sidewall. A curving ramp sloped from our perch toward the swarm of hooligans gathered below on the dusty floor, having arrived before us. A bridge of smoke from numerous flares wielded by the gang swirled under the gallery ceiling.

Several men appeared to be staring at something high on a portion of the wall hidden to me, muttering. Rudeboy swept his hand in a broad arc as if in appreciation

"Very paleolithic," he said. "Troglodytic—a caveman Banksy. Now, shut your yaps, and let's go."

Other ruffians had abandoned their shirts, chests and arms covered with iodine-colored streaks of grime and sweat. The Viscount was kneeling before a metal bin, striking its hasp with a chunk of ore. When the latch parted, he cried, gleefully, "An armory."

His forearm disappeared into the coffer, returning with blades dulled to mute reflection, handles black with a military-style brass knuckle guard. He spread the weapons upon the dirt, and the ruffians admired the various virtues of the cache. While they spoke, Aud, Snorri, and I ducked behind a low wall of rough planks that lined the ramp and crept crab-like down until we reached floor level.

Olaf lifted two more blades from the locker. He held one like it was an ice pick, ready to swipe down. The other he held in a saber grip and wheeled at the many corners of the vault. Something caught his eye, a blackness so voluptuous that it took me a moment to recognize it as a pit.

Olaf moved to the brooding spot and leaned over. He kicked a rock, and I heard it rebounding off the walls of the abyss for five seconds before silence indicated it had come to rest. "We can make use of it when we flush out the rats."

Directly, a terrible noise came, the furious haunted echo of the door to the side collapse room sliding on its rusted track, swift and decisive. The shrieking metal drowned out the startled shouts of the men, revealing a shelter, a proscenium sliced from the side of the cavity large enough for scores of men. There, the brothers stood, grey pelts at their necks, immaculate despite the filthy surroundings.

At the sight of his enemies, Olaf the Peacock clenched his weapons, knuckles white, "My heart is bursting with the need to hate." In an agony of rage, sweat, and exhaustion, he crossed his knives over his head and struck them against each other: Clang. Clang. The Viscount and Rudeboy joined in the blade-striking, and their faces gleamed with fury. The gang took up the beat, united in vengeance, and the cavern echoed with the ringing iron.

With a thin hand, Thorkill stroked his fur collar. "It's the boots-to-suits fellow. We never have visitors," he smirked. "Look at the welcoming gift we have brought."

On cue, Thorvald thrust forward what looked like three flares in his right hand. His left hand gripped a short metal cylinder with a shiny nozzle.

Thorkill announced, "These are not road flares; they are dynamite, a powerful Nordic invention. My brother also holds the culinary torch once owned by that fat mate of yours, now departed. Step aside and let us pass, or we'll turn everyone in this chamber into wet chunks."

Olaf's chest heaved. "With dynamite, the explosion would kill you, too."

"Why should we care? We're nihilists," said Thorkill.

"And fatalists," added Thorvald.

"Not an entirely consistent philosophy, perhaps, but you get the drift." Thorkill smiled. "We like violence of the most radical kinds: loud violence, crowd violence, episodic violence, boring violence, swift violence, slow violence, and violence because there is nothing else to do. Above all, we like very violent violence."

"Sorry about the girly in the lake," said Thorvald.

Aud stiffened beside me upon hearing the mockery, letting out a tiny peep of sadness that I hoped remained audible only to me.

"Well then," continued Thorkill, "the chalet. Urine—crass, but the mood comes on you."

Thorkill glanced at the black wall. "Euphoria and all that. We are disenfranchised, angry youth, not wealthy thrill-seekers like some. Never went to the right dinner parties, mate."

Olaf looked pale among the shadows, almost depleted. "Wealthy, me? Is that what you think?"

Thorvald balled his fists. "I see what you mean about the futility of reasoning with them, brother."

Thorkill snorted, "Ignorant devils."

Olaf the Peacock lowered his head and went on in a hoarse voice. "Why did you kill Nils?"

"He put a cover over the girl in the ice, sealed her up with a culinary torch. That corpulent fool made a fine display. Unfortunately, it caught the attention of the wrong people."

Raising his face, Olaf said, "That corpulent fool was my

son."

"That would make me bitter, too." Thorvald's smile gleamed in the flare light.

I had inched far enough down the zigzagging ramp to view what the men had been staring at before the brothers entered. A large rendering of a wolf occupied the stone façade, made in chalk, the beast's pelt stained in ochre, its body outlined in thick black strokes. To the side of the wolf stood a man in a fighting stance, caped in an ochre pelt and biting his shield—the portrait of an imagined history and manner of living whose disappearance the brothers mourned.

Eyeing the brothers, Olaf said, "You two have strange taste in fashion."

"Wolf pelt. The ancient garb of warriors in a battle frenzy. We live only to experience battle frenzy. Ours is a timeless, honorable way," said Thorvald.

Thorkill took up the remainder of the explanation. "Wolf-warriors, wolfmen. Berserkers. The impulse is involuntary, the ultimate power. A chase adds a thrill. Law and order, for what? Be barbaric. Barbarian life is one step from pure, joyful anarchy."

To my horror, I understood. Thorkill had voiced in some distorted way the reason for The Berserkers. Frenzy. Timelessness. Passion. In Viking metal, your senses quicken, and you achieve heightened awareness that cannot compare to anything you might do elsewhere. You soar, transcendent.

In such a moment, anything could be justified. The thought brought me up short, and I suddenly realized Olaf the Peacock had used the interval of speech to edge his way toward the black pit.

þ

Aud could no longer contain herself. She swiped the veil of matted hair from her brow. "Examine this well," she whispered, then rearing back, Aud kicked the wall of rough planks, which thumped onto the dust. As the giantess moved forward, she unfolded her endless frame like an oversized street-theater puppet, and the room fell quiet but for the sizzling flares.

"Who is that?" said Thorvald.

"It's the monster from the rally I told you about," said Thorkill.

"I think it's female," Thorvald said. "Kind of sexy with the fringe and tights. Nice shape."

"Regarding your mother," Thorkill said, returning his attention to Aud. "She was a dried-up old stick that crackled in flames like a summer campfire." He brought his hand inside his lapel. "And regarding that bird girl, well, all you had to do was look at her. The cheeks, the eyes, the hair. That foreign bitch should have gone to a border camp. Until Nils interfered, the plan was for her body to decompose before spring, undiscovered. She would have melted away like a block of soft cheese."

Thorkill drew his hand from his jacket and opened the palm to reveal a long skinny knife. "The look on her face. Beatific. I had removed my winter gloves to hold this sticker better. I felt the blood spurt on my hand, and she did nothing to defend herself. The blood was so hot that frigid day, and she looked at me in such a gentle way as if she pitied me."

"It was a holy moment," said Thorvald.

Thorkill disdainfully glanced upon his brother. "Oh, spare us your god-talk."

"I'm a berserker, a spiritual warrior, like my fighting man on the wall."

"Fair enough," Thorkill said, looking up at the image. "The artist does have a bold stroke I admire. But, of course, the artist is you."

"Thank you, brother.

When Thorkill spoke again, his voice went flat. "That girl in the lake, hers was not a life that deserved to be lived.

She was a creature devoid of value. The sound when I jabbed the blade in was just like cutting dry cork."

I crouched to my knees to get a better view of Aud. Her breath was wheezy and labored, her cheeks mottled as she sobbed in silence. She was about fifteen paces from the brothers. I saw her nostrils quiver; her fingers locked about the hilt of her sword. She took a step, then another, picking up speed with each pace, as the sword hissed from her belt.

Her eyes flicked to the low bulging ceiling as if to judge clearance. In a single motion, she stiffened her back and brought the hilt just above shoulder level, the tip of the blade jutting horizontally to her extreme left, the backside of her right hand almost touching her cheek. With unambiguous intent and charged with the rush of victory, the giantess then bellowed: "I shall weave a fabric of death about you with my sword and hunt you under clouds of doom."

The sword cut through the darkness. But before it had completed its sweep, there came a sudden clang of metal. Aud's upper body shook from interrupted motion. Pieces of metal flew about, lost in the black edges of the cavern. The blade had hit the wall of stone.

The giantess looked down upon the notched ruins of her weapon, shattered within an inch of the hilt. Her eyes welled, and her mouth twisted. Her judgment had been wrong, and, as if possessed by immeasurable fury, Aud leaped back and wrenched Snorri's ax from his hands.

Yet, even as the ankles of her turn-boots passed before my nose, something strange occurred. An insight expanded like a balloon inside me, a notion conceived in a flash yet seeming to bloom forever. The understanding was this: Ever since Snorri and I had encountered Aud at the mead house, I had felt a familial kind of love for this strange giantess, profound regard that seemed to predate our meeting. What I saw revealed in this dreadful moment was that the brothers' mysticism of violence was sucking her in. Violence romanticized, violence for fun, stirred into a cauldron of grievance. Such violence would and could only go on, fueled by resentment and revenge.

I knew how to act and did not feel flustered. Instead, I felt deep calm, as sure of myself at this moment as when I pounded a major chord on the keyboard. I did not know the full scope of what I intended to do, but I knew it was right. I could risk death for it.

I thrust my quarterstaff forward between her scissoring shins. Aud fell hard. The rake handle snapped from my wrists, cracking me below my right eye. Searing pain flashed through my cheekbone and jaw, blinding me in that eye. Meanwhile, the notched ax bounced across the lamplit floor and slipped over into the darkness of the pit. My quarterstaff stopped rolling at Olaf's boot.

I was lying full length on the ground, bleeding from an unknown area of my forehead. The walls ensconcing us had become black crags. Aud sprawled on the broken floor, unable to lift herself, and began to sob. She wiped her hands over her face, and her eyes narrowed. I had betrayed her. Did she know?

"You all struggle like children," Thorkill said.

Olaf's eyes widened. He scanned the fallen giantess. The scars on his cheeks were florid as he bent and gathered up my quarterstaff. "You do not have explosives; otherwise, you would have used them on her and killed us all."

The Viscount stepped to one side of Olaf the Peacock, Rudeboy on the other, and the three formed a moving front, as they might have seen police do at match riots. They were a dangerous moving barrier.

Thorvald said, "Your impudence is brave."

Thorkill smiled. "My brother believes in the old wisdom, that the only thing that will outlast a man's death is his reputation for bravery. And we have other ways to keep you in line." Thorvald flicked the culinary torch to life with this proclamation and turned up the flame, which snaked before him. Then, Thorvald Thorstein began to shudder. Tremors wracked his body, his eyes rolled, spittle fell from his lips, his face grew purple, and he howled wolf-like till his fury filled the room.

"Aooooo," he bayed. "Aoooo, ahhhhooooo."

"A ploy," muttered Olaf, as the distance between the adversaries closed to a few paces. The Viscount and Rudeboy kept a weather eye on the dancing blade of flame from the culinary torch. The Viscount fell out of step, and Olaf the Peacock glanced at him.

Seizing upon their distraction, Thorkill Thorstein vaulted from the collapse room rise, landing between the hooligan leader and the pit barely a yard away. Rocks clattered from his shoes into the black depth. Thorkill Thorstein delivered three jackrabbit strikes within seconds, his blade sinking in just below Olaf's left clavicle.

The victim looked down at the puncture wounds, his complexion turning the color of shale. Blood spread from the wound over his chest like a madly blooming corsage. Olaf stopped inhaling. His eyes narrowed as he touched the rapidly spreading stain on his t-shirt, black as pitch, and wobbled on his feet.

"Oh," he said, and then "Oh," as if merely assessing a fact.

The tableau remained intact for a moment. Then, Thorvald Thorstein began baying again, and the noise seemed to summon Olaf the Peacock back to himself. Quickly, even as the stain coursed over his chest, he regained his stance and swept the tip of his staff in a high figure eight. The descending strike cracked Thorkill Thorstein in his right shoulder with the force of a horse kick. The nearly equal backstroke smashed his brother on the spur of his ankle. Both strikes made a noise like wet laundry being clubbed, bones breaking.

"Brother," said Thorvald Thorstein, his long flat whiskers shivering, "I feel the gods have departed us."

Olaf the Peacock ended the whirling circuit with the quarterstaff parallel to the dirt floor. He gripped the weapon horizontally to his chest with both hands, assuming a defensive parry in the classic position of a policeman wielding a riot baton. Staggering forward a step, he blinked. Then, with no other words from him and no shriek or howl from the outlaws, Olaf the Peacock leaned forward with the staff like a man pushing an ox cart and charged. The weapon caught the Thorsteins as Olaf must have hoped; together, the assailant and victims sailed over the black edge of the pit, followed by irregular percussions ending within seconds in a trio of muted thuds.

21: Collapse

An eerie luminescence played far below from deep in the mine. An animated light reflected on the black walls, and the hooligans stood staring into the wobbling shadows.

"Should we try to rescue, Olaf," Rudeboy asked.

The Viscount ran his right thumb and forefinger over the wings of his mustache. "Olaf is dead, Rudy, as well as the two pissers in fur, and I say this as an optimist."

Nevertheless, a general brawl broke out among the ruffians over whether to descend into the pit to retrieve the bodies and who should go, each man threatening rebellion against his peers. As they disputed, a powerful sulfurous odor filled the cavern, the stink emphatic, and the bickering ceased.

"What a demonic stench," said Rudeboy.

"The fart of a mountain troll," the Viscount agreed.

While the confused flock debated, Snorri and I took Aud by her hands. Her broad, heavy fingers felt clammy, and her face was grey.

"I'm suddenly dizzy," said the giantess.

I said, "Me too."

Snorri sniffed the air. "Pitmen from old times called it mine damp."

"Mine damp?" I asked.

"Something has been stirred by their fall, releasing ancient gas deposits — a stone or shelf perhaps."

"The mine damp is vitiating the air," said Aud.

We helped the giantess to her feet. The archway loomed at the top of the rampart, our exit. I had just taken a step up the incline when Rudeboy cried, "These fumes are gas, and the kitchen torch still burns." Something exploded like a single clap of thunder, and bits of rock shot up from the abyss, ricocheting overhead.

Men galloped up the ramp, scrambling to escape back

through the mountain, and their voices disappeared once again up the passage.

"Let's go," Snorri commanded, darting ahead like a harrier in a field. Aud and I lagged, the giantess a pathetic sight after her ordeal. Her hair was disheveled, and she had lost the golden chain of fox teeth from her neck; the animal tails on her fringe drooped, and their number had dwindled.

The climb up was trying. A trickle down the center made a muck of the path. I forgot to stoop under the beams while Aud cursed at seemingly endless collisions, sometimes dropping on all fours. Worse, the rout up felt more labyrinthine than the descent, beset with blind alleys and convergences of tunnels that had been hidden on the way down. When we emerged from one such cul-de-sac, Aud stood staring at the rushing water, which had grown from a trickle to a hard-running stream.

Snorri considered the increasing volume of water. Before our eyes, the stream doubled in width, becoming at once a small river. His tone was grave. "The lake barriers are failing."

Immediately a distant explosion came, followed by a sequence of discrete booms, each closer to our position. Whether I heard the shrieks of the tormented souls who had fled before us, or I simply imagined them, I could not say. But the air pressure in the chamber changed, my ears rang, and my head felt light.

Snorri waved us onward. "A mine collapses in sections; if we stay ahead of the cave-ins, we might live. The trick will be to stay on the correct route."

The giantess lurched from side to side as we progressed, stopping to rub her bruised ankles. Large pouches of skin had developed under her eyes, and a blue shadow played at the edges of her lips. "I cannot figure how I tripped when rushing those murders."

Snorri's eyes had not turned toward me, so I could not determine whether he knew of my betrayal when he said, "Fate must have other purposes for you, lass."

We reached the narrow passage to the barrier gallery lined with timbers. Explosions had opened fissures, and the lake was gushing waterfall-like down the walls. Whether the gang was near or far, it was now impossible to tell. I felt my fingers curl into a diabolical formation on my invisible keyboard.

"The barrier gallery forms a basin," Snorri explained, "and water will collect there."

We heard nothing but rushing water and our voices. Stone visible on the way down was now hidden below the churning surface. Aud waded first into the frigid pool, Snorri held the hem of her skirt, I clutched his shoulder, and together we made a chain. The torn wood from the barrier beams hung sharp as spikes from the ceiling. A hundred meters lay between us and the other end of the gallery, where a black hole pierced the wall, our way out of this death trap. I plodded one step at a time, feet sliding along an unseen floor turned mushy by the torrent. The giantess advanced cautiously, the water rising to her navel. It rose to Snorri's armpits, mid-chest for me. Our little train pressed forward, and time blurred.

Suddenly, Aud halted. "Oh, my," she stammered and drew back.

A sallow mass bobbed in the uncertain light. The mutilated corpse of Nils floated, wedged face-up between fallen timbers. The torrent had washed his body down the passages, ending here, and the bloated form rocked in its watery cradle, red foam issuing from the wounds in his chest. My back stiffened.

We edged around the ghastly flotsam and reached the chamber head. The black hole I had spied from the other end of the gallery was a torrent now that we jumped at like salmon up a cataract. Water poured through the opening; my body was frigid, and I slipped repeatedly.

Aud grabbed an ancient wooden ladder floating near her and held it propped against the opening. One by one, we ascended, with Aud being the last. Her weight crushed two rungs before Snorri and I could hoist her right leg high enough to make the shelf.

Past the cataract, the icy deluge filled the entire width of the passage. "We shall never make it if we try to plunge through there," said Snorri.

The darkness and cold clung to me. Many collapse doors had been wrenched open by the hooligans, evidently searching for another route up. Snorri located an open door with a wide flat floor above the flowing river. We climbed up, shivering, our clothing drenched.

Aud and I dropped our weapons and sat on the damp soil, back-to-back with spines touching, as if facing out might add protection. Snorri disappeared into the dark, searching, while we rested. I felt the large bones of the giantess's back shift. She said, "What were you writing in your notebook the night we got to the island? You were scratching away like the devil."

The rune reading of three peculiar women had put me in a bind, impelling me to reveal that I was a musician, my closely guarded secret. I ran my fingers through the crumbles of the soil as that disclosure played over in my mind.

I faltered, "Just a, a, a…"

"A what?" said Aud.

"A melody."

"Let's hear it."

"I am too ashamed." And yet, heedless of disgrace, heedless of alerting hooligans up an adjoining shaft, manic with the survival instinct, I leaped into a slithering burst of the tune I had composed sitting on the overturned gig:

Warships

> *Warriors helm a warship,*
> *Sails aloft at midnight,*
> *Rudder dark as copper;*
> *Weary bodies bearing*

> *Plunder to the homestead.*
>
> *Warships bear the warriors*
> *Past a coastal fortress,*
> *Swathed in cloaks of starlight,*
> *Eye-beams bright with purpose.*
>
> *Ambush wakes the weary.*
> *Iron shears the darkness.*
> *Life drips from the dagger*
> *Edged with crimson threads.*
>
> *Cold, the hand of sorrow,*
> *Hot, the blood and marrow.*
> *Fortune is an arrow*
> *Tipped with silver moonlight,*
> *Whirling toward its target.*

Something very Viking in that tune, something the band would embrace—not happiness, rather, preparation, endurance, attack. My hands fluttered down like landing birds. Aud stared up at the black ore, marshaling her thoughts.

"A proper battle hymn," she said. "An anthem."

After what now seemed an interminable time away, Snorri's voice came ringing down the stone throat of the darkness, "This way, friends, it seems to be another tunnel, a different route."

"Where is Olaf's gang?" I asked.

Snorri circled his hand to usher us on. "Impossible to know; I didn't hear them, only the water. Maybe they have reached the exit already."

As we advanced up the new, dryer passage, the ceiling grew lower to our heads and the walls nearer our shoulders. Eventually, Snorri and I stooped to crouching, while Aud had to grapple along on hands and knees.

I looked back at the giantess. Aud was sweating

between her eyebrows and under her nose, her skin blotched and reddened. She pushed her hair back from her temples. "It is as though I have lived a thousand years already, yet my life may be extinguished in a heartbeat."

The rest of the route was a dark fog to me, punctuated here and there by the distant thuds of falling rock. The water sweating from the walls dwindled as we moved up the mine layers, and at some point, the flow ceased.

"We have passed the water tables," Snorri said with evident relief. Ten minutes later, I heard Snorri tapping metal. "Another door, the way out, I hope." When Aud leaned into the frame, it roared open with the squeal of old iron.

We had rejoined the main corridor, lit faintly by the chain of diode lights. To my surprise, the hooligans' screams boomed from behind us down that endless chasm of blackness — we were ahead of them.

"Listen to the direction those howls are coming from; they are back in the shaft. How could that happen?"

Aud let out a choked breath. "Some wicked necromancy."

Snorri wrung the wet from the tail of his shirt. "The place is a warren. They braved the main gallery against the river, but that route was gushing from the split barriers. The gang must have been held back somewhere along the way."

The voices reverberating behind us were like baying hounds, now rising, now fading. Still, I heard nothing to indicate the gang knew we were ahead in the same passage. Even if the booms of the collapsing mine did not suppress our voices, the rages and disputes of the mob likely drowned any sound of ours.

We rushed to stay ahead, Aud panting intensely. Six minutes later, I spotted a swarm of yellow moths; then, we came across a hanging shelf of brown and white fungus. The fungus patches became increasingly frequent, spreading in overlapping sheets of red and yellow or thick cords, while the moths turned furry grey or black. The pit door lay not far now. However, the last mile was anguish. I felt I might collapse at any moment from exhaustion. As I hung my head from weariness, I spotted a wedge of bright light on the dirt floor and looked up to the door through which we had entered.

"The moon," I murmured.

Aud swept the back of her hand against her forehead in what was a feminine gesture. "At last," she sighed. Snorri pressed his shoulder to the woven iron.

As I was about to pass through the doorway, a thunderous burst of recognition came from behind. "There is that monster bitch!"

Something clanged against the wall beside me. My ear stung. A chunk of ore lay near my feet, thrown from behind, and I glanced back to see the Viscount advancing with a squinty-eyed grin. Other faces glimmered beside him, dripping with filth. Several men had somehow retained their knives in the escape.

"We'll pierce your hides a few times yet," Rudeboy shouted. A chunk of ore sailed toward me, and I ducked too late. It split the flesh above my right eye, and blood ran into my vision. A stone hit Snorri between the shoulder blades, and he crumpled.

"We'll make you look like Fat Nils back there," the Viscount shouted from down the mine shaft.

"Perforated," added Rudeboy.

Fortunately, Aud had also made it to the woven iron door. I staggered away from the mine entrance, my arm about Snorri, as Aud shouldered the opening shut. She heaved a pile of beams and stones from nearby to barricade it closed. The hooligans cursed and hammered at the woven iron from within. We walked together out of earshot.

I asked, "What do you think happened to put them behind us?"

Snorri wiped a mucky hand over his beard. "They probably went up the main tunnel, which was flooding badly, and had to fight the torrent all the way."

"The troll of the mountain smiled upon us," said Aud.

Snorri stared at the ring on his hand. "Maybe so."

It was well past midnight, nearing dawn, perhaps four AM. The moon shone like a spotlight; the air was brisk though quickly filling with a grotesque plume of smoke and dust. The windmill rattled. I blinked and shielded my eyes from the haze. I fell to the earth at the top of the rim and ran my fingers through the moist crumbles.

Snorri took out his last packet of fish and handed it to Aud. "Here." The pack made it to me, and we ate in silence.

The giantess took a deep inhale, apparently summoning a last internal resource. To my surprise, she began to sing the song I had composed while sitting on the overturned gig. Her voice, though deep, was fluty and low. It seemed to echo inside her before coming out, and once out, to infuse the stone and penetrate the ground. Snorri stepped back and tilted his head up at the giantess, thumbs in his pockets, listening.

Perhaps from fear or exhaustion, or to accommodate her great torso, she had slowed the song down, transforming my metal anthem into a kind of folk tune. It was sweet but redolent with gravitas. It was not the song as I had written it; it was, somehow, better, and the way Aud rendered the tune felt just right. My hands fluttered down.

Snorri said, "The big lass can sing. She has the grandeur of Isolde."

Aud stared hard at us as if marshaling her thoughts. I felt the quake of her chuckle. The giantess tilted her long rectangular head, though her good humor barely lasted a moment. "I must sleep," she declared. Within seconds of lying down, she was snoring.

Snorri, too, placed his head on a flat stone and drifted into slumber.

I was preparing my bed when a sharp *kek kek* came from the darkness. Was Minne strutting upon a rock? She snapped her beak and flashed the white membranes of her eyes. I gestured toward her, and she jumped, landing on my forearm. Although exhaustion threatened to overcome me as well, I was glad to see her.

Minne made a long series of rasping high honks and pressed her head to the back of my hand, prodding. "What is this then?" I slipped my finger under a tough black ribbon at her throat. The ribbon had a plastic bobble, forming a collar of some kind, albeit with no marking.

I shrugged, ate a final handful of dried fish, and rested my head over my arm stretched across the grey soil.

22: Return of a Valkyrie

"She sings better than Bjork," a male voice rang out. "I heard her down the escarpment and across the shore."

Not long after I had lain down my head, I awoke. A figure stood atop the ridge of slag that capped the ravine silhouetted against an orange pre-dawn sky. The male voice sounded familiar, though I could not place it. Minne darted through the stubble of pines.

I called out, "Friend or foe?"

The shadow crouched as if to communicate better. "Friend."

The black shape descended the slope. After seven steps, I recognized the crisp, vibrant uniform of the Fulaflugahål police. Snorri had been roused, too, and chuckled. "Good morning, Patrolman Jerker," he said. "At least we got a little rest."

The patrolman peered round to Snorri and me, then up and down the length of the immense prone figure. His eyes glimmered cornflower blue. "You look like iron statues." I examined myself anew. All I could view of my body was this: grey with mine dust, I appeared as though forged of hammered metal. Snorri and Aud had the same coating.

Snorri hitched his thumb at the mine door. "We were in there a long time." Our conversation provoked blows from the mine interior before the door, followed by shrill demands.

"Who's in there?" Jerker asked.

Snorri said, "Prisoners."

"And who is imprisoned?"

"Acquaintances of the murderers of the girl in the ice."

Jerker turned toward the clatter. "Ah-hah. What about the murder suspects themselves?"

"The suspects are dead. The acquaintances—prisoners—have been detained for the police, that is to say, for you, Patrolman Jerker. Due process, the rule of law, and all that." Now that we were back in the world of light and fresh air, much to our relief, Snorri seemed to have resumed his predictably sententious tone.

Jerker placed his ear against the door. "Can the prisoner-acquaintances breathe in there?"

"Well enough."

Jerker pointed to the giant girl. "And this very large person, friend or foe?"

"A friend."

"A great friend," I added.

I abandoned the idea of sleeping as hopeless, despite craving it dearly. I took a place on the slag heap and clasped my hands to my thighs to keep them from leaping about. "Jerker, how did you get here to the top of this mountain?"

The patrolman spread an arm to the notch in the slag where Nils and then Olaf had entered. "There is an old paved track from the beach that switch-backs up the mountain. It is clear and easy; it took me perhaps forty minutes to hike up."

I stared in silence at Snorri, feeling a bit sick. "And how, Patrolman Jerker, did you get to the Isle of O?"

Jerker seemed to ponder the question. He indicated down the slope; there was a large rubber rescue craft half-beached on the shingle. "What an effort we went through to procure it, a maze of requisitions and a laundry list of approvals. Buddy, you would not believe the red tape. Securing that rescue craft was worse than wheedling entry to the Grimke courthouse."

"Are other officials with you?" I asked.

"Sergeant detective Bergthora is still making her way up the hill." Jerker patted his sternum. "Too much smoking." Even as the patrolman finished speaking, the stout form of the policewoman appeared at the crest. Her dark office suit had grown shiny with dirt, and there was something shabby and run-down about her. She glared at us without speaking.

Patrolman Jerker approached her. They conferred in low tones, heads bowed, a duration that seemed unmeasurable though filled with dramatic feints and vigorous gestures. Finally, Bergthora said loudly enough for us to hear, "Alleged perps are dead, eh? Acquaintances of the perps are trapped in there, the so-called prisoners, eh?"

She did not mean for us to answer. Jerker said, "The records clerk asked how we knew to come to this island."

Bergthora paused to light a cigarillo. She inhaled, blowing a stream of blue smoke through each nostril. As she addressed us, she examined the giantess sleeping on the soil. "Point one, Kolbitter and Sturlusson. A shop girl at the harbor said you fled in boats; gave the whole story about motorcycles and burning the village. Point two. The Constable claimed he held some inkling the island would be your destination. Some mysterious prescience. His hunch was confirmed when a tremor was registered by Grimke seismographic equipment, at which point your whereabouts were extrapolated based on a minor earthquake centered at this very spot."

Bergthora grinned with roughshod vigor. "Fortunately, there was no tsunami. The Constable was wild and out of his head upon hearing all this, and I, well, I felt it my duty to do first reconnaissance."

Jerker puffed his chest. "I was designated to assist."

Bergthora extended a plump damp hand for me to shake. "Congratulations, Kolbitter. I'm certain the Grimke magistrate will be intrigued by this apprehension of suspects, this farrago executed by a retiree, a giant teenage girl, and a records clerk."

Though I could not tell by what logic of goodwill, Snorri said, "Grammaticus is a musician." Then added, "And this giantess sings beautifully, too."

Bergthora tapped the ash from her cigarillo. While she appeared to be working toward additional trenchant observations, a mechanical *whomp-whomp* interrupted her, reverberating through the air. Snorri let his gaze scour the pit entrance: "Is the mine still collapsing? A collapse can stretch over days."

Jerker snapped his thumb and forefinger as if confirming a notion. "The sound is coming from the sky. It is the Constable."

I searched along the indigo horizon—a flash of glass, a rising din. Soon, the fuselage of a helicopter became visible, swooping, yellow and blue, toward shore. As it passed overhead, the sky rent with its noise. On the belly, between the rails of the undercarriage, were tall letters: G-R-I-M-K-E.

Snorri groaned, "Usch."

The machine blasted grit and pine needles as it settled like a beast on its hocks; the blades shuddered to a halt on a flat spot near the postern. Jerker held his ears, shouting, "How thrilling to see an aircraft land."

Time moved rapidly. Freja leaped easily from the cargo door; her wide brow swept the terrain, long yellow hair swaying like a ceremonial fabric down her back. She exuded robotic competence, as though she had seen the same loop tape far too often. Within moments, six officials in black livery were spreading over the mine postern. Peering around the dismal ravine, they rattled the metal door and listened to the echoing complaints. The tape went up; photographs were taken.

Jerker laughed and slapped my shoulder. "It's like the Ride of the Valkyries, Grammaticus."

Admiring Freja's efficiency I said, "She is graceful and precise, but ever out of place, a mermaid cast from the sea."

Jerker's eyes narrowed. "You are a peculiar man, Grammaticus."

The Constable stepped next from the helicopter, a bottle-green cravat limp at his throat. He looked old and weary, as though he had been through a great ordeal. A glossy black raven flew out from the hatch over his head.

The Constable strode toward me, thumb wedged

between the pages of his beloved blue volume. A yard off, he stopped, pressed his good eye shut, tilted his head back, parted his lips, and ran the tip of his tongue over them as if summoning an effort.

He opened his good eye. "Hello, boy. I believe justice can yet be wrenched from this catastrophe." The Constable flung open the covers of the manual and read aloud to me in a manner that was suggestive of a prepared speech. "When future historians lament a poisonous atmosphere of city government, the crooked secrets of state administration, the confusion, bloated sinecures, and corruption ever and again…"

He inhaled.

"Not that bit," he grumbled, then hunted page after page. Finally, the Constable's back stiffened, and new words fell from his lips:

"*It is all in the art of administration.*" A rhapsodic glow overcame his tired face. "There we are; we're done."

I said, "Sir?"

"Kolbitter, trust is the strength in all official relations. The investigating detective must create the conditions for trust. Clear cut responsibility. Deploying resources. Executive discretion." He swatted his thumb on the antique manual with a savage *thock.*

I said, bowing my head. "It was anarchy, sir. Worse. I have nothing to show for it."

To my surprise, the Constable did not hesitate, his voice quiet and gentle. "Well, boy, one can manage to preserve trust within this crazed hodgepodge, this hugger-mugger; within this cataclysm of idiocy called human history." He seemed not to be listening to me. "Yes, yes, yes," he affirmed.

Meanwhile, the uproar of the landing helicopter had roused Aud. The giantess stretched out her legs and was massaging her shins. She said, drowsily, "Grammaticus is a paragon of trust. Look what has come of this adventure, sir. The acquaintances are entrapped and . . ."

"And?" coaxed the Constable.

The glossy black raven that had escaped the helicopter swept past. At the sight of the bird, blood rouged Aud's cheeks, and she regained her tongue. "Tanke."

Tanke streaked away again and executed three high corkscrew twists. Minne shot back a *rap-rap*, and the ravens met on a pine bough, beak to beak. Minne then bent her head and made long *oooo* calls. Tanke, in turn, preened her, probing her neck feathers one at a time. Aud added in a subdued voice, "I was deprived of your solace and counsel too long."

Recognizing the opening created by the giantess's distraction, Snorri pressed himself into the conversation, picking up where the Constable had left off. "And, Constable? And this: we know that Fat Nils used a culinary torch on the ice, a culinary torch that also ignited the mine gasses."

The Constable raised an open hand to the bird near him, "Minne, can you confirm that?"

"*Kwork*," said Minne.

The Constable lowered his hand, "I offer no admonishment."

Snorri's brow was corrugated. "The sergeant detective Bergthora mentioned you had an inkling we would be here."

Bergthora stepped over the giantess's long limbs. Something in her impatience suggested she wished to ferret out any further blame of me. I said, to head her off, "Yes, how did you know to find us on this godforsaken lump of rock, Constable?"

The Constable extended his forearm and trilled a long *rrrrr*. Minne flapped to her perch on his wrist. The Constable slipped his finger under the black neck ribbon I had discovered earlier. "Remote tracking."

Bergthora grunted and crushed her cigarillo butt with the toe of her right shoe.

þ

Under the supervision of Freja, the captives were frog marched from the mine to the landing spot. They sheepishly mulled about on the scrub, in torn black and yellow uniforms and all manner of ragged jeans and T-shirts and boots. Their skin was grey as iron, too. The Viscount had rolled down his one-piece suit and cinched the arms of like a belt, stripped to the waist, his chest hair a matted pelt. He immediately understood the situation and herded his companions up the stone chute to an impromptu enclosure, where interrogations commenced.

It was concluded all were present but Nils, Olaf the Peacock, and the Thorsteins. Aud, Snorri, and I were spared the humiliation of questioning this time and were free to lounge. We consumed every morsel of the food rations from the helicopter, drank quarts of bottled water, and washed our faces with the water we did not drink. The Constable looked about as if the goings on were no longer quite his concern. For Freja, directing her team meant executing the forensic duties with clinical precision. No procedural detail was unworthy of her suspicion or correction.

The inmates were bound at the wrists. Freja directed Bergthora to process them down to the shore. "Sergeant detective, there are too many prisoners to fit in the helicopter. Use the requisitioned craft." At a nod of Freja's head, a Grimke officer retrieved two black weapons from the helicopter. Jerker received a truncheon, Bergthora, a service pistol, a sleek metal gun, and a black holster.

"An Ogleworthy P370," she murmured. She swung the weapon to feel the heft, peered down the sight, and gave an appreciative cluck of her tongue before saluting Freja with a smile.

A mysterious rapport seemed to be burgeoning between the women.

Under Bergthora and Jerker's command, the hooligans

tramped off. Jerker tapped the edge of the herd with his club. My eyes roamed over the tiny paper-pink flowers that edged the ravine and then out to the lake's perpetual transformations.

Aud said, "I do not know how those men could hate someone different. If they do not recognize a common humanity in another human, they cannot know themselves."

Snorri replied, "I fear they know themselves too well."

I wandered around the side of the helicopter, where I found the Constable. He was staring at his knuckles as if they were strange to him. He said, with dark satisfaction, "I have been on this planet a long time."

"Are you okay, sir? You look exhausted."

He waved a hand. His thoughts seemed miles away. "The apropos question is this: Have we settled the matter to your satisfaction, boy?"

I surprised myself even as the words passed my lips. "Not entirely, sir; in fact, not at all."

The Constable cast his black lens at me. "A shame. It is the nature of great things to rise and melt away. Aimlessness leads to the aim. Have a good think on it." He disappeared behind the panels of the Grimke aircraft, and Minne and Tanke followed after.

In pursuit of her winged friends, Aud approached and stopped, seeming to detect something sour in my mood. "Come, Grammaticus, pluck up your heart."

Freja whistled a high note that made me think of a bird call; one felt the weight of her beck. We boarded the helicopter.

þ

More tired than I had ever been, my head flopped against the flat, institutional aircraft seat as if it was a down pillow. My thoughts scattered in a disordered cadence, and I wanted only to let sleep consume me. I stirred, in brief moments of wakefulness, my perception growing increasingly fragmented as the machine whirred its rhythmic sequence toward Grimke.

I roused to Aud's voice mourning the dead girl in the lake: "My dear friend, yes. She would have been condemned to a life more or less close to death. A bare life." I could not fathom how the giantess was still awake after such a harrowing ordeal. It eventually dawned on me she was caught in the mania of victory, a spirit in extremis. She was a young woman buffeted by bitter sorrow and the energy of triumph. Aud, poor Aud, magnificent Aud.

The Constable said, "The mine explosion was remarkable."

"A very Viking solution," Aud said.

Freja had composed her face in unnerving stillness. "You are a scoundrel, Aud," she said, with only the quickest of winks to hint at her dry humor. Pursing her wide lips, the giantess laughed a long silent laugh.

Then, again, blackness. Another void of time, an ancient blurriness. I emerged from sleep once more, with my face pressed to the glass of the helicopter window. I saw my reflection, the wide puffy face of slumber, hair in scraggles.

I raised my head to look around. Snorri, still caked with grime and looking like a garden gnome, was gesticulating madly to his seat companion, a man in black strafe gear. His elbow drawn back Snorri was demonstrating how to melt ice with a kitchen torch.

23: The Song that Brings Everyone Together

I had slept enough on the helicopter to manage what I knew had to happen. The roommate who answered the door had the same mascara-black eyelashes as Fadlan. He nodded wordlessly and backed into the shadows, leaving me standing in the darkened foyer, clutching my papers tightly, waiting. Gudrid had started up a sing-song beat on her drums; the band was practicing.

There was another voice, too, a rough male voice I did not recognize, followed by the sound of Fadlan's v-body guitar being lifted. I held myself in the shadows of the hall, hands on the plaster, and peered into the room. The man must have been six-five and three hundred pounds with a pumpkin-colored beard cinched at the bottom with twine.

"I'll use this monster," he swatted the guitar body.

Fadlan flinched, saying, "I haven't tuned it yet, Skallagrimsson."

"Tuning? No problem." The man then smashed out a monotonous drone on Fadlan's beloved instrument. He wasn't a suave baritone like Egil, and when he let out a raw-throated howl, it sounded like he had a head cold:

> *I kill the warriors!*
> *I murder them all*
> *And gobble their flesh!*
> *Ja, ja, ja, ja!*
>
> *The dead are so ugly!*
> *I feast on the ugly dead!*
> *My stomach is bloated with warriors!*
> *Ja, ja, ja, jaaaaaarrrrgh!*

Someone in an adjacent flat banged on the wall. Gudrid said, "What is the song called?"

Silence for a space. Then Skallagrimson said, "I call it *Dragon Snack*."

Fadlan said, "Proper Viking material there," though the way his tone dropped belied his claim.

Egil stepped back. "Look, mate, I do the howls."

"You guys said you wanted to shake things up."

"It's about pitching to our strengths."

"We should have a saliva war," Skallagrimson said, unheeding. "We spit, and the audience spits back—fans love it. And we gotta rename the band Pus Brigade or The Ass Fudge Front or something, shake off the nasty old vibes."

Gudrid said, "How will people know we're Viking metal?"

"We make a demo recording. I have a song about bed spins." Skallagrimsson disappeared from my view, as I heard him stomp to the kitchen and open the refrigerator. "Got any food? I'd love a ham sandwich right now."

Fadlan sucked in a breath. "I would never eat ham."

Lone, roaring laughter from the huge man. He stomped out of the kitchen and headed toward the front door. "I'm so hungry right now," Skallagrimson panted. "I got places to be and women to screw, and you guys gotta raise money for the demo recording." He turned the corner of the hall just as I pressed into the shadows out of view. His hands were like red balls of meat, and he brushed by me, banging the door closed behind him.

A concentrated silence. Then Gudrid said, "Usch."

Fadlan said, "Demo recording?"

Egil said, "He lacks nuance."

"Aisle or window seat?" Grudrid asked.

"Send him steerage class," Egil replied.

Fadlan twanged a string on his base. "Nothing wrong with steerage, mate; it's getting kicked in the ass all the way back to Grimke I'd find shameful."

There was nothing for me to do but live in the moment and face the impossible truth. I stepped out of the darkness. Fadlan and Egil had their backs to me, heads down, but Gudrid was full-on. She wore a leather vest with shiny grommets. She had shed her cloche, and the pink and green twists in her hair made her look like a confetti popper. She spotted me instantly but was momentarily silent, scowling, trying to weigh her words. She did not pause long. "Fuck off," Gudrid said.

Fadlan and Egil spun around. Neither disputed her words, and Egil grunted like a man lifting a heavy weight. "The song writer who ghosted."

"You guys fired me." I walked forward.

Gudrid said with steely precision. "Don't come back until you can spend the time."

"It was the case," I sighed.

Fadlan's brow darkened. "We went over this. That's all you have to say?"

Gudrid sent a drumstick whirling, and it nipped my left ear. Egil said, "It's not funny until you put someone's eye out."

"The case is over," I pleaded and wrung my hands, seriously contemplating weeping. But tears were not a Viking thing, and, instead, I told my bandmates what had happened, at least as much as made sense for the moment. Then, I repeated what I had said to Snorri. "There has to be one thing, one thing so important you would do it even on the most horrible day of your life. That's what makes an artist."

I loosened my fist and pressed the stave-marked pages into their hands.

þ

"Right proper Viking material." Fadlan's eyes shone like water at the bottom of a well.

"You blew up a mine?" said Egil.

"This has been one of the odder times of my life," I said, strapping on my keyboard. I started my new song at a breakneck tempo and plowed in twenty bars before realizing Fadlen had not taken up the rhythm.

I rested my hands. "What's up?"

"Grammaticus, I am going to use an acoustic guitar. Part of the band remake. I have been thinking, what we play is folk-rock, but folk-rock at warp speed."

"Hmm," I said. "Fair enough; that's the acid test if the song can survive the transformation to acoustic."

Egil said, "You think it will sound *dinky?*"

"Not," Fadlan replied, "when the melody rolls in with your voice and Grammaticus's keyboards, mega-textured."

Gudrid played with a green hair twist. "A song will only reach its final shape as a result of being performed."

Fadlan stroked the whiskers of his chin, so dark they appeared blue. He seemed pleased by Gudrid's statement, "Our music should be like subatomic particles drifting on a solar wind. A fusion of chordal and rhythmic pallets, sardonic, but also sincere."

I said, "Sometimes you guys talk like a bunch of rock critics."

"I just want to sing," said Egil.

We went back to my song, the song I had unfolded to them, but slowing the tempo way down. Gudrid started slapping the drum skin with her bare hands. I could hear Egil breathing waiting to hit just after the beat. He lifted his eyes now and then to watch my hands, Fadlan giving subdued support on his acoustic to suggest melancholy.

"RagnaRock, full throttle," I said.

Egil attacked the lyrics with the relish of a B-movie actor announcing an invasion from Mars. Fadlan's guitar and Gudrid's drums roared in.

Epilogue: RagnaRock

We must love one another in Art,
as the mystics love one another in God...

—Gustave Flaubert

We are on stage at RagnaRock. I am wearing iron earrings and a leather jerkin. My straight black hair sweeps over my shoulders. My skinny arms gleam bone white.

Gudrid and Egil thrash their helmeted heads. Fadlan whirls his pick down across his electric bass, his pupils huge, sweat raining off the tip of his nose. He is part technician, part mesmerist, a fusion of skill and spirit. I worry whether or not Fadlan can deliver in the next few seconds. He is a little too ecstatic. But of course, he comes through with his signature icing of seventies funk, ironic but charming. I am relieved and burst forth on the keyboard.

We, The Berserkers, make a glorious Gotterdammerung of noise.

Beyond the ticket booth and cyclone fencing, a fake medieval farm village casts its shadow over the audience. Longhouses, outbuildings, grass pathways. Lumpy thatch roofs. A replica ship with a dragon-carving bow. Visitors have been arriving at the festival all week. Men wear brown tunics, wooden caps, chain mail sleeves; women, hooded flounces and sashes at the waist or something to push up the bust.

The Berserkers have come to execute our scorched earth policy of fun. I see a stack of the brightly painted round shields dancers have piled against the barricades so that they can mosh in the pit amid discarded cups emptied of beer.

We are seventy seconds into the piece that makes us famous, at least in the Viking metal world. It is not the song I had written on the overturned gig, which Aud had rendered gorgeous. No, we are executing another tune: hard, Viking. The lyrics are simple. The ideas are simple. We sing a saga of a wizard who tricks a giant, a dwarf and an elf into slaying evil trolls that live in a mountain. The three heroes win glory and renown. Our song goes on for seven harrowing minutes, a shriek-metal epic. My voice grows hoarse with hero-shouts, my keyboard fingers immanent with god-death. We hit the chorus:

> *Forged in fire*
> *And made to pierce,*
> *I'm deadly sharp.*
> *My bite is fierce!*

Egil sucks a mouth full of liquid and spit-blows it through a flame in his clutched hand. Two meters of butane-scented fire spew from his lips. He gives a feral roar. I break from the practiced routine to shout, "So this is RagnaRock. Let it go on forever. Welcome to the greatest Viking-metal gathering on earth, the party at the end of time."

Gudrid snaps to on her snare: militant percussion. We conjure images of warriors clashing, witches prophesying, flames roasting the earth to cinders. Battle fury. Fire and friendship. We then melt into a glacier slide of guitars and drums and keyboards. The crowd is transfigured, hitched to a vapor trail of rapture. Together, we make our raid on Valhalla and our soul-shot at fame.

The song mounts toward closure like a set of spiral stairs, revealing itself in ascent. Most of the song is in a minor key, yet its progression plays hope against loss. Hints of melancholy and chaos faltering to silence end, at the last moment, in joy. The lasers and dry ice fog shut down. The universe collapses upon itself into the size of a soundstage. Our metal opera has ended. We bow. Roadies hand out towels to dry our faces.

þ

I step with the rest of The Berserkers across the stage to accept our award. I look at all the cameras, now remembering that the concert is being broadcast on TV9. I still cannot believe our good fortune.

The trophies are transparent acrylic corkscrews of sculpture, high modern and long out of date. The Mayor of Grimke, where the RagnaRock contest is hosted, hands us the award. He is all smiles and gracious bows. In the front row sit the prigs from the Grimke violence squad, who had grilled me about everything, over and over; they look appropriately awed. It is now my turn to get a corkscrew. I flick the bangs from my face and adjust the leather sheaths on my forearms.

"Thanks," I say to the Mayor. The award feels lighter in my hands than I had expected. It is also cheaper looking. "A lot of sacrifice has gone into this, a lot of wonder and astonishment. But you have to recognize something about our band, The Berserkers. Seriously, you have to understand this."

The Mayor looks puzzled.

"We are more popular than . . ." I fish after the thought. Then, I realize that because I am on TV9, I am speaking not only to the Viking nerds in the audience. I am speaking to tens or hundreds of thousands, perhaps even millions, of Scandinavians. The moshers in the pit have stopped. The Mayor lifts his hand to the perfect knot of his tie, uncertain. Perhaps I will do a John Lennon and reveal my smartass ingratitude with a snarky comment like, "We are more popular than Jesus?"

I do a regional version of the same. "This is much better than listening to ABBA, don't you think?"

I have uttered the impossible, yanking the sword of

Scandinavian pop music from its stone. The Mayor of
Grimke props his cheeks into a grin and wings his hands
around his face. Big, fake smile. "Mama Mia, you will have
a Broadway show soon," he mugs for the cameras.

The moshers stomp and applaud. Someone in the
audience farts a note on a vuvuzela. The Grimke prigs rise
to their feet as if on cue, clapping. The band members
scatter from the stage to all four corners of the festival. I
stumble over Snorri in the wings; he faces a woman I can
only see from the back.

"You've got to love the ancient wisdom. Even when you
think you know it, something new pops up." Snorri is
eating from a catered herring and cheese plate. He is
wearing a linen shirt with a densely embroidered pattern
and a collarless neck, sleeves tight at the wrist, sash around
the belly. He blithely ignores me, engaged with the blond.
The woman's long hair hangs in pigtails that obscure her
face; she is dressed in a muslin blouse and short tartan skirt.
There is a distinct Euro-model feel about her. Dangling a
wooden prop bucket with a rope handle in her hands, she is
nodding her head at polite intervals.

Bergthora approaches, carrying two plastic drinking
horns of mead, and the pig-tailed woman turns. Her
neckline sweeps downward like an alpine vale—it is Freja.
The women clap eyes on each other and Bergthora hands a
mead horn to Freja.

"Bothering the lady, disgraced sergeant detective
Sturlusson?"

"Tak," says the dairymaid.

The women gaze at each other as if reading the final
phrases of a poem neither wishes to end. Snorri shovels
more cod into his mouth. Finally, Bergthora says, "Have
you seen the blacksmith's forge, dear friend?" She offers
the tall woman a forearm to clasp.

"My gallant," approves the dairymaid.

Bergthora smooths an imaginary flaw from Freja's
cheek. "Anything for a damsel in distress." There is an

untamed flicker in Bergothora's eyes. The women depart, arms entwined. As they disappear into the crowd, Bergthora drops her hand lower on her companion's back and twirls a finger near the base of her spine. I see Freja smile for the first time.

Snorri scoffs, "Gallant. Damsel in distress. That's not from the Viking sagas; it's from those campy French romances." He stares at the syncopated gait of the receding women and says, "Did you see Bergthora's hand nearly on her haunch? The tall filly doesn't know what she's missing."

"What could she possibly be missing?" asks Patrolman Jerker.

I do not know where Jerker has come from. His earth-tone tunic barely covers the crotch of his tights. He has a full beer stein in one hand and, strapped to his cap, a can of beer covers each ear. In his other hand, he totes a plastic vuvuzela.

"No pockets," he grins, mildly drunk. Swaying, he fixes his eyeballs on Snorri's collarless shirt and dense embroidery. "You look like a Cossack on summer holiday," he says and blows a discordant B-flat on the horn.

"That is an instrument of the devil," says Snorri.

A worn soccer ball has strayed from the festival green, finding a home at Jerker's feet. The patrolman gives Snorri a perfectly weighted pass. Snorri, in turn, toe-pops the ball straight up and bounces it rhythmically on his forehead. With a final punch of his brow, the little man sends the ball flying back to the green.

"Come on, old geezer, let's play," Jerker says, and the two mates disappear into the festival crush.

I weave behind the bandshell to where there is another mosh pit, but no one is moshing. Aud towers over a throng gathered near her. Children gasp in astonishment, their noses to her knee. She circles her hand to bring the attention of the crowd to herself.

"Examine this well," she instructs; then adds, as though

addressing a gaggle of journalists, "I shall take questions."

"How tall are you?" says one.

"Tall as a mountain."

"How much do you weigh?" asks another.

"What the earth commands."

"Where were you born?"

"In an enchanted glade."

"Faraway? You're a foreigner?"

"Only insofar as every foreigner is a monster or a miracle. I hope you will not be disappointed that I am of local stock, friend."

"Are you related to Andre the Giant?"

"I am his spiritual cousin."

"Can you have babies?"

Aud stands there, immense, one hip thrown out, and a hand upon it bent back at the wrist. "No boy has the fortitude to endure my pleasure."

Men grow pale. Women snigger.

Another question from the audience. "Any regrets?"

In her speech, there is a hiatus, during which Aud repositions her hands, fingertip to fingertip, the toe of her vast left boot pointing upward. "That I am on this globe too short a time to know life with the zest of which I am capable." The giantess straightens, a pillar of pride. "I am a rarity hewn rough from nature's stock, mortal excess, and therefore an exile. I have nothing but my glory to trade upon."

"I see," the last questioner says; it is plain enough this person does not see. Children begin to wander away. Wrestlers resume wrestling. A moment of silence passes. When she sees me, the giantess says, "Thank you for the IOU for my sword poem. I'm pleased you put it in your song lyrics, Grammaticus, and the cash will come in handy."

"If we make any money. Even if you win, the RagnaRock festival is not exactly a bubbling cauldron of album offers," I caution. For reasons beyond my comprehension, I decide to confess to Aud about tripping her. "My friend, I must speak to you about something else."

Aud scans the vicinity. "I feel the place thick with watching eyes."

"Perhaps it can wait," I say.

She draws me toward the skirt of the tent apart from the people. "Let's us not delay, Grammaticus. We must address the most important news swiftly."

"I agree."

"To ease the pain."

"The pain?"

"It is written in your eyes." Aud is not smiling. The blood runs from my face. Has she realized my deceit? The way the giantess stares down gives me an uneasy feeling. "Ever since we left the station house on our quest, Grammaticus, I have known there are things between us that we shall not understand. Perhaps we do not wish to; doing so would be to spoil what goes deeper than comprehending." The giantess compresses her lips the same way a woman does to test her lipstick, trying on coyness. Is she flirting with me? I step back.

"Do not retreat, Grammaticus. There is greatness inscribed upon me; I must render that back upon the world. My destiny, my destiny calls me to be me." A strange welter appears in her deep brown roving eyes. Her hand falls gently upon my skull, a huge spider, fingers stretching from one ear to the other. Bending over, she kisses me on top of my head as one does an infant.

I abandon the notion of confessing. I recognize my non sequitur only after my words come out, though I am happier with these words, anyway.

"You have altered me, Aud," I say. "I had very little sense of identity, and my start in life has been slow. You have changed that. You are a miracle, a friend, and more than Fulaflugahål can contain."

The giantess seems to see something over my shoulder. She withdraws her hands from my skull. "Constable."

I am relieved at the distraction. My eyes seek upward and see the Constable high on a catwalk behind the bandshell. Aud clamps her over-large jaw and sashays her way back to the mosh pit. "Adieu, Grammaticus." She knows the Constable and I require privacy.

The Constable is wearing a plush scarlet blazer with a braided gold belt at the waist that resembles an old bell pull. His collar is wide, missing the cravat, the neck open. A large sleek black bird sits on each shoulder, Minne's white feather bright in her tail, Tanke dark as midnight. With one hand, the Constable drinks a portion of frothing mead from a RangaRock Festival ram's horn.

"The bird, Minne, she wore a tracking collar," I say.

"Yes, Kolbitter?"

I see in his other hand the Constable carries the antique blue volume. I continue, "She seemed always to know where to go, even to lead us."

"I see. 'Perception or fact?' you are asking. Perhaps, Kolbitter, perhaps some gifts one cannot explain. Well, boy, did you rouse yourself from your drowsy embers?"

"Sir?"

"Ages ago, you gazed possessively into the flames in the hearth before my table, as if to escape into dreams. Now, you and your lot have won a musical contest."

"We have."

"You are good at that noise? Is that what you have been dreaming of ages ago, that racket?"

"Very good at it. We are The Berserkers."

The Constable sighs. "Say no more, boy."

"I have a matter to discuss, Constable, the matter you took up rather than pursuing the killers with us."

"Good lord."

"Have you found the king's letters?"

He looks at me as though I am trying to be clever, then brightens, "Missives recovered. The dignity of the nation is preserved."

"Wonderful, sir."

"Amazing adventure. Sorry, you missed it." He flips open the blue volume and plucks out a heavy sheet of cream-colored stationery, elaborate insignia, smart crease. He stares down his nose from the great height and reads to me:

> *My little cherry, if only you knew how I revile them for preventing me spending all my time with you. Why do they separate us? Scamps always entertain false notions that they are important. I could banish them with one stroke of a pen.*
> *Yet by the time you read these pages, I may be dead, having expired of grief, and my heart surely will wither to nothing without you near. I feel a lacuna; your absence is draining my soul. Where are you? When will you come to me? Without you, the dregs of time are bitter. Do you recall those fleeting delights we unlocked that weekend when we fled to Paris to meet at the Café Huysmans? Nothing exists for me but you, my grasshopper. My gosling. My amorous cloudberry. Believe me when I say —"*

The Constable chuckles into his sleeve. "On it sails, page after glorious page." He flips a few sheets more. "And then there is this:

> *You may accuse me of being in love in fits and starts. I cannot deny it. What do we do with this gift of ecstasy, lifting us from ourselves and letting us peer into the souls of others? Life is strung together with desperate acts, a daisy chain of catastrophes, and buried ruin. Only art can render love truly, over time. Some speak of revolution to throw off mortal failings, but the violent have left off care for the souls of others, and the flies of their doubt sup upon the wounds of*

grievance.

"The king wrote that letter?"

"It would be the gravest professional breach for me to say." He leans over the catwalk rail, as if with the air of the confidant. "The declarations strain credulity, perhaps, but the detail is lovely."

Maybe I have a companion in the king, I think to myself. The Constable is about to turn away with the letter and the birds, an actor retreating beyond the footlights. However, he stops in his steps when I call after him. "On the theme of credulity, Constable, your autobiographies. Two of them. Why did you give me those fake stories?"

He turns back to me. "Still gnawing that old bone."

"The autobiographies, one asserts it is such. The fairytales, or legends, or whatnot. People who turn to statues of glass; men are shooting from canons; eyeball slashings. Wild escapes, mad adventures. Who was the mysterious nemesis who haunted your life? Does any of it correspond to fact?"

He studies me with that dark ancient eye. With the recognition I have stepped beyond my accustomed zone, I persist. "I mean, only one autobiography can be true. Right?"

He sighs.

I continue, "I believe you enjoy persecuting me, sir. You seem to make a sport of it."

"A duty elevated to an austere art."

"In the service of what, sir?"

"Your spiritual transformation."

I wonder what strange abandon has taken root in him. I want to say that if such a thing as a spiritual transformation has stirred within me, the giantess would be the prodigy behind it, not him. But I do not.

The Constable takes my silence as an invitation. "Sometimes," he says slowly, "a fable tells the greater truth. Not easy to get your head around, but poetry takes a little bloodletting. Look at the changes wrought in you since that day on the frozen lake."

I consider the assertion. My heart begins to beat harder, my cheeks to grow hot. Still, I am silent.

"Don't be impertinent, boy," says the Constable. "One lends another a quandary for no reason other than to cultivate durability and a sense of cunning. We know each other through our dissimulations, Kolbitter. We are travelers in a mountain pass, strangers saluting each other over a crevasse."

Then I recall those unfortunates left in the mine: Nils and Olaf the Peacock and the Thorstein brothers.

"Those who died on the isle, sir, they are buried forever?"

"Entombed till the end of time."

"All that ferocity from them, to what end?"

"It is a curious reaction. One might rather savor differences: a good shock, the congenial twist. Paint the broad canvass. Perhaps train for an acute and immediate perception of what must be an eternal kind of contrast: a self, another. That would make the human experience richer."

"What about the dead girl in the lake—Misty, the friend of Aud, the giantess?"

"Ah, yes."

"Did anyone figure out where was she from? Did she have family?"

"These facts, too, we concede are lost to the sands. This girl, Misty, with no last name and no known country of origin, was buried in a pauper's grave along with the remains of others, a standard procedure in Grimke, I'm afraid."

"Such cases…"

"Of the indigent and homeless, the unidentified or unidentifiable."

"No genetic analysis."

"Impossible now."

"What about the shape of her eyes? Can anything be determined that way?"

"The fold in the eyelid."

"Yes."

"Epicanthic. Many peoples the world over have that fold, including some Scandinavians. Nothing to cling to there."

"After all that, no identity unearthed. Things are not fair that way."

"They are not. You are fortunate, boy. What you wrought was after all a bagatelle, a contretemps."

I draw a breath. "I suppose."

"The expense of an investigation, trial, and incarceration would have been extravagant. The Grimke magistrate is too busy to hear such a matter. Case dismissed. Funnily enough, the magistrate recognized you, Kolbitter."

My glances leap from Tanke to Minne as I try to assuage my panic. "Me? How?"

"Your personnel photo. Apparently, you made a big show of a lost express ticket, frisking yourself, searching the suddenly problematic chambers of your wardrobe on a train she was riding. She did not take much of a liking to you."

"I am surprised I am not in a penitentiary."

"Jurisprudence is its own beast. Under our national constitution and the sovereign laws of the state, and by the spirit of Nordic justice, responsibility devolves to the mining company."

I shake my head, confused. "I thought the pit was defunct."

"Yes, boy. The Linkoping Mining Company, founded in 1794, was dissolved generations past, and the pit on the Isle of O permanently shuttered." The Constable's good eye roves about the scene as if he is expecting ears that should not hear him, before announcing, "The site was said to be plagued by noxious trolls and sinister bewitchment."

When I do not answer at once, the Constable plunges on. "There is joy in variety. An ability to conceive otherwise."

For an unearthly moment, I think I have understood. I stagger back. All the uncanniness of time rushes upon me. For once, I now feel I am exactly and unambiguously where I am meant to be. "Conceive otherwise… That is what musicians do, Constable."

The one-eyed man, as if sensing my embrace of a disarming mood, raises the golden horn and swirls it, squinting at his drink as though looking back through fathomless whorls. A toast. A clash of embers; the sweet, icy drafts of life. He says in a low, conspiratorial tone, "We must do our best with this ever-diminishing fragment of time."

Two black streaks plunge between the Constable up high and me below. It is our pair of heralds, the ravens Minne and Tanke, who, in turn, rise and circle above the festival, tuck their wings, plummeting earthward. They split and shoot over the singing crowd at the last moment, then sweep up once more. Soon, the birds merge in my eyes into a single black speck far overhead. The speck reaches its zenith, two ravens, one tiny point—a point that might contain, I marvel, all other points. Now, the dark grain grows larger, returning, yet the birds do not separate back into two, and I see her emerge, the dead girl, as in a vision. The ravens have become one in her. The girl races nearer in her exquisite contrivance of feathers and rolls like an acrobat, catches a thermal, and swoops, wheeling on airy drafts, beating her mighty wings under an apple-red sun. Her face is an inverted teardrop: a seeking face, tender, and of infinite dimensions. A strange creature from a strange fable, yet so familiar, so human.

THE END

Acknowledgments

A novel is not created in a literary vacuum. I would like to recognize my debt to Bill Buford's classic on hooligan life, *Among the Thugs*, which furnished a foundation for the present novel in so many ways. I drew insights about Nordic culture from non-fiction works by Michael Booth, Roger Boyes, Robert Ferguson, and Sarah Moss; about indie bands from Michael Azzerad; and about ravens from biologist Bernd Heinrich. I also turned to the following authors for literary inspiration that sometimes reveals itself as homages "in the style of" those writers: J.G. Ballard, Patrick DeWitt, Charles Dickens, Alexander Dumas, Robert E. Howard, John Gardner, Saxo Grammaticus, Lee M. Hollander (translator of Norse sagas), Christopher Isherwood, Phillip Larkin, Emanuel Levinas, Hillary Mantel, William Morris, Hakan Nessir, Rudolph Eric Raspe, the writing team Anders Roslund and Borge Hellstrom, Aksel Sandemose, the writing team Maj Sjowall and Per Wahloo, Snorri Sturlusson, and Johan Theorin. This novel's mine journey owes much to George Orwell's *The Road to Wigan Pier* and Emile Zola's *Germinal*.

And, of course, my family and friends whose love gives me strength.

The Author

Vic Peterson was educated at Kenyon College, the University of Texas (Dallas) and the University of Chicago. He worked as a business executive and now divides his time between Lawrence, Kansas and Northport, Michigan.